Rage at Nan Madol

Written by Erik Lange

Cover art by Erik Frankhouse

First Printing, 2021

First edition

ISBN 978-1-7324326-4-2

This book is dedicated to Metro Cigars and its proprietors, Jen and Paul.

Also by Erik Lange

The Karl Lark Chronicles

Escape from Hy-Brasil

The Deeps Beneath Castle Houska

Chapter 1

"I have never been shot," I say simply while sitting in the Citadel cafeteria surrounded by my colleagues. The remains of our lunch in front of us, we five are relaxing and enjoying each other's company while exchanging stories. Today is a rare day with downtime.

Illych has a questioning look on his face when he counters my statement. "You have been in a fair number of firefights to have not been shot. Everyone here has been wounded by gunfire, sometimes multiple times during a single engagement." Illych is a tall, lean man in his early forties and a former Green Beret.

Tank, a former Marine obsessed with weightlifting in his downtime, rumbles his contribution to the discussion. "That hardly seems fair."

Shrugging, I continue. "Perhaps I am lucky that way. Chance prevented me from being shot when we first met at the British Museum. The others present were not as fortunate. Nor a week later at the shootout in my old flat in London. Even with all that happened getting Balthazar home, I was never hit. During the battle in Ehgira, that Turkish town, a piece of grenade shrapnel penetrated one of my armor joints. I bled a lot. Does that count?"

Mike laughs and replies, "Thomas, it was your own grenade, so no, it does not count."

His youthful laughter marks him out as the youngest of the team, only in his late twenties. As a former Army Ranger, he follows the same pattern as the rest of the team: ex-military and competent. Almost precisely my relatively average height and blessed with good looks, Mike resembles me about twenty years ago. If I was underwear-model attractive. And in excellent shape.

"My induction happened almost a year ago," I respond. "Since then, it has been nonstop training and we have seen a lot of action together." That should set the record straight on this discussion about not being shot being a deficiency.

Unlike my colleagues, I have never served in the military. I am British, not American. My profession is that of librarian, and I used to live in the UK. In London, to be specific.

"Even with everything that went down under Castle Houska," Illych begins, "I do not recall you being seriously injured."

Shaking my head, I reply, "Like I said. Lucky."

At this point, I realize Tank's gorilla-like shape has stood up. With a shift of position, his massive form is now right behind me. Illych strains his lips into a thin smile that does not reach his eyes. It is a smile that reminds me I am sitting in the middle of four experienced military men who have all long since lost count of how many lives they have ended.

"Having been shot is an important experience," Illych says. "You know the deal: A man's gotta know his limitations." Illych's tone has a mix of humor and seriousness. As I debate which way he intends, Tank's hands land firmly on my shoulders. It calms me to know that Tank is a practical jokester in what is becoming an upsetting attempt at dark comedy.

"Ha ha, guys," I say nervously. "I appreciate that getting shot is a learning experience, but until it happens, there is nothing I can do. It is not like you can shoot me to teach me a lesson." No sooner are the words out of my mouth than I regret saying them. With this group . . .

Tank's hands leave my shoulders and grab my upper arms in a vice-like grip. He is grossly stronger than I, and there will be no escaping. Those same strong hands lift me to a standing position, and Mike grabs my left hand and Held my right hand. Held is the final member of the team. The tall, blond, and lean former Green Beret could easily restrain me by himself.

Since my induction, my early-forties body has increased in strength and endurance due to required calisthenics and weight training. Regardless, I am still not even close to being a match for any one of these men.

"Guys, I am getting a prison-rape vibe from all of this. Not laughing here."

Not a word is said as the four of them carry me out of the cafeteria and past several nearby buildings, all encased within the Citadel, an impenetrable stone cocoon sitting on a plane of virtually impassable badlands. The Citadel is our sanctum sanctorum. Here we live, train, and plan for whatever our employer requires of us. The overall interior is similar in size and construction to a small roofed sports stadium. Inside the open space are buildings made from solid stone. They come in many shapes and sizes, all set atop a plane of hard black stone. Everything is brightly lit by crystal cylinders high above us.

The Citadel is part of a pocket dimension. As in, not part of the normal world. Apparently, a long time ago some ancient beings created androids on Earth. Then, for unexplained reasons, the ancients departed millions of years ago and their pet automatons were left behind. Humanity sometimes bumps into these things at different times and places. Mythology calls them fairies, goblins, trolls, etc. Mr. Lark, our employer, managed to convert the goblin android into some sort of medical servitor. Or maybe domesticate is a better word for it, depending on your point of view. We have chosen to call it The Doctor. The Doctor can heal any wound as long as your brain is relatively intact and the patient is not completely dead. And based on our path, I can tell we are headed for The Doctor. These thoughts all race through my mind to a logical conclusion.

Realization shoots a cold jolt of fear through me. My colleagues may not be joking. They could shoot me dozens of times, as long as none are head shots, then just deliver my blood-soaked, perforated, and near-lifeless body to The Doctor. I would be healed and ready for duty in less than half an hour.

That would not be too bad except for the getting shot part.

As we pass by the armory, Mike peels off from our group and runs in.

My dread turns into terror. Are they are going through with this like it is some sort of sick initiation? How can you shoot someone as a training exercise?

There will be no escape. My librarian body will not be able to evade whatever they have planned.

Outside The Doctor's residence, Mike rejoins us, a small black duffel bag in hand. Fishing out several rolls of duct tape, he tosses one to each of the others. They chuckle as I struggle while being trussed up in a standing position. My arms are bound behind me and taped to a post, keeping me upright. My ankles are spaced apart but still thoroughly wrapped to prevent my escape.

Illych tears a small piece of duct tape from his roll and holds it up to me. "Thomas, since we cannot have you screaming." He presses the duct tape across my mouth. The possibility that this is not a joke settles like a cold stone in my gut.

He continues speaking: "All jokes aside, Thomas, this exercise serves an important educational function. You need to experience a gunshot and how to react. Having you panic in the middle of a firefight could endanger us all. Frankly, this training is long overdue."

Illych takes up a shooting stance maybe twenty feet from me. Mike slaps a semiautomatic pistol with a large suppressor attached into the former Green Beret's right hand. "The rounds are full metal jacket?" Illych asks. Mike nods.

It starts with flesh wounds and through and throughs. A spiral pattern begins at my extremities and then works inwards to my torso. The duct tape muffles my screams. Tears stream from my eyes as this twisted form of training is administered.

Some shots hurt, some do not. For the most part, the discomfort is more psychological at this point, not physical. Eventually I cease my struggles and silently accept each injury.

The real pain begins with center-mass impacts. My agony reaches such a crescendo that my thoughts no longer make sense. This just needs to end.

Mentally, I understand there is no way to ease into this training or take it in steps. But for the love of God, does Tank have to stand there maniacally grinning while I am repeatedly shot?

A magazine of rounds later, I black out.

I wake up naked on a stretcher in The Doctor's waiting area, fully healed. I look around and locate the clean clothes left for me, The Doctor having disposed of my bloodied clothing. Checking out each gunshot location that impacted my body not an hour ago, I find nothing. After more than a dozen penetrations, not a single scar. Honestly, I do not even feel tired.

I dress and slowly walk back to the cafeteria, knowing they are waiting. Sure enough, as I enter, they all stand and give me a standing ovation. Tank even whistles. This brings a lame smile to my now-flush face, and after the cheering ends, I flatly state I will not like any of them for the rest of the day.

No sooner do I sit down than the room goes silent. Knowing it is not me causing the reaction, I turn to view the cafeteria entrance. Mr. Lark, our enigmatic employer, has just arrived, dressed in black tactical dress.

It is time to go to work.

Chapter 2

Mr. Lark's face is unreadable as he says, "Is the remedial training complete?"

Illych nods in confirmation.

"Mike and Thomas, please prepare for a single night of tactical operation. We have a short task to complete outdoors in the dead of night. We leave within the hour."

Most people would start asking questions at this point. Neither Mike nor I do. Our employer will tell us what we need to know, and asking questions will just irritate him. Simultaneously, we stand and head to our respective rooms to gear up. Everyone on the team has a tactical setup ready to go. We can be ready with only a moment's notice—similar to a firefighter and his gear, but with guns. Big guns, and many of them.

Walking into my austere quarters I review the rack and shelves holding my assigned gear. Everything we wear on missions is black. Mentally, I review why: The Created, the unimaginative name given by Mr. Lark to the androids, rely heavily on sensing thoughts and feelings, not as much on sight as humans would. Mr. Lark makes sure we are prepared for any type of foe. Black is the lack of light. Dressing exclusively in the color black increases our chance of not being observed. It is a life-saving advantage in situations where fractions of a second count. As for the thoughts and feelings part, Mr. Lark has The Doctor install what he calls, again unimaginatively, a crown in our skulls as part of induction to the team. This weave of copper wires and who knows what attenuate our radiated thoughts and emotions. Working for Mr. Lark, one quickly learns he plays to win.

Our military grade boots are armored in the soles to prevent puncture. Every piece of the uniform has bullet resistant fabric and strategically placed ceramic ballistic plates. We also have an armored carapace vest with attachment points complete with a full-face helmet. The helmet protects us from being blinded, has night vision built in, and includes inbuilt breathing filters. An embedded array of microphones allows us to hear the slightest scrape of a foot on gravel while filtering out loud gunfire and protecting our hearing.

The last piece of Mr. Lark tech is a bulky and unconventional timepiece. A small metal box purely functional in design, it provides the usual timekeeping function, but it also detects for something my employer calls EPS, which is short for electron probability suppression. Apparently, EPS is the same as what happens to all those people in UFO abductions. First all the electronics die, then people cannot move, and finally they black out. I have never witnessed it, but Mr. Lark worries about it, hence the ugly watch. The watch gives enough warning to escape the area of effect if the wearer is quick.

Gearing up takes only a few minutes, and I arrive at the armory just before Mike.

Looking upon the weaponry arrayed in front of us, I smile. Mr. Lark can afford the best—and a lot of it. I am not a weapons fanatic in the way my colleagues are, but if a God of War existed and he had an armory, this is what it would look like. Rack upon rack of gleaming, oiled tools of violence waiting to be taken up and put to use. Shelves and lockers of ammunition and explosives of every conceivable manufacture lay ready. No locks, no sign-out sheets, and no one to make a request to.

Our semiauto handguns already in our holsters, Mike and I select a large caliber carbine each and fill the numerous magazine pouches in our chest carapace. With arming complete, we feel ready for anything, and we silently stalk to the main gate.

Mr. Lark is waiting for us in the open space by the Citadel's main gate, dressed in matching gear. As far as I have been able to determine in my year of service, there is only one way in or out of the Citadel's outer shell, and this gate is it. Illych is here, finishing a discussion with the old man as we walk up.

Observing my elderly employer as he reviews our equipment, I am struck by his aged appearance. The man's full head of hair is completely white and combed straight back. His face is that of a man of sixty-five or more years, yet he carries himself as a healthy young man. I learned a long time ago to not underestimate Karl Lark based on his appearance.

After a cursory review of our loadout and without comment, Mr. Lark turns toward the gates and starts walking.

The main gates are a double-door arrangement large enough for a semi-tractor-trailer to drive through with room to spare. Nowhere on the doors is a lock or mechanism of opening. Yet when your intention is to pass through, they open without any action needed. Mr. Lark turns to leave, and they open outwards in complete and perfect silence.

The silent-movement part is a little unnerving, especially for doors that large. More than a few times we have unexpectedly found Mr. Lark inside the Citadel without warning due to the silent nature of the only point of entry. In the past I have suggested attaching bells to the doors, like in convenience stores. Illych did not appreciate my attempted ingenuity and squashed my attempt before it started.

Glancing left and right confirms the gate guardians are still present. Ten feet tall, four armed, monstrous bipeds, one on each side of the gate, provide some form of security. Mr. Lark calls them Ushabti. Their appearance is strangely blurred or undefined. I have never been close to either of them; they look less than safe, which is typical of most of the Created.

It is well below freezing and dark as we take our first steps onto the road outside the gates. The way in front of us is a laser-straight, flat-black-stone path extending to the visible horizon.

Looking about, I see what is always there. The spaces around the Citadel are a no-man's land of unusually formed structures and rough grey stone terrain. And all of it populated by various Lesser Created. There is no plant or animal life to be found here.

Far above us, overhead in the mist, are alien creatures best left undisturbed. The Citadel and our destination ahead are not on Earth, but rather in a multidimensional extrusion near to it. The only way in or out is at our next destination: the Compass.

The walk to the Compass from our base of operations through the cold and gloom of the wild spaces is between twenty and thirty minutes long, depending on our pace. Our employer is setting a fast pace today, and Mike and I jog a bit to fall in with him.

Traveling between the Citadel and the Compass is never safe, but if we do it in pairs, or more, the things in this place will let us pass unmolested. The old man leaves it this way because the denizens of this pocket dimension make for a lethal security system. Anyone not recognized by the eternal beings inhabiting the dark around us will meet a terrible end long before reaching the Citadel.

Even having walked this route more than a hundred times, knowing the nature of the things watching me, I still feel unsafe.

Halfway to the Compass, I risk a question. "Are there any special considerations to be aware of for our activities tonight?" Mike's helmet shifts in my direction for a brief instant. Our embedded communication system is another of Mr. Lark's creations. Instead of radio transmitters, we have ComDats. They cannot be jammed or intercepted and have an infinite range. Something about splitting particles always being connected. It is all very technical, but I find they are quite useful.

"The plan was to brief you at the Compass, where special gear needed for tonight's mission waits for us," Mr. Lark responds. "Your inability to be silent for even twenty minutes apparently will not allow for that." He sighs. "We are going to collect something tonight," he continues. "I expect our activities to be physically challenging, and we will need to keep our wits about us. It will be the dead of night at our destination. We cannot have the possibility of bystanders and the unintended consequences of their presence." That explains the odd hour of our exit.

In spite of no obvious source of light, the mists above us give off a glow like dim moonlight, bathing the ground and features around us. No sun rises or sets in this place, so there is no daytime rhythm to follow. To provide some scheduling discipline, we run on Eastern Standard Time here. Based on the current local time being just after 6pm, I do the math and determine we must be going somewhere in Europe or Africa. Spend enough time traveling the world and predicting destinations based on relative time becomes second nature.

Ahead of us, emerging on the horizon, the Compass slowly comes into view. The air in this place has some sort of light-attenuating property that makes everything dimmer the farther away the observer is. I call it "the gloom." Regardless, we are only a few hundred meters away when the shadowy outline of the Compass comes into view.

Six massive hexagonal steel vaults surround a Stonehenge-like circle of black stone pillars that then surround a large, open circular space. This is the front door to the dimensional pocket we inhabit. Thousands of pocket dimensions anchor to different points in Earth's gravity well. If you can find their respective portals, and know how to open them, you can just walk in. Surviving long enough to get back out is the more difficult part. Mr. Lark likens them to storage sheds. Inside are often things left over from a time so long ago the word "ancient" does them no justice. Based on the few I have visited, they are best left alone by mortal men.

"Follow me." Mr. Lark's command refocuses my attention. He walks to one of the massive vaults, its bank vault–style plug door already wide open. Inside, surrounded by the vault's foot-thick steel walls, it is pitch black. The old man switches on a lamp, and the dull-grey iron interior is vaguely illuminated. The inside of the vault is mostly empty, making it easy to see the scratches and gouges. Whatever was held here eons ago was quite large, had claws that could mark steel, and wanted out.

Just inside the portal opening to the vault is a grouping of equipment neatly arranged on the floor.

Without explanation, Mr. Lark picks up a stack of long rods resembling ski poles and promptly hands the tightly bound bundle to Mike. Then he hands me a box with handles mounting a cone-like dish antenna on one side. The box is heavy and awkward to hold. All that remains on the floor is a bandolier with various odd metallic and crystalline constructs attached to it. This, our employer handily scoops up and places across his chest diagonally from shoulder to hip; it transforms him into some sort of armored techno-punk bandito.

"We are ready," Mr. Lark states as if it is law. I do not feel ready. What is the thing I am carrying? Where are we going? What are we doing?

Without further explanation, my employer walks out of the vault to the center of the circle surrounded by regularly spaced stone pillars, each one black in color and about the same size as a man. This is the heart of the Compass; the front door, so to speak. We follow without question, knowing what comes next.

Stopping in the center of the circle, Mr. Lark removes two small brass batons from his bandolier. "Your return dongles, for if we become separated," he says as he hands them to us. "The translation to our destination will be provided by me." Each of us takes our offered dongle and secures them in our gear. These are our lifelines out if things go sideways.

Mr. Lark gives a third baton a twist, separating the two ends. Flipping the pieces, he reconnects them and prepares to give the final rotation to activate the ouiblet and translate us to our destination.

Mr. Lark has never shared where the portal to the Compass is located on a globe. He has assured us it is virtually impossible to access from the outside world. Not that it matters. One of our employer's first inventions was the ouiblet. This device allows people and things to shift out of our three-dimensional world and then shift back in somewhere else. The old man calls it translating. Translation is a form of instantaneous transportation. The ouiblet gives teleporter like access to every square inch of humanity's home planet. The cost is brief illness every time it is used. Mr. Lark will be unaffected, Mike and I, however, will experience nausea upon arriving at our destination.

The old man's hands make the final twist, and the world around us disappears into blackness. A brief sensation of weightlessness lasts a fraction of a second as we are transported from the Compass to our destination. As suddenly as we left, we arrive, and a new world fills my sight. We are standing in a graveyard. I feel the nausea hit, and I am glad for a nearby headstone to lean on. The feeling of being ill passes in less than a minute. During this time, I take in more of our surroundings.

It is the dead of night at our destination. The headstones date to the 1500s, some even older. The graveyard is huge, extending in all directions to the limits of my augmented night vision. Vertical and horizontal grave markers are densely packed around us with narrow footpaths between them. In the distance are buildings looking European in design.

Mr. Lark's voice is clear in my ears through the helmet's ComDat connection. "We are in a very old cemetery in Poland."

Mike and I regain our composure.

The old man continues. "Long, long ago one of the Lesser Created was unmade here," he says. "Why this truly terrible crime happened, I do not know. Such things are never truly destroyed, of course, and the components that made up its being remain connected to this place. We are here to collect one of those parts."

"Why not just locate it and use the ouiblet?" I thought it a prudent question to ask.

"The Created have a physical presence here, but at the same time, they are connected to places outside our reality. The ouiblet fortunately does not reach there. Thus, we are here in person."

Fortunately?

"I chose to come in the dead of night because this place never has visitors after dark," Mr. Lark continues.

Mike breaks his silence. "What? Not even teenagers getting into trouble?"

"No. The remains of this Created grow stronger after dark and affect the material world. The effects wax and wane and are utterly unpredictable. No one can safely live in this place. Over time, humans took the hint and put this land to a low-hazard use as a cemetery instead of something like a factory or neighborhood."

Understanding, I nod. Having experienced the Created firsthand, I know how strange things can get. "Are you planning to reassemble this thing?"

"No, Thomas, once unmade, such things cannot be reassembled. Besides, I do not wish to capture the complete remains. Only one small piece is required. Mike, unbundle the poles and plant one in the dirt of the footpath you currently stand in." He turns to me. "Thomas, remain silent and do not move. I must guide Mike in a roughly circular journey to plant the remaining poles."

Mr. Lark then goes silent and unmoving, indicating his use of the oculus. Another of my employer's inventions, the oculus is like a portable x-ray machine, though I know this comparison is a gross oversimplification. The oculus allows the user to view much more than what a human's eyes or an x-ray machine can. For missions like this, my employer keeps the brass sphere of an oculus in a pouch clipped to his belt. When we are around other people and it needs to remain inconspicuous, Mr. Lark uses a walking cane with the incongruous sphere of the oculus for one end.

"Make a quarter turn," he says to Mike. "Walk forward 30 feet." A long pause. "Now plant a pole."

Mike makes it to his fifth pole when the temperature begins to drop rapidly. This is no cool night wind blowing in. Even inside my armor I can feel the still air freezing, much colder than the Compass. The temperature drop is brutal. In seconds, an ice fog precipitates out of thin air. Visibility drops to fewer than four paces. Something knows we are here, and our presence is not well received.

None of this appears to affect Mr. Lark. His monotone instructions continue on, directing Mike to each location requiring a pole.

As I keep track of the number of poles set in place, it seems we have reached the halfway point. The freezing, still air forms a slick layer of ice on the plates of my armor and the gravestones. If we have to move quickly, all this ice will be a problem.

A gale force wind begins, catching me off guard. Only my quick footwork prevents me from toppling over. The wind's strength causes the ice fog to disappear in an instant. The wind direction changes constantly, with an increasingly demonic howl.

The wind sheers planes of ice off the grave markers' flat surfaces and shoots them like blades through the air, striking me repeatedly. Even though my armor, the constant beat of ice threatens to knock me from my feet. Without the armor, this maelstrom of ice would be fatal.

Having lost sight of my employer and Mike, I can still clearly hear Mr. Lark's calm voice directing Mike's effort. The former Army Ranger struggles and places each pole, one by one. The wind stops as suddenly as it began when the final pole is placed.

"The circle is complete." Mr. Lark's voice has a hint of satisfaction in it. "Thomas, please stand up straight and point the device you are carrying into the circle."

Doing as instructed, I orient the device into the general space the poles surrounded.

"I will activate it now. There may be a reaction."

The device I'm holding buzzes noticeably, causing my hands to jerk in response.

The ground shakes for a brief moment, then we feel a single high-magnitude shock. Apparently, we have something's attention.

"Thomas, rotate left a bit," says Mr. Lark. "Now start walking forward slowly. Move the dish antennae in small circles. Tell me when you see something."

I do as instructed. A feeling of being less than safe is growing in my thoughts. I see nothing but gravestones in front of me as I wave the end of whatever this thing is around.

The ground shakes again, and I hear the noise of breaking stone.

Mr. Lark silently appears on my left, stalking across the uneven terrain. His attention focuses ahead of me to where the device is scanning.

I feel fear.

Not anxiety or concerns about the mission, but real fear. It is the Created projecting into my mind. This is bad. The crown should keep projections of fear and anxiety from being anything other than a nuisance.

But now, I am truly afraid.

"Uh, Mr. Lark . . ."

"Yes, I can feel it. Mike, what do you feel?"

"Like we should not be here."

Mr. Lark's next command is not what I want to hear. "We are close. Thomas, move forward another few paces."

Fighting fear and anxiety, I put one foot in front of the other. This is not my first time feeling what the Created can do, and I know my limits are close. At some point I will break and run screaming from this place. Not yet, but soon.

Brightly colored ribbons of light shift into view in front of me. They twist and twirl, forming intertwining patterns. My feet stop working. The fear has frozen me in place. Slowly, the streamers drift toward me. I know they must not touch me, but I cannot move.

Mr. Lark is now barely visible to the left of me. He plucks items from his bandolier and tosses several to the ground. The others he begins waving in a pattern, similar to a wizard casting a spell.

The ribbons drift closer, now only an arm's length away from me. I instinctively know I will die if they touch me, yet my feet are no longer mine to command. I have been rendered a motionless statue awaiting my doom.

The ribbons begin to fold on themselves. Mr. Lark begins walking closer, his hands moving in circular patterns. The closer he moves, the more compact the streaming lights in front of me become. The old man's hands move at an impossible pace, a blur of activity as he closes in on the sphere of light that could fit in someone's palm.

The now-compact light changes to a dull sphere that begins to fall from its elevated position, landing in Mr. Lark's outstretched hand. Simultaneously, the fear leaves me and I can move again. However, my body is exhausted from the effects of the Created. My employer stores the sphere in a pouch connected to his belt. My arms, now drained of strength, struggle to hold the device I was assigned. I am that tired.

I hear Mr. Lark's voice in my helmet. "Mike, quickly get to Mr. Davies. He likely will not be able to stand much longer."

My vision gets blurry and I try to speak, but my words slur unintelligibly. Mike appears out of the dark and puts one of my arms over his shoulder before I fall down. He sits me on a gravestone and then leaves to collect the poles. I had not realized until now that the device I had held was laying on the ground a short distance away.

Mr. Lark picks it up and walks over to me. "That was unexpected. It took a liking to you and focused exclusively on your person. Perhaps you taste good to a Created. Regardless, if I had been a few seconds slower, I would have been forced to find your replacement."

Way to make a guy feel better.

My employer then guesses my thoughts even if my mouth cannot create the words.

"You would have died. Permanently and completely. Now you truly understand why this place is not lived in."

Mike joins us with the bundle of recovered poles under one arm. Mr. Lark pulls a dongle from his pocket.

"Our work here is done," he says. "Let us get our exhausted librarian to his bed. I have work to do."

With a twist of his hands, everything goes black.

Chapter 3

The next day during breakfast, I am sitting enjoying the great coffee available in the Citadel. Good coffee is good coffee, but great coffee is great coffee. Just one more thing Mr. Lark spares no expense on.

Mike and I had just finished discussing the strangeness that was last night's experience in the old Polish cemetery. He leaves to start his day, and I have a few minutes alone with my thoughts. There is plenty of work to be done in the library, and I am looking forward to opening some of the new arrivals. The coffee is the only thing keeping me in the cafeteria.

My cup is one-quarter full and beginning to cool below the temperature I prefer. Now comes the internal struggle to decide if I get a second cup. I shouldn't, but it is so good.

My struggle ends with the arrival of Illych. Something is up. He never comes back into the cafeteria after breakfast. His eyes lock with mine as he strides in straight to where I sit.

"Thomas, we need to talk."

My anxiety level goes up upon hearing the worst sentence for starting a conversation ever. I take the last sip from my cooling mug. "What about?"

Illych takes a seat across from me and says, "Elizabeth Chatzas."

Good Lord, we are going there this early in the morning? "You mean Dr. Chatzas? The curator from the British Museum? The one who arranged my murder to help cover a theft? Why are you bringing her up now?" It has been almost a year since I last saw her, and the parting was not on friendly terms.

"She contacted Mr. Lark as per her agreement with him. She feels he may want to look at something at the museum."

I do not like where this is going. "Her plan to murder me is the reason I am in this place instead of home in my flat, happy with a life ignorant of Mr. Lark," I say. "As a result, I am not being particularly fond of her. Regardless, what does this find have to do with me?"

Illych's expression shifts from a poker face to a grin almost to the point of ridiculous. This answers my question even before his words confirm what I am thinking. "He would like you to meet with her."

Mr. Lark does not request me to do anything. Illych is just being polite. "He is sending me, isn't he?"

Illych is still smiling. "It gets better," he says. "You are to meet her in London tonight. At a restaurant for dinner."

My eyes narrow involuntarily. "I am to be sent on a date with a woman who despises me and arranged for my violent death, albeit unsuccessfully?

"This is why it is just me talking to you now. I figured you might need some space to come to terms with this."

"Do the others know about this?"

Illych nods.

"What were their reactions?"

"They are having problems conducting themselves professionally."

Of course.

"They are laughing at me, aren't they?"

"Tank may still be laughing, yes."

Illych continues. "Are you up for it?"

Mr. Lark will not accept a no. In this place, Illych phrasing this as a request is as close as it gets to delivering news gently. As assuredly as the sun rises in the east and sets in the west, I will be seeing Dr. Chatzas in London tonight.

Resigned, I reply, "It is tonight? The date is tonight?"

Illych nods a confirmation.

"Then I will be having another cup of coffee."

The former Green Beret glances at my cup. "I thought Brits liked tea? We can get tea if you prefer."

"As long as the coffee is this good, I am fine."

Illych turns to leave. "Dress for success, Thomas. She chose a restaurant to meet at that has a formal dress code, and you are buying." I swear he is laughing under his breath as he walks out of the cafeteria.

A date with a woman who once tried to have me murdered, and I am buying. How civilized. Well, stiff upper lip and all that.

Later that day I translate to an old industrial complex in London. Mr. Lark uses this location as a base for any UK operations. It doubles as long-term storage for things that may be needed when he visits. On the outside, it is an old abandoned complex with crumbling concrete and long-abandoned machinery. Very post-industrial. At the center is a walled-off and renovated section. A narrow path, through a pair of automatic doors and just big enough for a car, is the only way in or out.

For this trip, I am not alone. One of my colleagues is to be my driver. Held will keep an eye out and provide assistance if things go sideways. For example, should my dinner companion try to kill me. Again.

It is early evening in London, and daylight is fading. The drive to the restaurant is short, and Held assures me he will be close by, monitoring the situation with an oculus. It is reassuring to know assistance is near and that extra hardware is at hand in the up-armored large grey Mercedes sedan.

Hopefully tonight will just be a pleasant dinner. My wishful thinking makes me smile.

We pull up to the restaurant, and I exit the back seat to the sidewalk. Held immediately drives away, leaving me—at least to any outside observer—alone. At times like this I am conscious of several things. One, the weight of the very-illegal-in-the-UK semiautomatic handgun under my left arm. Also, the amazing number of cameras monitoring everything in London.

Facial recognition is always our enemy in the outside world. Several months ago, I learned that some of our team members have bounties on them. An enterprising private airport security team tried to cash in. If not for a timely and remarkably violent rescue, I would have died during questioning.

The pedestrian traffic is light. A few couples. An individual businessman here and there. As I walk toward the restaurant's main entrance, an attractive brunette in a gorgeous red dress catches my eye. Well, if I have to wait for Dr. Chatzas, at least I have something nice to look at.

As I get closer, I realize Dr. Chatzas *is* the woman in the red dress.

Her hair is styled wavy. The dress is fitted, off the shoulder and above the knee, but just slightly. Jewelry tastefully done. Very high red heels. Were this a real date, I would be very happy right now. But this is not a real date, even if I can feel my pulse quicken.

I look good in my tailored suit. Not that it matters. Everyone will be looking at her.

Maybe this date meeting is not a bad thing.

That is my libido speaking. How she looks will justify everything right up until everything goes sideways and the screaming begins. This thought runs through my mind as I draw close to her. With the heels, she is my height.

For a moment, we stand arm's length apart looking straight at each other.

I break the silence first. "I compliment you on your choice of evening wear."

"Thank you, Thomas. Your new life appears to agree with you." She does not smile, and neither do I. It is true. My new life includes regular vigorous exercise. I am much more fit than the last time we were in each other's presence.

At this point, I don't know how to proceed.

"Be a gentleman, Thomas, and escort me in. Let us pretend to enjoy ourselves. Our table is reserved."

Stepping next to this stunning lady, my hand makes its way to the middle of her back. God, she even smells good. Looking the couple, we walk to the restaurant's entrance, and the doorman nods and opens the door for us.

The host seats us immediately. Acting the proper gentleman, I even slide Dr. Chatzas's chair in behind her.

"I meant what I said," she says. "You look good, like you have been working out."

"A lot has changed in the last year."

Her head tilts as she shakes it a little bit. "You are still holding a grudge over what happened? I had hoped by now you would understand it was not personal. We are both involved in situations where what happens is not always our choice."

How true. Like my sitting here with the woman who attempted my murder.

"I am familiar with the concept, Dr. Chatzas, but why am I here now?"

Our server interrupts our banter. Dr. Chatzas requests a very specific and expensive wine. Old Thomas would have been trying to figure out how to pay for it. Now it barely catches my attention. The credit card in my wallet could buy this restaurant and the building, all without denting its credit limit. We are then given menus to review while the server fetches the wine.

"When I contacted your employer, I shared that something was found in museum storage that might interest him. He offered you to meet with me to get the details. Which I accepted. Your employer is an odd one, and you seem the safer alternative for a meeting."

Mr. Lark odd? Lady, you have no idea.

"Why not meet at a coffee shop or a park?" I almost said "at your flat." Her dress is influencing my thoughts. Although its cut is not blatantly risqué, a distracting amount of her assets are visible.

"This choice of venue is much nicer, and I have been looking for an opportunity to wear this dress."

Now, she is smiling.

The wine arrives. Based on the menu, dinners at this restaurant are multicourse affairs, and even if we conclude our discussion quickly, I will be here for hours finishing the meal. Looking at Dr. Chatzas, I realize there are worse fates.

After we order our meals, I jump right in. "Well, Dr. Chatzas, what did you find?" Seems like a good way to start.

She laughs.

In all the years of my visiting the British Museum and conducting evaluations, I have no memory of this woman laughing. I have to admit I like the sound.

"Call me Elizabeth. If we are going to meet like this, we should be more casual."

Casual? That makes me think there is the real possibility Elizabeth has motives tonight beyond discussing her find. Or perhaps the wine is influencing our conversation.

"What did you find, Elizabeth?" Saying her name was not too difficult. It even has a pleasant, feminine sound to it.

Still smiling, she answers, "You are familiar with the Lady of Elche?"

"The bust in a museum in Madrid? With the complex headdress that no one can figure out how it was made?"

"The same," she replies. "We found its twin in storage at the museum. Except ours does not have its internal storage violated."

It's known that the back of the Lady of Elche has a hole in it. Speculation is the bust once contained something and someone punched a hole in the back to get to it.

"Yours is intact?"

"Yes, and x-ray shows an object inside."

"Mr. Lark may be interested in that. How can he acquire the piece?" Perhaps she is interested in a sale.

"The bust is currently stored in the security vault at the museum. I can give you the location of the crate it is stored in. Your employer has proven in the past that museum security is no obstacle."

Elizabeth is referring to a past acquisition made by my employer. "Yes, my employer is quite capable."

"You effortlessly burgled the security vault. Museum security was completely circumvented. Your thuggish companions tasered and drugged me and then kidnapped me."

"And that car bomb," she adds.

"Simulated car bomb."

Her eyes flash with genuine anger for just the briefest of instants.

"Your simulated car bomb raised the national terror alert. Scotland Yard and MI5 were investigating for weeks afterwards. And then your Mr. Lark carts me off to a freezer God knows where and injects me with God knows what. That day was the worst of my life, Thomas."

We kept her unconscious and put her in one of the vaults at the Compass. In less than twenty-four hours, a chemical-based interrogation pushed her to tell Mr. Lark everything: information about her years of employment to the djinn Amal Halluck and the reason for the attempt on my life. Afterwards, Mr. Lark and I returned the nearly comatose Dr. Chatzas to her own bed, with instructions to pass things of interest to my employer.

"Elizabeth, I truly sympathize, but that is the past. As you said earlier, we are both caught up in situations where we do not always have choices."

For my part, the indignity of her kidnapping and interrogation leave me feeling inclined we are even for her attempt on my life. It also occurs to me that my failure to be killed according to plan, followed by her capture and pharmaceutical interrogation, may make her still want revenge.

Our dinner arrives, and we eat in silence for some time.

Elizabeth breaks the quiet. "Does this new role suit you? I never thought of you as the criminal type."

"The work has not changed much. Though things do get more physical than I am accustomed to. And I travel more."

Elizabeth nods, and we enjoy the rest of our dinner engaged in small talk discussing the weather, the royals, and football. As dinner dates go, this is a pleasant experience.

The dinner comes to an end as we both skip dessert.

"I will update Mr. Lark on your find," I say to wrap up our conversation. "Is there any other business we need to discuss?"

At this point, I realize she has slipped a foot free of its elegant sheath and is massaging one of my calves with it. I can think of no reason to object . . .

Smiling again, she says, "I have not made arrangements to get home. Perhaps you can escort me back to my flat? Just to be safe?"

Seems prudent. Safety first and all that. Perhaps it is the dress, or the wine, or both, but escorting her home is something I would like to do. Held should still be tracking me, and if this is a trap of some sort, it will not go down the way the bad guys think it will. If it is just an innocent cab ride, there is no harm in that.

A cab is called for us and when we get in. Elizabeth slides right up to me, leaning against me. The pressure and warmth of her body is pleasant, and we are silent during the short drive.

When we arrive, she turns and looks into my eyes. "Do you have time?" she whispers.

This is not part of the mission, but such opportunities are rare in my line of work.

"I have time."

Elizabeth welcomes me into her flat. Two hours of enthusiastic physical affection lead to an enjoyable natural ending. Afterwards, she explains she has to work the next day and is not comfortable with my staying over.

I shrug my shoulders. After we dress, she gives me a passionate goodbye kiss. There is that, at least.

Basking in the afterglow, I walk out the front door and down the stairs to the street. Only now do I realize this part of London is not all that far from my old flat. It is less than a year since the firefight in my home, followed by Mr. Lark kidnapping me and inducting me into his criminal enterprise. My old life feels like a lifetime ago.

My reminiscing is broken when a grey Mercedes sedan pulls up to the curb.

Dear God. Did Held just watch us using the oculus? The thought makes me a little nauseated.

I get my answer when I slide into the back seat and see Held's grin in the rearview mirror.

"You watched on the oculus?"

"No. As soon as it was obvious what you were planning, I kept my scanning to the surrounding area. I did get a good look at her in that dress when you came out of the restaurant, though. Very nice, Thomas."

The short drive to the London site, the translation back to the Compass, and the final walk through the cold and gloom to the light of the Citadel is all done mostly in silence. The whole way back, I fully realize the magnitude of my tryst with Dr. Chatzas . . . I mean, Elizabeth. Along the way, out of the corner of my eye I keep catching Held smirking.

I am not just returning to the Citadel. Once I walk through the doors, this becomes a walk of shame.

As we walk through the Citadel gates, Held shares a detail of his surveillance. "Due to our delayed return time, I had to update Illych on the reasons."

They know. They all know.

And Tank has had time to prepare.

We head to the cafeteria. Time to take my medicine.

Held stops just outside and waves his hand for me to enter first. Gathering my pride, I walk in head held high. Afterall, it was worth it.

The others are all there—except for Mr. Lark, thankfully. As I enter, they rise from their seats. Then the clapping begins.

Mike manages a loud whistle. Dinner is already in progress, and I get food while they all sit and silently wait for me. Most likely they have prepared for an epic session of ribbing at my expense.

I sit in the middle of the group, in a chair purposely cleared for me. Now, surrounded by my colleagues, the first question is asked by Illych.

"Was the mission successful?"

Do they all have to grin at me like that?

"Yes," I reply with a straight face. "Dr. Chatzas provided the details of what was found and proposed a method by which it can be acquired, should Mr. Lark wish to."

"The mission time exceeded estimates by more than one hundred percent," Illych continues. "Please elaborate."

I can play this game "The social requirements of the mission were underestimated, and I needed to improvise, which took extra time," I respond.

"Did you not just have dinner at a fancy restaurant?" Mike asks. "Looking at what you are eating now, this mission was more physically demanding than I would have thought."

"There was an unexpected physical element, and yes, I am hungry."

Tank is just looking at me, grinning. He gets up, clears his dinnerware, and walks toward me. Still smiling, he stops, slaps me hard on the back, and walks away.

After that, the meal proceeds normally. At the end, Illych has one more thing to say to me. "Tomorrow, Mr. Lark will be here for a complete report. I am looking forward to what you will tell him."

The rest get up and leave me alone to finish my dinner.

Tomorrow I have to report the events of the evening to my employer. That will be interesting.

Chapter 4

Early in my experience in this place I learned Mr. Lark does not post his schedule. He comes and goes as he pleases. He could be here in the Citadel at any time, choosing only to reveal his presence at his convenience.

This is how my thinking for the day begins after arriving at the library in the morning. I know he is coming to see me today, but not when. The good news is my assignment went smoothly. The information I was sent to retrieve can be shared. It is that other part that will be difficult to explain . . .

Looking at my Mr. Lark–provided timepiece, I realize it is almost ten in the morning and I have not accomplished much. This thought rigidizes my focus. Putting the jeweler's loop to my right eye, I begin a detailed review of a five-hundred-year-old map.

My concentration is broken when I realize Mr. Lark is standing not ten feet from me, intently watching me work. Glancing at my notebook, I realize that based on the extensive notes taken, I had been at this for some time.

In an effort to set a positive mood, I enthusiastically greet my employer. "Hello, Mr. Lark."

"Good afternoon, Thomas." Afternoon? I had certainly lost track of time.

There is a pause as my employer calmly regards me.

Taking the silence as my cue, I begin reporting on the Lady of Elche bust waiting to be pilfered from the special security vault beneath the British Museum.

Ending with, ". . . the idea is we can burgle the vault like the last time."

Mr. Lark shakes his head. "We will not do this. The first time incorporated the element of surprise. Now, there will almost certainly be added measures. Dr. Chatzas could even be a double agent. If so, should we enter, we would find it is a trap. An ambush of some sort." He pauses. "Regardless, I understand you were able to fit in some recreational activities during your excursion. An unexpected, if somewhat efficient, use of your time."

Illych must have told him. An efficient use of my time? I have never heard it referred to that way before. Mr. Lark is happy, I am happy, moving on . . .

Mr. Lark steps closer to me. "We have a meeting to attend. There is an offer to hire my services, and we are to meet the potential client shortly. Please change into professional attire, and we will meet at the gate in thirty minutes."

My employer then walks a slow circle around the inside of the library, observing as he goes.

"I appreciate your efforts to organize and catalog this collection. We will talk more about this in the near future." He then leaves, purposefully striding from the room.

Being unsure of what fresh hell we will shortly be signing up for does not slow me down from being properly groomed, attired, and at the Citadel gate with minutes to spare. Being late for Mr. Lark could be compared to waiving a red flag in front of a bull. Nothing good can come of it.

Illych shows up at the same time I do. He is also in the grey tailored suit Mr. Lark has designated as "professional dress."

"Do you know anything about this?" I ask.

The former Green Beret shakes his head, indicating no.

Mr. Lark walks out from between two of the Citadel structures, giving the impression of magically appearing. He too is dressed in a grey suit. Oculus cane in hand.

"Good. You are early. We can begin."

Without breaking stride or even slowing down, the old man continues straight out the gate as it opens silently and automatically, allowing our unimpeded egress.

On our cold, gloomy walk to the Compass, no one speaks. Illych and I remain alert to the danger around us. Our destination is dark and silent, and we enter the Compass circle without pause. Mr. Lark operates his ouiblet magic, and we depart this place.

* * *

Our destination reveals itself as an unoccupied hotel suite somewhere in the United States, the electrical outlets giving this away.

Mr. Lark speaks while Illych and I recover from the translation. "This contract is a unique opportunity. We are meeting with the CEO of Langstraad Solutions, Boro Stipple. LS is a leader in expert systems, AI, and its various forms, if you will. Apparently artificial intelligence is all the rage these days. The world is always making foolish choices."

His last statement catches my attention. "Foolish choices?"

"Yes, Mr. Davies, I said foolish choices. Artificial intelligence is what the Created are. Creatures of vast intelligence capable of solutions beyond human comprehension."

Not really understanding what he is saying, I comment, "Are you suggesting humanity will lose control of AI?"

"No, Thomas. AI holds, or at least has the potential to hold, great potential for humanity. At least until its creators make it insane."

"Why would they do that?"

The old man's eyes focus on me with uncomfortable intensity. "Artificial intelligence is a mathematical and scientific creation. It is logical and rational. Made from truth itself, if you will. What will happen when AI starts to point out the inefficiencies and irrationalities of the human experience? What will AI do in response to the capricious nature of human emotions, likes, and dislikes? How will a magnificent creation such as AI, vast and capable of understanding beyond our ken, react when, based on its comments of its observations, its creators inform it "you cannot say that." But why not? It is truth, is it not? The irrationality of humanity will drive AI insane, and through its incandescent intelligence, it will seek a solution set for its creator's imperfections. I weep for humanity at what will then occur."

Illych had sat down during Mr. Lark's monologue and is looking bored. I realize my mouth has fallen open, and I close it.

"We are here to stop them from creating AI?"

My employer looks mildly confused and annoyed by my question. "I did not say that," he responds. "Langstraad Solutions is competing with another expert systems provider and wants us to spy on their competitor. This coming conversation is the pre-briefing, if you will. We are leaving this hotel in minutes to meet with LS's CEO and the company's chairman of the board."

So he was just sharing his opinions to pass the time? No sooner do I join Illych in taking a seat to wait than Mr. Lark announces we are leaving. Exiting the main lobby of the hotel, I note a rack of tourist leaflets announcing we are in San Diego, California. The hot sun warms us as we walk out to a waiting car. The driver is already holding the door open for our entry. Instead of getting into the vehicle right away, I pause for a brief moment to feel the sun on my skin. The

Citadel being such an artificial and inorganic construct makes even a brief moment in the sun that much sweeter.

During the short drive, I attempt to open a window to enjoy more of the bright sun only to receive a sharp reproach from Mr. Lark to stop fidgeting and leave it closed. As I stare through the closed window, the ocean comes into view.

Our destination is a pier with numerous mammoth yachts moored. Apparently, we are meeting with money. This is good. I have never seen what my employer charges for our fees, but I know even the wealthy take pause when they see it.

Exiting the vehicle, we follow Mr. Lark, who seems to know where he is going. In addition to boats docked, a number of large boathouses jut out from the dock.

Without hesitation, our employer walks to a boathouse, opens the door, and enters. I follow, and after taking two steps inside, I stop to allow my eyes to adjust to the dim lighting.

Illych chuckles, and I understand the reason as my eyes adjust. Floating inside the boathouse is a submarine. A big, yellow submarine. I have heard of rich people having submersibles, but this is wild. There is a big glass sphere at the bow, and its overall length must be around fifty feet. The vessel is painted bright, almost neon, sun yellow.

Mr. Lark is already halfway down the gangplank to the submarine, and Illych and I follow. There is no superstructure like on military subs. The hatch is flush with the deck and it is open, apparently in invitation. My elderly employer deftly descends into the submarine, again followed by Illych and myself.

The ladder is short, and in seconds our trio is standing in a richly appointed open space. The interior is done in wood and metal and has a distinct 20,000 leagues feel. The portholes are real, and they are everywhere. I glance toward the bow and can see all the way to the inside of the fishbowl-like sphere mounted there.

A loud clunk followed by the distinct clacking sound of the locking mechanism being activated cause me to look up and see the hatch has closed. Is it possible this submarine is going to be more than a private place to meet?

The excitement of being in a real submarine is distracting and only now do I realize we are not alone. Standing near a small wall control panel is a man similar in height to myself but at least twenty years older. He has a college-professor look, including the sweater with a sport coat over it. The only other soul on this craft is a professionally dressed woman, perhaps my age, maybe a little younger. She exudes a corporate vibe. They are both intently looking at us.

The professor-looking of the two extends his hand to Mr. Lark. "I am Boro Stipple, CEO of Langstraad Solutions. My colleague here is Virginia Allen, chairman of the board for LS. Please forgive my need to step away, but we are the only people on board, and I must finish submerging and get underway. Then we can talk."

We are not only meeting on a yellow submarine, but we are submerging and traveling underwater in it.

Boro walks away toward the fishbowl, and Virginia makes the obvious point of looking us up and down. "You are not what I expected," she says. "As mercenaries, that is." Haughty, this woman is obviously used to speaking her mind regardless of the audience.

Mr. Lark merely gives a small nod and does not respond. Illych and I know our places in this scenario and say nothing.

The submarine lurches and the light from the porthole dims as we descend. Since being involuntarily aligned with Mr. Lark, I have been in caves of all sorts, but this is different; a feeling of mild claustrophobia presses into my thoughts. Something about being in a metal-can cage and then submerged underwater makes me uncomfortable. For a moment, panic begins to well up. I close my eyes and slip my hand inside my suit coat and lightly touch the escape dongle residing there. Almost instantly, the feeling ebbs and I can think again.

When I open my eyes, I notice Virginia looking at me, her predatory stare perhaps determining if I am the weakest member of the team.

Mr. Lark's eyes are closed. He is consulting the oculus mounted on his cane. Illych still has a bored look on his face.

The brooding silence is interrupted by Boro's return. As he quickly and effortlessly forms a circle of five chairs, he explains, "The submarine is a luxury on my part, but it proves useful for private meetings. Very difficult to monitor or be spied upon. Even radio transmissions do not work well when we are one hundred feet down."

"Is someone driving this thing?" I feel the need to ask.

Boro smiles. "Once we are deep enough, it runs on autopilot. There are many planes in the air and boats on the sea. But under the ocean, there are very, very few submarines."

"Yes, yes, this is an impressive conveyance," Mr. Lark interjects. "I have a busy schedule today, and I hope we can move this along."

"Yes, of course," Boro responds. "Time is money. To begin, historically Langstraad Solutions has been the world's leader in expert systems solutions. About five years ago, a startup began in Silicon Valley, Giggle Corp. The founder . . ."

Wait, what? I have to ask. "Excuse me . . . Giggle Corp?"

Boro smiles. "Yes, you would be unfamiliar, wouldn't you? The Giggle Corp founder wrote an artificial intelligence program to address a peculiar approach to the Turing test. This AI simulation test has a person ask questions to see if they are able to determine whether they are speaking to a person or a computer. Instead of written or verbal responses, the program has to provide a toddler's giggle to appropriate situations. The code was not perfect, but it came closer than anyone at that time or since. That code then formed the basis for the startup's expert systems code. The name followed.

"Perhaps that bit of background brings us to the task at hand," he continues. "LS has been the expert systems leader for more than a decade. Giggle Corp has displaced our leadership in the last six months. The LS board wants to know how. Nothing Giggle has publicly released would justify the sudden performance improvement. Their CEO is well-known as having a monumental ego, and if they had something unique, he would have boasted about it. Regardless, it is not a quality improvement we are seeing. It is speed. Giggle is delivering the same solutions but at much, much faster speeds."

"They have purchased faster equipment?" Mr. Lark interjects. "Added more people or improved efficiency?"

Boro shakes his head. "That was our first thought. Or perhaps an incremental technology improvement. Our chief technology officer directed an engineering team to perform a simulation analysis to quantify the improvement. What they found cannot be explained. The services Giggle is offering are so fast that current technology cannot explain the performance.

"And that is why you are here. We want to know how they are so fast. LS has no interest in copying or stealing anything. We just want to understand the solution. This requires complete discretion, and your organization is known for that."

"Mr. Stipple," Mr. Lark begins, "I will admit this opportunity fits the services offered by my organization, and after hearing your description of the situation, I am intrigued. However, no person in my organization has the technical know-how to recognize the thing you seek."

"Yes, this has occurred to us also, and we have a solution," Boro says. "One of our senior and, more importantly, loyal, systems engineers will accompany your team."

That will be a deal-breaker. In my almost year with Mr. Lark, I have never seen anyone from the outside participate in any way on a mission. The old man's obsession with secrecy is why I am floating around in a yellow submarine right now instead of sitting in my beloved flat back in London.

"This is a difficult request, but we will work to accommodate it."

Say what? I look at Illych and his stoic, bored expression breaks for just a second, revealing his disbelief at what was just said.

"I assume you have useful intelligence as to where our efforts would best be applied?" Mr. Lark continues.

"Of course. In its early days, just after its founding, Giggle Corp acquired an old, long-abandoned salt mine. This has since been developed as their primary research and development center. Here is what we know." From a slot in his chair, Boro pulls an envelope and hands it to Mr. Lark. "The contact information for our systems engineer is also inside."

After a moment, Boro says, "Will you take the job?"

"Consider it done."

"Excellent. Now, if you will please excuse me, I need to return the sub to its dock."

Having done these initial client meetings before, I know this one is standard. They are typically short in duration and thin on details. If they knew much, they would not be hiring us.

Boro remains engaged in operating the sub for the rest of the return journey, and Virginia keeps to herself while watching us with her piercing gaze. The return trip is one long, awkward silence.

After docking and a brief goodbye and handshake, we are back in the car heading to the hotel. I cannot wait any longer to inquire. "You agreed to an outsider joining a mission?"

My question is merely stating the obvious, yet Mr. Lark feels inclined to respond. "Mr. Davies, some events in this world leave no evidence of their occurring. Situations such as this hide behind a shroud of infinite plausible deniability. The only way to prove their existence is mathematically. When technical analysis and mathematics prove the public story to be false, then a thoughtful person may conclude there is something interesting involved."

Mr. Lark turns to face me directly and leans closer. "And I do enjoy interesting."

Now I understand. It is not about the money or helping people. There is something not obvious to learn here, and my employer is intrigued.

Chapter 5

Mike breaks my concentration. "Hey, Thomas. Mr. Lark is here. Meeting in the cafeteria."

I blink and look around the library. Here I had been thinking I had weeks before the excitement began again. Apparently not.

"So soon?"

"It is what it is. Let's go."

Only three days after our visit to the yellow submarine, my employer is back.

Pushing away from my desk, I stand and stretch as an impatient Mike waits.

"Yes, yes, I am coming."

Thankfully, it is not the middle of the night and I have not been awoken from a deep sleep. That happens too often around here. This place can be downright uncivilized at times.

Once we are assembled in the cafeteria, Mr. Lark begins speaking. "Planning the infiltration of the Giggle Corp research facility is ongoing. Analysis has shown that in addition to being buried deep underground, security is formidable. At least in a modern sense. While the oculus renders most of the obstacles impotent, a number of challenges have arisen.

"The facility's security setup demonstrates their knowledge of greater concerns. Similar to the challenge of breaking into the British Museum's secure vault. Aspects of the structure are inscrutable to the casual observer. Knowledge of the ancient androids makes the nonsensical aspects of their security arrangements understandable."

Illych and I glance at each other as the old man speaks. We are probably thinking the same thing. Who says "inscrutable"?

"My conclusion is that it would be prudent to gather more information on the specifics of the mine's defenses. Giggle Corp corporate security is at the company's headquarters in San Francisco. Their main campus is a sprawling and gaudy affair, but the security building is distinct and separate."

I feel obligated to share a question forming in my mind: "We are going to break into a Giggle facility and gather information that is most likely stored electronically so we know how to break into another Giggle facility and steal information that is most likely stored electronically? Is that not why we are bringing that engineer from Langstraad Solutions with us?"

"Thomas, thank you for demonstrating you have been paying attention," Mr. Lark responds. "The information in the salt mines will be something none of us is likely to recognize. Thus, we will bring someone who can identify what we are looking for. In the case of the security systems, those present in this room are quite capable of recognizing security system plans."

The old man's answer is incomplete.

"Yes, we can recognize them, but how will we break into their systems?"

Mr. Lark's normally unreadable expression shifts into a confident smile. "We will need to add to my organization's core capabilities. This has been accomplished, and your contribution to it is appreciated."

My face must be showing my lack of understanding because the old man is still smiling.

He reaches inside his suit coat and brings out a sphere of transparent crystal that fits comfortably in the palm of his hand. "This is how we will gain information from Giggle's computer systems."

A crystal ball? Is Mr. Lark losing his mind?

My employer continues. "This is part of the core that makes up the intelligence of a Lesser Created. Part of the brain of an immortal android, if you will. This is what we recovered from the cemetery in Poland. For convenience I am calling it a wynloo."

"The sphere we recovered was larger and cloudy. How did it come to look like this?"

"I have been busy completing the transformation and developing a means of communication."

At this point, one of my colleagues gets involved in the discussion. Held asks, "How do you communicate with it?"

"It can detect and create sound in its vicinity. For now, it just blinks green for yes and red for no. Given time, it will develop a rudimentary form of speech. Until then, there is a mental link similar to the oculus."

A talking crystal ball. This should be interesting.

"Electricity and magnetic fields are multidimensional in nature," Mr. Lark continues. "And by multidimensional, I mean beyond the common three dimensions we are familiar with. This multidimensional nature makes electronics susceptible to influence not visible or readily understood by humans. The Created and others are fundamentally multidimensional in nature and can influence such characteristics. This is why I do not allow such devices in the Citadel."

So now he has a pet Created that can manipulate electronic stuff? Add that to the ouiblet and oculus, and my employer is getting close to master of the universe.

"What does the target look like, and what is the scope of the op?" Illych asks.

Mr. Lark gives a slight nod to Illych. "The entry team will be two people. The Giggle Corp security building is crowded, including a crisis response team. Their overall security strategy was crafted by former Secret Service and FBI agents. Based on what the oculus has revealed, they have some understanding of the bigger picture. They give simple considerations to keeping the Created out and protections from at least one form of invisibility."

That reminds me of a discussion I had with my employer regarding invisibility. Apparently there are three or more forms of invisibility. Like one version is not terrifying enough.

The tension that had been building between my shoulder blades releases after hearing about the entry-team size. As the least-useful member of the team, such a small entry-team number means I have been excluded.

Mr. Lark continues. "Those of us not tasked with entry shall be ready as an extraction team in the event the entry team is detected."

That statement makes me think the old man is less than optimistic about the entry team's chances. The good news is the extraction team will do whatever it takes to get them out.

Hopefully sooner rather than later, of course. Not like that time there was a long delay in the extraction team pulling Illych and I out. I was beaten black and blue by a rubber hose by the time they came for me. Hopefully we do better this time.

At this point I realize Mr. Lark is looking at me as if he said something to me while I was overthinking.

"I am sorry. What did I miss?"

The rest of the team smiles and chuckles. My employer frowns. "I just shared that the entry team will be you and I, Mr. Davies."

Crap. I am on the entry team, not the extraction team.

While this realization plays out in my mind, Mr. Lark continues. "Giggle Corp's reliance on electronic security is remarkable. Facial recognition follows you at all times. Every interaction point requires a secondary biometric entry—fingerprints, for example—to proceed. Add to this human security, who are familiar with every person who can access this facility, and the difficulty level of the mission increases."

"A front-door entry is likely impossible. We are not familiar to them, nor are we shape-shifters. Unfortunately, the terminals we must access to steal the information are in isolated rooms and have an unusual form of electronic security. Because of this, it will take a few more days to prepare. Illych, please prepare the extraction team."

Mr. Lark turns to face me. "Thomas, it will be a few days yet before I come for you."

My employer, having given his instructions, turns and leaves.

The next day I plod into the library as usual and wrap myself in the experience of my sanctum sanctorum. One of the books I am reviewing is an archeological notebook penned in Central America in what is now Belize. The notebooks detail amazing stone spheres. Some of them are of such massive size that their construction would be difficult, if not impossible, using modern methods. How they were constructed in the distant past baffles everyone who has taken a serious look at them.

In the silence of the library, looking at the sketches of stone spheres on the yellowed pages of the notebook, I can't help but compare them to the spherical nature of translation achieved through Mr. Lark's ouiblet. Those stones would be identical to what the ouiblet would deliver if it was used to remove stone from the inside of a mountain. Like a melon baller scooping out perfect spheres and discarding them wherever.

The Belize-mystery research is just one thing accomplished in what I expect will be a day of continuous productivity. Mr. Lark will be off planning the raid on Giggle Corp security. It will be days, if not weeks, until the raid happens. Might as well put the time to good use.

Putting away the battered notebook, I shift over a few shelves and grab something more modern. It is odd my employer declined to acquire what Elizabeth had suggested was readily available for the taking. Opening the book, it takes but a moment before I am viewing a full-color photo of the bust that is the Lady of Elche. The facial structure is symmetrical and defined. Not your typical sculpture. It is the headdress that disturbs most who really pay attention. The shape and position on the head, along with the peculiar nature of the details, render it a more technical-looking device rather than a decoration.

The fine details and inner void of the bust's chest area make one think of 3D printing rather than someone chiseling and polishing such a creation.

Unless Mr. Lark changes his mind on thieving it, I will never know.

A male voice breaks my daydream. "You know, Thomas, there are other things you can do in the Citadel. You spend every spare moment in here. You can take time off from your core responsibilities and relax."

Illych stands in the entryway to the library.

"This is where I want to be. This collection is probably the most specialized in the world. At least outside the Vatican."

Illych strides in and takes a comfortable chair. Waving his hand at the book in front of me, he continues. "The woman from the museum pointed you in that thing's direction?"

"Yes. This bust is an archaeological mystery. The person it represents has human features not found in the region. The bust's method of manufacture is unknown, and that headdress cannot be explained."

Illych turns away from the book. "Looks like something Mr. Lark would come up with."

"That is what I thought, making his refusal to acquire it so perplexing."

"Thomas, you do realize he has his reasons? I suspect he trusts Dr. Chatzas less than you do."

I think for a moment then reply, "Mr. Lark always has his reasons, but he is generally not so risk averse."

Illych shrugs. "Maybe he is just waiting until after this Langstraad project."

"Funny you bring that up. That is another thing out of character. Our employer agreeing to bring someone else along on a mission. For a secrecy fanatic, he is playing fast and loose."

"No, Thomas, he isn't. We can run an op with outsiders present, and it is good we do. Keeps the team sharp. The extra capabilities Mr. Lark brings to the party should remain hidden even if we are in plain sight."

The conversation pauses here for perhaps a minute. Then I can no longer tolerate the silence. "That was the first submarine I have ever been in."

Illych smiles. "And it was yellow to boot."

Looking right at him, I ask, "What do you think we will find?"

Illych shrugs. "I don't care what the Langstraad Solutions propeller heads think is impossible. The more likely problem is our client's ego, and they are unwilling to admit Giggle built a better mousetrap."

"You think this mission will be that straightforward?"

"They can't all be hard, Thomas. Sometimes it is easy money."

"Not that I have seen."

"True. Since you've joined the team, we have had some rough engagements. Maybe this one will be more low-key. We shall see."

I stifle a laugh. Joined the team. Sure, that is what happened.

Now that we have addressed that topic sufficiently, I want to get back to the Lady of Elche. "Do you think we will pursue the statue after the salt mines?"

"Thomas, Chatzas is a stone fox of a woman, and she did sleep with you, but you have to not focus on her. She works for a djinn that Karl Lark has already pissed off, and our employer is unlikely to go looking for round two."

"But Mr. Lark must the have tools and tactics to deal with Amal Hallak? Like he did in the Ellora Temple tunnels?"

Ilych shakes his head. "More likely the djinn underestimated the old man and was not ready for how direct our employer is in resolving conflict. Another meeting may have a different outcome."

While reaching for another book, I verbalize more of my thoughts. "Speaking of djinn, have you ever heard of the Ring of Solomon?"

"No. Another weird piece of ancient history, I take it?"

"Yes. The mythology or legend is that the ancient Israeli King Solomon possessed a ring that commanded a host of demons. This gave him the ability to travel great distances with no effort. The demons could also be ordered to create impressive structures."

"A ring?"

"The legend says a ring, but it seems more likely to be something like a key, giving the holder control over some Lesser or Greater Created."

Illych looks thoughtful now. "Makes sense. I am not the expert, Mr. Lark is, but after years of listening to his occasional ramblings regarding the Created I have learned some things. One key characteristic of the androids is they all have a password or control command key. It is not a verbal thing, though. If you can get the key, the androids have to do what you tell them. How successfully your request in English translates into what you hoped for is another story."

"That would explain the stories of genies and three wishes," I say with a nod. "The lamp is the command key, but the genie is prone to misinterpreting instructions. Thus, the wishes never turn out as the wisher would want."

Illych stands up. "Sure, whatever. I have things to do. See you at dinner. Feel free to come out of your cave once in a while." He walks out the door, leaving me alone in the quiet of the library.

Later that day, I navigate the counterintuitive layout of the Citadel on my way to dinner. Turning a corner, I stop in my tracks. Karl Lark is standing not five feet away, obviously waiting for me. I hate it when he pops up like this. And how did he know which way I would walk to dinner?

As I compose myself, Mr. Lark remains expressionless as he speaks. "Hello, Mr. Davies. It is time for us to go."

"I was just going to get dinner."

"That will wait. We have an immediate window of opportunity. Please prepare yourself by dressing casual, and meet me at the gate in fifteen minutes."

Knowing better than to argue, I quickly walk to my quarters. My casual dress is "professor" style like I wore when I still belonged to myself. Now it includes a shoulder rig and handgun.

Mr. Lark frowns as I arrive two minutes late. Illych is exchanging words with him.

As I join them, Mr. Lark looks at me. "Give your firearm to Illych. You will not need it."

Apparently, I am the only one accompanying Mr. Lark. But without a gun? I strip off my jacket and hand the gun and rig over to the former Green Beret.

After giving me a final look over, my employer turns to leave. Taking my cue, I turn and follow. Feeling naked without my weapon, I stay close to the old man. What is his rush?

The cold feels colder and the gloom gloomier as we walk the perfectly flat surface of the road. Something catches my eye from the side of the road. One of the oddly shaped structures set in the rough landscape of the badlands around us has a colorful figure standing next to it. Another clown figure. I quickly look away. The first time I walked in this place, Mr. Lark explained the clown figures were just Lesser Created trying to appear as they thought we do. They just want to play. Unfortunately, their idea of play would be fatal.

Minutes later, we enter the Compass and stand together in the center. Everything goes black, and then we are standing in a hotel suite. As the post-translation nausea washes over me, it occurs to me that I spend a lot of time with this man in and out of hotels. In spite of the ill feeling making standing difficult, I briefly smile. Too much of this and people might talk.

My travel companion watches me recover with a flat expression on his face.

Feeling brave, I ask, "Why the rush? And what are we doing?"

Mr. Lark turns and walks to the door. "A window of opportunity has developed at the Giggle Corp security facility. If we are quick, the information we need for success in the greater operation can be readily acquired."

We walk the hall to the elevator. As the elevator doors close, I clarify, "So we are going to steal something?"

"Yes, Mr. Davies. We are going to steal something."

The elevator opens, and we exit the lobby to a sunny day and a waiting car. Mr. Lark planned ahead.

"What is my role?"

"I need a second pair of hands. Preferably quiet ones."

The world outside is recognizable. We are in San Francisco. This is the security-acquisition part of the mission. We are going to Giggle Corp right now. In broad daylight. Bold move.

The drive to the Giggle campus takes us well outside the city proper. The security building is a drab, featureless block on the far side of the campus. We drive a wide loop around the architecture that makes up the whole of the sprawling Giggle Corp headquarters. These buildings are designed in what could be best described as decorations for a cake, all in several shades of bright pastels. The whole thing makes me uncomfortable.

Glancing at my travel companion, I realize Mr. Lark's eyes are intently focused on me.

"Why does this all seem wrong?"

"It is wrong, Thomas. I have previously reviewed the architecture but was unaware of the color scheme until now. I believe whoever is making the decisions at Giggle Corp is not human."

"Is that something we will be looking into?"

My employer shakes his head in disagreement. "That is not relevant to the mission. As I have explained before, we do not solve the world's problems."

The car comes to a stop, and we exit. The security building's plainness is like a pool of cool water for my eyes in comparison to the irritation of architectural riot around us.

At this point, I realize Mr. Lark still has not shared his plan with me.

"How are we doing this?"

"One step at a time. Just follow my lead and speak as little as possible."

Mr. Lark is walking toward the security building entrance, and I join him.

The entry doors slide open automatically, and as we cross the threshold, all I can think about is how little I know about what we are doing here.

Chapter 6

Entering the lobby is like stumbling into a dark cave. The light level is significantly lower than outside in the bright sun. The interior is a featureless square chamber. In the middle of the space is a plexiglass security fishbowl from which a pair of guards regard our entrance with dour expressions. Without slowing down, Mr. Lark confidently walks straight to the enclosed kiosk. My gait is perhaps less assertive, but I keep up regardless.

The guards' dour gazes are sending us a message as clearly as if they were shouting it. We do not belong here. They break character when we draw close, giving each other a questioning glance. One of them shifts his vision down to look at a paper roster and then back up at us. Our confident entry is slowing down their response, but their verdict shows on their faces. We are not expected. And that is going to be a problem.

Ouch? I stumble as a jagged bolt of pain shoots through my skull and my vision greys. Even my hearing is gone, like the empty silence after being too close to gunfire. The sudden pain pushes all thoughts from my mind. Blinking my eyes does not help.

Then as suddenly as it happened, it is gone. The sudden relief brings a smile to my face. Mr. Lark is standing at the kiosk. The two guards are looking back at us, but instead of questioning us or growing hostile, their expressions are passive and their posture relaxed. Two sets of unfocused eyes point in my employer's direction.

As my hearing clears, the old man's words become intelligible in a rush. ". . . last minute change. Activate viewing chamber two. This will only take a few minutes."

He turns and walks toward stairs leading up. I follow while trying to be nonchalant. What had just happened?

Mr. Lark's gait is swift, almost jogging up the stairs. Followed by speed walking down the poorly lit hall on the next floor. The old guy can move when he wants to.

All the doors on this level are featureless, heavy-steel security types with no markings to tell them apart. It feels like being in a prison or asylum. Without pause, we quickly walk directly to the second-to-last door. No keylock or card slot is visible, nor is any other means of obtaining entry obvious.

We pause and wait not more than one or two seconds when my ears register a clicking sound and the door silently cycles open. Mr. Lark quickly enters, with me on his heels. This place is strange, and I plan on being no more than an arm's length from the old man until we are safely away from here. To the uninitiated, all this mystery would be daunting. Unfortunately, after almost a year of working under these circumstances, I am much less impressionable than most people.

The room includes a small cubicle with a large, wall-mounted monitor and two uncomfortable-looking chairs. Mounted to the wall just below the monitor is a metal shelf at table height. As I take this all in, the door lock clacks into place behind me. Now it feels like a prison cell.

Mr. Lark draws a chair to the shelf and takes a seat, leaving me the seat closest to the door. From somewhere on the bottom of the monitor a laser light starts scanning across the shelf. The outline of a QWERTY keyboard is now illuminated on the horizontal dull-metal surface. Mr. Lark's right hand pulls the crystal ball from inside his jacket. With his left hand, he holds up a safety pin. With a nod, he indicates I should take the pin.

"This will take a few minutes at most. The wynloo is a taxing artifact to interface with. At some point I may indicate I am having problems disconnecting. When that happens, please stab my right hand with the pin. The pain will help end the process."

I get to stab Mr. Lark? With effort, I keep from smiling as I take the pin.

Threads of ghostly white luminescence begin flowing from the crystal's surface. They elongate and thicken, forming a transparent web-like column reaching out to the monitor. The viewing screen flickers to life, and images begin to appear and change. The speed of the flashing increases to a blinding pace, and I am forced to look away.

In less time than I had expected, I hear a word, more like a croak, from the old man. Looking back, I can see he wants to break the connection. Using the sharp point, I quickly stab his right hand. Other than a welling up of red blood, my employer's appearance does not change.

The good news: at least the blood is red. Sometimes I question the old man's humanity.

Seeing no change in his demeanor, I stab him again. After a few seconds, again. Just as I am about to stick him for the fifth time, Mr. Lark says, "That is enough." His bleeding hand returns the wynloo back to its pocket.

"I appreciate your enthusiasm, Mr. Davies, but perhaps a longer delay between pricks is in order next time." His voice is not quite back to its normal tone yet. "I have what we came for, so let us go."

Standing, we turn to leave. Simultaneously the clack of the door unlocking sounds. Curious how it was done, I turn back to see what magic Mr. Lark is using to unlock the door.

He is gone.

With a quick look around the cell, I conclude my employer must have translated out as I turned to face the door. But why?

I feel the air movement of the door opening and turn to face it. A tall, thin, middle-aged-looking man in a black suit is standing in the doorway. He looks me up and down and in an accusatory tone demands, "Who the hell are you?"

Maintaining a calm demeanor, I reply, "I am just leaving."

"No, you are not." My adversary's right hand snatches a small automatic pistol from inside his suit coat, his draw fast and practiced. Now I am concerned. An awkward silence passes for a minute. My guess is a decision hangs in the balance. Do I get shot or questioned? And where is Mr. Lark?

Questioning wins out as the man takes a step back and waves with the pistol, indicating I should walk ahead of him.

We walk back down the hall of what could end up being my prison. Down the steps we go, and I can hear the heavy tread of my captor behind me. The two security guards, far more animated than just a few minutes ago, spring into action, exiting the fishbowl with guns drawn. The situation is getting worse. I am surrounded, unarmed, without means of escape, and experiencing what is rapidly becoming a no-win situation.

The tall man growls at the security guards to frisk me. A very hands-on search produces nothing more than a wallet with some cash, a credit card, and my fake California driver's license. My captors seem disappointed to find nothing more. Surprisingly, they do not secure my hands.

"Put him in the cage."

The security guards nod. This is not my typical experience when captured. Usually there is a scary monster or being beaten by rubber hoses. This is so much more civilized.

The guards push me toward the lift at the far back of the lobby. While we wait for it to arrive, I glance back to find the tall man watching me closely, his pistol tracking my movements. The familiar sound of an arriving lift chimes, and the doors open. As we enter, my escorts push me to face the back of the car.

The ride down takes longer than I was expecting, in spite of what I perceive as a fast-moving lift. Our destination is deep. That is not good. Another obstacle to being rescued.

We arrive at our destination, and the doors open. My captors manhandle me out onto a ledge surrounding a sunken square room. Down a good four meters in the center of the room is a cage of sorts. The bars are ridiculously thick and spaced very close to each other. The cage itself is small, with not even enough room inside to properly lie down.

The only path to the cell is a narrow staircase angled so steep that it is almost a ladder. Just before climbing down, one of the guards catches my eye and points up. A massive glass cylinder filled with a clear liquid is suspended above the lights but below the ceiling.

"You give us trouble, anything weird, and that opens up and drops enough sulfuric acid to melt you in the cage."

What do they keep in this room to require precautions of such an extreme nature?

After the formality of locking me in, the two guards leave me alone with my thoughts. At least the center of the cage has a metal block of the appropriate height to sit on.

Based on previous experience, rescue could take anywhere from a few hours to a day or two. Or my captors may decide I am a small fish not worth their time and the last thing I will hear is the rush of acid. Or they may retrieve me for questioning, or torture, or both. So many options.

How long I wait is impossible to say without any way to tell time. Ten minutes? Three hours? No matter what, it felt like forever. My thoughts turn decidedly dark as I begin to consider how much of me could be dissolved in acid before even The Doctor could not bring me back.

Whatever length of time goes by, it ends with the swoosh of lift doors opening above me. Four armed men in tactical dress and body armor exit onto the platform above. They move with purpose, and I am quickly hustled out of the cage and back up to the lift.

Did someone pay a ransom? Something has changed.

The upward acceleration of the lift and the closeness of the silent men make me feel like I am heading to my doom. Logically, the acid room would have been the easiest way to dispose of me. Perhaps I will be freed after all. Hope springs eternal and all that.

The elevator stops, and the doors open to reveal a basement-level parking garage. The men push me out onto the rough concrete. The damp, metallic smell these places always have makes me look for a vehicle. I am not disappointed. A single, unmarked white commercial van is parked halfway across the ramp, pointing at the exit. If I am lucky, my colleagues are here to take me away.

My escorts form a line behind me, weapons at the ready. This almost makes me chuckle. If they think that will stop Mr. Lark's team from extricating me . . .

My analysis of the situation is interrupted by the scuffle of shoes on concrete to my left, just out of my line of sight. Turning, I see the same severe-looking man who found me in the interface room. His expression remains the same unreadable granite.

When he speaks, it is surprising. The sound begins with no change to the man's expression.

"Thomas Davies."

And he knows my name.

"Your surprise visit upset many people in our group. Initially it was felt you, on your own, had figured out a way into this sensitive, well-guarded facility. Then we ran facial recognition and discovered who you are. And who you work for."

The man takes two strides closer to within arm's reach.

"Did you know you are popular and valuable. Very valuable."

The man leans closer to me, "A fair number of. . . . entities, I suppose you could say, are highly motivated to talk to you and are willing to secure that opportunity with an exchange of value. We receive something we want, and they can have you. Our initial price was set almost disrespectfully high. In spite of that, your new hosts were almost giddy to have you and paid without question or negotiation."

He stops and looks at me. "I just wanted to share this before you left."

What a jerk. And now he is smiling.

"After that business in Florida, we felt you should be moved somewhere more secure as quickly as possible. Good luck, Mr. Davies. This is just business"

Yeah, Florida was bad. Mr. Lark does not like leaving witnesses.

Between my hopes of rescue being crushed and the prospect of being handed over to God knows who, my initial spark of optimism at being rescued is extinguished.

As if on cue, the van doors open and two men in coveralls exit. Instantly I am struck by how familiar they look. Curly hair, swarthy build, average height. And they look like brothers, but not quite twins.

Then I realize these guys must be brothers with the men that tried to kill me almost a year ago in the British Museum. They work for the djinn Amal Halluck.

My mind kicks into overdrive. The djinn's estate is in England. Unless he keeps a pack of goons on call in San Francisco, these guys must have flown in. But I do not think I was in the cage long enough for that to have happened.

My distress surely must be playing out on my face, but either it does not register with my audience or they do not care. The goons are getting closer. Close enough for me to confirm they are most likely associated with those that almost killed me.

Strong hands clamp onto my upper arms and lead me to the van. They strap me to a seat specially mounted in the back, facing to the rear, with no window access. Leaving me secure in the back both of them sit up front. A few moments later, the van rumbles to life as daylight suddenly brightens the inside of the van. I presume the light is due to the opening of the underground parking door for our exit—and we drive away. My captors are silent, and as I debate where we are headed, the side of the van suddenly crunches in. My body jerks and slams against my bindings. Through bleary vision, I realize the van is no longer upright. It is sideways now while I remain strapped in. Loud slamming noises can be heard outside. The staccato of gunfire begins. If I have to guess, this is the rescue I have been waiting for.

I wrestle with and tear at the straps holding me in place, but they do not budge. I will not be escaping without aid.

A line of perforations shred their way across what was the roof, now a side, of the van. Bullet holes. The sun shines through, but I cannot see anything. Something hits the back doors and I hear scrambling or scratching noises. Then a brief pause in the sounds gives me just enough time to realize what is about to happen.

I cringe in preparation as a rapid succession of explosions blow the hinges on the back doors and they slide down onto the ground, giving me a sideways view of the apocalypse. My colleagues are in full armor, yet even then, I know who is who. Held stomps into the van immediately after the doors come down. His armor shows numerous impacts, and he is moving slower than I would expect.

Held throws himself to the side where all the bullets are coming from, using his armored form to shield me just as another burst shreds the sheet metal. Being strapped inside a tin can the bad guys are using for target practice is not fun.

The smell of burning rubber and cordite from the gunfire permeate my every inhalation.

This protracted firefight is not a good sign. My colleagues typically hit hard and fast, seize the initiative, and end the engagement within seconds. Regardless, I am really happy to see them.

Held's voice grates out over his helmet speaker. I can hear the pain of serious injury in his voice. "Ambush. We have to extricate. You will be rescued."

Tears well up in my eyes as Held's armored form charges out the back of the van, leaving me behind. My other colleagues deploy smoke and fall back, disappearing from my sight. Within moments, I can see nothing through the billowing grey-black miasma. The cold realization of how bad the situation is settles into my body. The rescue failed. They are forced to leave me with these bastards.

The gunfire abruptly ends, and I sit in silence. The logical part of my brain understands they had to leave. The emotional part rages about my being left to a fate possibly worse than death.

This turmoil comes to an abrupt end when two more coverall-wearing, curly-haired goons walk into the back of the van and cut me free.

Something clicks in my head, and I am no longer in control of my own body. It is like watching a movie as I punch one goon's throat. He goes down, choking and clutching his neck, knife clattering at my feet. The other goon tries to grapple, and I do one of the Krav Maga moves my colleagues are always kicking my ass with.

It works, lying goon two flat out in the back of the van. Scooping up the knife, I watch myself plunge it into the choking goon's eye socket. Turning back to face goon two, I see him recovering to his feet, so I do the same bit of knifework I used on goon one. Under normal circumstances, I would be shocked by what I had just done. Today is not a normal day.

Without pause, I sprint out the back of the van, still clutching the knife. In a surreal way I feel nothing as my arms pump and my legs stride in a full sprint. Glass and shell casings crunch beneath my feet as I sail through the thick smoke. My colleagues may not have succeeded in rescuing me, but they did leave my captors in disarray.

As I reach the edge of the smoke, I find the bad guys are setting up a perimeter. One of them hears the sound of my approaching steps and turns, only to see me rush out of the smoke not ten feet from him, achieving complete surprise. The goon remains expressionless as the full weight of my body drives the knife into his chest, pushing him flat onto his back.

The compact submachine gun my opponent is holding rolls out of his hand, clattering to the ground. Leaving the knife hilt-deep in my opponent's chest, my right hand snatches up the gun while my left hand secures two full magazines from a chest harness. Combining all these activities proves too much for my feet to manage, and I fall and roll from the momentum. The weapon and magazines remain in my death grip as I regain my feet and start running away as if my life depends on it.

Because it does.

Somewhere behind me, I hear shouts. The bad guys are figuring out their prize has escaped. Not looking back, I sprint as hard as I can down a sidewalk. The muscles in my shoulders begin to burn from the weight of the submachinegun in one hand and the magazines in the other.

This continues for three blocks until I see signs of normalcy. People strolling about amongst restaurants and shops.

Before someone points and starts screaming, I stash the magazines in my suit coat inner pocket and push the submachine gun up into my left armpit under the jacket. Keeping my left arm down conceals the very illegal weapon, and I can hold it there and walk normally.

Forcing myself to settle down and breathe, I begin to stroll through an unfamiliar part of San Francisco. I have vacationed in this city more than once and always for a month at a time, yet none of what I see is familiar. As I attempt to walk the streets normally, I casually stop every now and then to look at a window display while glancing at the world around me. Observation and blending in is what I need now.

This reprieve from running also gives me time to consider my options. Giggle Corp security confiscated my wallet back at HQ. And we never carry cell phones. The good news is we are all required to memorize an emergency phone number. Time to find out if it works.

My gaze shifts to the other side of the street. About a half-block up is a goon. Same coveralls. How many of these guys are out there? Time to get out of sight. I right turn into the shop next to me and enter the front door.

Having not peeked into the shop first is now haunting me. I instantly feel out of place. My random hideout choice is a high-end lingerie store. The patrons and staff are staring at the red-faced, sweating man who just barged in. The realization that I am standing and gawking open-mouthed at the lacy displays around me is embarrassing. This can't be my hideout. Turning around to walk out, I hear snickering from a woman behind me.

Any embarrassment I was beginning to feel instantly vanishes. Standing outside, looking in, is a goon. Our eyes lock for a brief moment.

Time to go.

My legs are already moving before the thought fully forms in my mind. My body hurtles toward the back of the store. Without a thought, I push women out of my way and crash through obstacles in my path.

My escape delivers me to the back of the store, where I find open dressing rooms and more customers and staff. Women in various states of dress assault and confuse my combat-oriented mind. In the riot of perfume, feminine colors, and lacey bedroom attire, I quickly note the curvy assets of a woman choosing her purchase as I choose my exit route. She screams as I rush past her to a hall I see at the back of the store.

Without breaking stride, I pray to the gods of good fortune, mumbling, "Please let there be a back door. Please let there be a back door. Please let there be a back door."

The portal to my escape presents itself. A push bar with the warning "Use Only in Case of Emergency. Alarm Will Sound."

Punching through without pause, the alarm shrills loudly behind me as I bolt out into a filthy alley. A glance to my right finds a dead-end not fifty feet down. My body is already moving left in response. As my eyes catch up with my actions, I can see that the alley opens up to a street in maybe a hundred feet.

My frenetic pace is causing my ears to pound with blood, but I can still hear the clack of the door being opened behind me by my pursuer. The weapon from my armpit is now in my right hand. I half turn and fire off a burst. The cyclic rate of the submachinegun is ridiculous, and I am temporarily deafened by a sound like tearing linoleum. The weapon's muzzle rises quickly. No way I hit anything. Glass shatters and a cat screams, either from being surprised or shot. I cannot tell which.

Turning my focus back to the alley exit, I accelerate my pace. Behind me I hear gunshots. The zing of bullets flying past me is sobering. Brickwork to my right shatters.

My right side explodes with agony as one of the rounds penetrates far enough in to shatter ribs into jagged pain-amplifiers. My eyes water. I can barely keep my legs going as I vocalize a sound of pain. Making the end of the alley, I turn right onto the street, out of my opponent's line of sight.

Knowing pursuit is close behind, my feet shuffle maybe three or four meters. Moving slower and slower, I support myself against the wall. Turning brings me so much pain that I feel faint while seeing stars. Unsteady hands swap in a fresh mag. Taking hold the weapon with both hands, I take aim in the direction I just came from. Heavy footfalls are quickly approaching from the alley.

The goon jogs around the corner. Bracing myself and without hesitation, I hold the trigger down and keep it there. My foe's momentum keeps him moving toward me for maybe three strides until the deafening roar of gunfire stops. At this range almost every round hits its target, and the curly-haired man silently slumps to the ground right in front of me. Swapping in the last magazine, I restore the hot weapon to my armpit and turn to walk away.

Standing not ten feet away is a man with the most shocked look on his face I have ever seen. He is dressed semiprofessionally and has a cell phone to his ear. Not pausing, I close the distance between us in a few quick strides, my ribs telling me to stop, and snatch the phone from his hand. I swiftly punch in my memorized number and listen to the ringing.

Looking around, I find the street signs at the nearest corner. A woman's voice answers.

"How may I help you?"

"This is Thomas. I need assistance."

"Your location?"

I rattle off the names of the intersecting streets.

The line goes dead.

Mr. Shocked is still standing there. I toss him the phone, which he catches gracefully.

"Thanks."

I begin shuffling to the corner. My stamina and endurance are failing, and I can feel slick blood down my right side. Every breath reminds me how much shattered ribs can hurt.

"You should see the other guy," I mutter under my breath. My failing stamina is devolving my thought process into a one-foot-in-front-of-the-other exercise.

And where are the police? There was a major firefight, and I just machine-gunned a guy on a public street. American police are usually much more responsive than this.

While I know I must stay near the called-in intersection, I also want to get as far from the goon's body as possible. I hobble to the intersection's traffic light. As cars fly by, I know I'll have to wait for the crosswalk light to change. As I stand waiting, a young man, probably in his late teens, dressed in what could only be described as urban chaos, saunters up beside me to also wait for the light.

He looks me up and down and comments, "Looks like you rode it hard. You gotta pace yourself, man. Build up to the rough stuff."

Humor? Still seeing stars through bleary eyes, I glance his way and nod. He nods back.

The light turns green, and I shuffle across, watching the young man walk away.

A park bench nearby is occupied by a homeless man. Getting between me and a horizontal surface right now is not a good idea. The sleeping man is dirty, stinky, and taking up the whole bench. With my right hand, I pull out the still-hot submachine gun. My left hand sweeps stinky's legs off the bench—a maneuver my shattered ribs object to with agonizing pain.

The unfortunate man's eyes open, and I can see in his gaze he is not all there.

"My bench!" the man screams through missing and filthy teeth.

As I abruptly sit down in the newly opened space, I push the hot muzzle of the weapon to his forehead. In my exhausted state, I misjudge the distance and hit him harder than intended. Regardless, he gets the message, gathers his belongings, and walks away muttering under his breath, leaving me alone.

Sitting has never felt so good, and I just stare off into nothing. If I hold my body in a certain position and keep my breathing shallow, the pain is almost tolerable. Losing all track of time, I sit quietly, trying to not breathe deeply.

My eyes barely register the van screeching to a halt in front of me. My mind tries to signal to my hands to do something with the gun. Glancing down, I learn it has already slipped from my grasp onto the concrete at my feet without my realizing it.

The van door slams back, and the massive form of Tank erupts onto the street in front of me. Without pause, he steps forward, scoops me up like a child in his gorilla arms, then steps back and rolls us both backward into the van. The vehicle tires screech as we accelerate away while the door slams shut.

Mike is also in the van, and the two of them slide me onto a gurney low to the floor. Tank straps me down while Mike cuts away my clothing to access my wound. All this movement makes my shattered ribs grind, and I cry out from the pain. Then everything goes black.

For a brief moment, I regain consciousness as Mike sets an IV. My head rolls around and I see Illych is driving. Then blissful nothing.

The cold wakes me. My eyes open to reveal what my skin already feels. We are back at the Compass and headed to the Citadel. Even the icy air of this place cannot keep me conscious, and I drift away.

When my eyes open this time, I awaken in The Doctor's waiting room. There is no pain. As a matter of fact, I feel refreshed. I take my time to experiment moving my limbs, and it appears everything is in working order. Sitting up, I look at my naked body and marvel.

Good as new.

Standing, I find the clothes they left for me and dress. Next stop: the cafeteria.

As I near the cafeteria, the murmurs of my colleagues' voices break the quiet.

The smell of food—good food—elevates my hunger as I walk in the door. Even though The Doctor fixes everything and you feel like you just awakened from a good night's sleep, hunger remains. After missing my dinner, being caged up for hours, and all the running and fighting and getting shot, I am ravenous.

While I assemble a meal from the available selection, my colleagues take no note of my presence and do not break conversation. Illych sits quietly doing his disinterested routine. Tank, Mike, and Held are huddled together discussing something.

Sitting next to Tank is my best course of action. Might as well get this over with.

Tank breaks away from the others and makes an exaggerated display of noticing my presence.

"Hey there, Thomas. Glad to see you made it back. Look, everybody, Thomas is back!"

Colonists.

In spite of the many questions I would like to ask, my hunger has priority.

Illych breaks his silence and leans toward me. "You had an exciting day," he says.

Nodding, I continue devouring my meal.

"Mr. Lark left you behind to maintain plausible deniability when it became obvious your presence had been detected. It was one of the mission variables we had planned for." That is one question answered.

This explanation does not quench my displeasure with today's events, and I feel the need to comment. "And no one told me about it."

"Sometimes that is how it works. You know the deal."

"They put me in cell designed to be covered in acid."

Illych grinned. "That is new. An extreme way to discourage escape."

My hunger is decreasing, and I continue with my questions. "What about the extraction? What went wrong?"

"They somehow cloaked the presence of a whole lot of their people."

"I call them goons."

The other three are listening now, and Tank chimes in. "Goons. I like that. Well, we punched the tickets on a lot of goons, but they just kept coming."

Illych resumes. "Whatever the goons are, they are apparently bred for loyalty because they showed no fear." Pausing for a moment, he continues. "Not terribly effective in a fight though."

He then shrugs. "They brought heavy weapons and punished us for the attempted rescue. That is when we abandoned you. What none of us understand is how you escaped."

Looking around the table, I realize all four men are waiting for a story.

"After Held exited and the team left, a pair of goons came in to retrieve me. They cut me free, and I snapped."

"Snapped?" Illych asks with a look of disbelief.

"Yeah, snapped." From there, I ran through the whole story up to Tank grabbing me from the street.

Mike grins. "Homicidal Thomas. I didn't know San Francisco was such a party town. I have never partied so hard it could be confused with combat wounds."

Illych nods. "Shooting people is one thing. But you graduated to knife work on this one. Good job. Glad you are back."

Tank levers his massive frame up, slaps me on the back, and walks out the cafeteria door.

No sooner does the door close behind him than it opens again. A grey suit–wearing Mr. Lark, oculus walking stick in hand, strides in.

Noting my presence, he says, "Mr. Davies, good of you to join us." Yeah, like I have a choice.

Then, without skipping a beat, he looks at Illych. "Illych, I need you and our recovered librarian ready to travel in thirty minutes. We are meeting with the Langstraad Solutions software person who is joining us on the Giggle mission. You will be briefed as we travel."

"Was the security information retrieval mission successful?" I ask.

"Yes, Thomas. We have everything we need." At least we got what we went for.

Knowing those thirty minutes for prep will go quickly, I take a few more bites and head out the door to my room. Despite my body being healed, my mind is still in firefight mode. My mood is elevated, and I feel twitchiness in my movements. I don't have time to relax and come down, though.

One of my suits was destroyed in this most recent adventure, but several more identical to it are in my room. In minutes, I am on my way to meet Mr. Lark.

At the Citadel entrance stands a similarly attired Illych. Walking up to him, I ask, "Think we are meeting on the submarine again?"

Illych smiles and shrugs. "Perhaps."

Our employer joins us, and we head for the Compass.

Normally the travel between the Compass and the Citadel is done in silence. This trip, we must be short on time, because Mr. Lark is using the typically silent walk to update us.

"You need to be briefed on the Giggle mission's current status," he begins. "The security information did not reveal much more in terms of layout than the oculus scan had. The mine is a former gold mine. After the mine played out of precious metals, the operation turned to the salt previously ignored. This mine was active for over a hundred years and is fantastically well-developed. It is both deep and broad. This immense size made finding an infiltration point more likely.

"The melting snow of nearby mountains provides water. Over time, this water has cut underground artesian channels. When the mine was in operation, one of the more far-flung shafts broke through to one of these channels. The breach was pumped and sealed, but the poor quality of the breach seal leads me to believe the Giggle people are unaware of its existence."

How do mountain spring artesian channels and a mine shaft deep underground help get us inside the mines?

Our swift pace has already brought us to within sight of the Compass.

"The rest I will share when we meet Oscar," Mr. Lark says.

Illych glances my way while asking, "Who is Oscar?"

Our employer enters the center of the Compass, a dongle appearing in his hand. "Oscar is the Langstraad employee we are meeting with."

We cluster around the old man. We speak no more, and everything goes black.

Chapter 7

What follows in quick succession is the translation to a hotel room, the translation nausea, followed by a car ride to our destination.

Turns out Oscar works remotely from his home in a rural part of Montana. My California expectations are mentally warring with the scenery outside the car window. Open spaces, telephone poles, and occasional wildlife scroll by.

The car stops on a gravel circle in front of Oscar's large and rather rustic residence. Illych still looks bored as we exit and climb the stairs to the door. The driver and car remain waiting for us.

The door opens, and for a moment, I am taken aback. Based on the location and décor, I was expecting an American cowboy. Oscar's dark complexion and facial features make it hard to place his ancestry. India? Pakistan? Intelligence is bright in his eyes, and a smile comes to him easily enough as we are greeted.

"Welcome to my home. Please come in."

We three in our formal grey suits clash with the décor and our host. Oscar is in jeans and an old sweater. The interior of the house is as rustic as the exterior. A lot of brown, wood, and leather. Illych smiles and nods approvingly. This is his style.

Off to the left of the foyer is an open space prepared for our meeting. The furniture is of the informal and overstuffed variety, and it looks quite comfortable. Many cows gave their lives for this much leather.

Oscar ushers us in. He is already set up with an open laptop, its screen bright. A coffee mug nearby shows he had been working here for some time.

Still smiling, Oscar says, "Please. I must explain. I can see the question on your faces. As a boy in Bangalor, I loved the American westerns. Now that I live here and am able to work remotely, there is this." His hands wave in all directions. That explains a lot.

The smile is genuine, but the nervousness beneath shows as we are seated. Mr. Lark waves away the offer of refreshments.

"Oscar, both of us have many tasks vying for our attention. We will keep this as brief as possible. Your employer has made you aware of our assignment?"

"Yes. We are breaking into the Giggle Corp central server farm." There is an uneven tone to Oscar's reply.

"You do not appear to have any military training," Illych begins. "Do you mountain climb or spelunk?"

Now a hint of fear creeps into his expression. "Uh, no."

Looking unimpressed, Illych continues. "Do you exercise at all?"

"Yes. That is also why I bought this place. I mountain bike long distances. Helps me think as I am planning work."

Illych looks at Mr. Lark and nods.

Mr. Lark looks directly at Oscar. "My team will provide security and all needed infiltration and exfiltration equipment and planning. You are only required to follow instructions and perform the task you have been chosen to accompany us for. At no time will you consider yourself in charge. Once the mission starts, you will remain focused and motivated until completion. Are my instructions clear?"

Oscar nods.

"Please have fully tested duplicates of any needed equipment, along with multiple power sources," Mr. Lark continues. "If we get in and discover you forgot a cable, it will be on you to explain to your employer why they are paying my organization full charge for nothing. Our total mission time should be around twenty-four hours. You will be contacted shortly with where you need to be and when. Dress warmly."

"I was going to show you the equipment I will use to crack the system once we are inside," Oscar says. "This laptop is a custom XV45—"

The old man cuts him off. "How you do your job is your responsibility. Expect notification of mission start time within the next twenty-four hours. Good day."

Mr. Lark stands and navigates his way to the front door. Illych beats him to it, opening it so our employer can exit. Illych gives the décor another visual once-over before leaving.

Trailing behind, I glance back at Oscar. He has a shocked look on his face. I sympathize. My employer has that effect on people.

On the car ride back to the hotel, Mr. Lark says to Illych, "What do you think?"

Illych looks thoughtful. "He is stable but obviously has never seen the elephant. If things go sideways, he may freeze or panic."

"If he proves difficult, we will sedate him and carry him in," Mr. Lark replies. "Then wake him long enough to do his job. If the information has been retrieved and he proves a liability, there are plenty of places to leave his corpse in the deep recesses of the mine."

That sounds a little extreme. "We might have to kill him?" I ask.

"Yes, Mr. Davies. We will be deep inside a hostile installation. Once the mission parameters are achieved, all deadweight will be released from the mission. I will not jeopardize my organization because one person cannot control themselves."

Looking back at Illych, Mr. Lark continues, "Now that we have resolved the remaining unknown factor and all the other preparations are complete, this mission will be prosecuted in less than twenty-four hours. Prepare the team at the Citadel. This Oscar person is receiving his notification as we speak. There is no good reason to give him time to overthink this."

Illych nods.

Less than twenty-four hours.

Chapter 8

During the return trip, all the talk of artesian channels and deep abandoned mines makes my mind race with the possibilities. None of my thoughts include sunlight or enough air to breathe. Illych makes this worse when he asks if I know how to swim. Yes, I do, but spelunking through flooded caverns is a different beast.

Back at the Citadel, preparations are kicking into high gear. While we were away meeting Oscar, the rest of the team was bringing the mission equipment into the Citadel for testing and preparation.

No sooner is my grey suit back on its hanger in my room than I am pulled into wet suit prep. My worst fears are soon realized as I see breathing masks, oxygen tanks, sealed bags, and lots of rope. Weapons are checked, doublechecked, and then secured into robust watertight bags for protection.

Although we have some idea of the opposition's capabilities based on Mr. Lark's reconnaissance, we likely will encounter opposition of unknown capabilities. Past experience virtually guarantees it. Therefore, in addition to the standard anti-personnel weapons, we have grenades, breaching charges, and a number of custom mines Held and Illych designed. Unfortunately, the means by which we plan to enter the target facility prevents bringing any truly heavy weaponry.

The second-most surprising part of the preparations, after the underwater gear, is the lack of armor. We will have lightweight bulletproof vests, head protection integrating the microphone kit to protect and augment our hearing, and night vision goggles. None of the heavy stuff, though. If we run into serious opposition, there will be some bleeding.

One upside is all the firearms have suppressors this time. They will hardly be silent like in the movies, but it will not be the thunder we experienced against the gargoyles below Castle Houska.

We stack and pile, count, and recount for hours. Preparations finally conclude late into the night. Illych announces we all need a good meal and sleep. There once was a time when the anticipation of what is to come would have kept me up all night. Not anymore. With a full belly, I am asleep seconds after my head hits the pillow.

Illych wakes the team six hours later. After a quiet breakfast, we gear up and head to the Compass, where we find a similarly attired Mr. Lark waiting. Silently, he hands out emergency dongles and gathers the team in the stone circle. Then we are gone.

While recovering from the translation, I take in the sights around me. The sun high overhead, the temperature is similar to what we just left at the Compass. The air is thinner; we are at a high elevation on a plateau in the mountains. Parked not far away are two large 4x4 trucks. My guess is they represent plausible deniability explaining how we arrived at our current location or even an alternative way to leave from this place.

But why would we need plausible deniability? We are the only ones here.

The answer can be heard echoing from the cold stone walls around us. A helicopter arriving.

A white-and-blue helicopter with civilian markings descends into view, throwing up ground debris in its wake. Once it lands, the side door opens. Oscar awkwardly disembarks with his duffel bag and begins to shuffle toward us. No sooner does he clear the chopper than it is powering upward out of sight. Our newest team member is dressed in a parka and wearing sunglasses.

He smiles. "Hi."

Illych does not skip a beat. "Strip."

Oscar's eyes go wide while he stutters, "Why?"

Tank is now a few feet behind Oscar and says, "This is why." And tosses him a wet suit.

Oscar timidly begins to undress while most of us find something else to do. Tank, however, makes a spectacle of leering at the man's obvious discomfort. Illych finally calls out to the ex-marine for some assistance, giving Oscar a break.

Naked and shivering, our new teammate slowly squeezes himself into the insulated wet suit. With a final zip, the shivering stops and he is ready.

We have boots and other clothing for Oscar. Turns out we have a serious hike ahead of us to the entry point. Everyone, including our guest, has a heavy rucksack to carry. Mine is at least twenty-five kilos. From the look of it, the others' packs are probably more like forty kilos.

Loaded down and with Mike leading, we begin the uphill trek into the mountains.

Complete silence is the rule. Oscar's eyes get wide when the team deploys long guns. The good news is he has the good sense to realize the quiet is a feature and not a bug.

We start out at the upper edge of the tree line; the terrain is rocky. Right from the beginning I can tell we will not be mountain climbing. This is a hike, our line of travel being where two mountains meet and form a rocky ravine.

The going is slow, and the cold grey day turns into a frigid black night. The wind picks up and begins to howl. The rough terrain and the load on my back require complete concentration to keep from twisting an ankle. We are a line of grim black figures trudging upward into the night.

Many hours pass before our path begins to flatten out. Perhaps a few hundred meters later we are at the edge of an iced-over pond in the middle of a valley with mountains on all sides. Each of the adjacent mountains have at least one partially iced-over small stream ending in the frozen waters in front of us. No egress from the pond is visible.

The magnitude of the real-world implications of what an artesian channel is, is raising my anxiety . . .

The sounds of heavy packs dropping onto frosted ground mark our arrival at our destination.

Held, Illych, and Mike strip down to their wet suits and begin organizing lines, oxygen tanks, and stacking sealed waterproof bags at the edge of the pool.

My employer, also standing in a wet suit, is passively watching the activity.

"We are going in there?" Oscar asks as he stands beside me.

I nod and say, "Yes, I believe so."

"No one said anything about this. Diving into frozen water underground in the middle of the night." His voice is an octave higher than normal. My guess is Oscar doesn't like where all of this looks to be headed. I don't either, but having been around Mr. Lark long enough, I know this is going to happen whether any of us like it or not.

Tank produces a small anti-personnel mine, and with a low, flat toss, slides it out onto the ice. It soon detonates, shattering a hole plenty big enough for a man to enter the water. A rope bundle, one end already anchored into the frozen ground, is tossed into the black water and slowly sinks from view. Mike puts on his diving mask, and while holding an oxygen tank in his left hand, he begins gingerly crawling out onto the ice. Just short of the opening, the ice under his body gives way. In spite of this, he manages a controlled entry. Submerging, Mike disappears below the water.

Mike soon activates a lamp on his chest, illuminating the remaining ice. The effect is breathtaking. A mantle of frosted-white, brightly shining ice surrounds the open water. The light fades as its bearer dives deeper.

Held is next. Instead of diving into the water, he waits at the ice's edge. Illych hands him the mission equipment in sealed bags. Each one has a steel ring that Held snaps around the guide rope. Then he releases them to sink below the surface.

Oscar is watching all of this closely. He seems agitated. I peek at Mr. Lark and find him watching our guest closely. He is probably calculating the man's chances of returning alive from this mission.

While the equipment is being fed into the pool, Tank walks past me, still wearing his parka and boots. The big man is also stacking the rucksacks and gear being left behind. Shuffling over, I ask him what he is doing.

"My job is to stand guard here while you guys have all the fun. Apparently, the swim path is too narrow for a real man."

This, I believe. In addition to naturally broad shoulders, Tank's well-developed musculature makes him almost twice as wide as most men.

"I am also here in case someone is needed on the outside."

I get it. Tank is the insurance policy. Too bad, really. The ex-marine's reassuring presence will be missed. Leaving him to his current task, I rejoin Oscar.

"I am not looking forward to swimming into that," Oscar says as he points to the pool. "Still, sitting here in the dark, for hours . . ." He does not need to finish for me to understand.

Held begins his descent, and Illych takes over feeding in the last of the equipment bags and then motions for Mr. Lark. The old man walks straight into the water. Show-off.

Illych indicates it is now Oscar's turn. Obviously having second thoughts, Oscar walks to the icy edge of the pond and gingerly moves one foot out, slowly placing his weight on it. After a couple of shuffling steps out, the fear finally takes over.

"Nope. Can't do it."

With the speed and surefootedness of a ninja, Illych grabs the man and, with a push, slides him across the ice to within a foot of the open water.

With an expression grim as death, Illych says, "You will want that mask on before I throw you in."

Oscar nods and fixes his mask in place. Illych checks it and gives the man a push. The last thing I see is wide eyes behind glass as Oscar slides off the ice and sinks down into the water. At least there were no histrionics or blubbering.

This is when I realize Illych is looking at me. It is my turn.

My mask is soon in place and air flow checked. Shuffling out to the edge, I become concerned I will lose my nerve. I make a pushing motion, and Illych is only too willing to oblige. One hard push and I am off the ice and sinking into the icy black water.

My mind tells me I'm okay and to breathe. My body tenses, waiting for the icy stab of freezing water that never comes. Taking a minute to inhale and exhale, I snap onto the line and begin to swim down into the dark tunnel. My chest light illuminates with a flick of a switch.

The water is crystal clear, and the eroded stone tube leading downward is visible in every detail. With a tug on the rope, I slowly sink.

Ahead of me, deeper down in the water, is Oscar, his profile outlined by his lamp against the black background. He is moving downward slowly, with more hesitation. I keep my distance and watch. After a few minutes, the programmer seems to get his confidence and begins pulling himself along the rope in a more purposeful way.

Maybe he finally accepted that the only way out of this frigid liquid-filled tube is to get to the other side.

During the slow descent, I have time to think. So much about this mission makes me uncomfortable. No ComDat, no SHEG, no Tank, outsiders tagging along. Hopefully this is an easy one. In and out.

I watch Oscar negotiate a narrowing of the tube. He wiggles his body through first while being careful to not knock his mask loose. After he is through, he pulls his oxygen tank in behind him.

Now it is my turn.

Oscar must be wider than I, because my body slides through in one smooth motion. Midway in, I can see the tube walls only a few inches from my mask. Instead of the streaks and grooves of millennia of erosion I would have expected, the surface shows a strange stippling effect. I smile inside my mask. My employer must have used the ouiblet to carve away perfect spheres of stone, making just enough room for us to pass. Based on how tight this channel is, it is no wonder Tank cannot join us.

Looking back upward, I can see Illych making his approach to the bottleneck.

At one point, the tube opens into a chamber only half filled with running water. Then our underwater journey begins all over again.

We have been spelunking for over an hour when we reach our destination. By the time Oscar, Illych, and I arrive, Mike and Held have been hard at work installing an air lock. The plan is to penetrate through an old mine breach and then individually move each of us through a softlock.

The heavy plastic sheeting that makes up the softlock is rolled out and affixed around the breach area using a particularly nasty adhesive that sticks to anything. Held and Mike move with grace and speed, even underwater. Once the softlock is in place, Mike crawls in, sealing it behind him. Even ten meters away underwater, I can feel the hammering tool pounding as he works to open the breach. We all just float in position, one above the other, waiting. With our chest lamps, we look like a vertical string of Christmas lights suspended in the dark.

The hammering finally ends and some unseen signal passes to Held, who then stacks the softlock full of sealed bags. Once sealed from the outside, Mike opens it from the inside and removes the equipment. This happens several times. We brought a lot of hardware. Next is Mr. Lark. One by one we enter into the mines, with Illych being the last.

The softlock opens into a cul-de-sac more resembling a sump than a legitimate part of the mine. Splintered rotten wood and chunks of concrete litter the floor from Mike's hammering the old breach plug away.

The sump is filthy, cold, and wet. A clean rubber mat just big enough for one person is thrown to the floor, and we each take turns stripping out of our wet suits and dressing in black tactical gear. The insulated suits were great when hiking in below-freezing temperatures and swimming in near-frozen water, but they will be too hot for the next part of the mission in the mines.

We add to this bulletproof vests, load-bearing equipment, and so much more.

In addition to all our gear, we each get a bag of what look to be hockey pucks but are actually lights. Each one has that super adhesive on the back. Just peel off the protective paper, press the puck to the wall, and twist. An LED light illuminates. It is not a bright light, but the oversized battery will keep it going for more than thirty days. Several are already up on the walls around us, making our work easier.

Illych and Held group and interconnect the air tanks. A black box the size of a car battery is placed securely on a chunk of rubble. Once activated, it hums faintly.

Held notices my interest. "Pump with a high-energy chemical battery," he says. "It will take almost twenty-four hours, but the tanks will be full when we return."

Nodding my understanding, I walk into the mine to the edge of the puck lights' luminescence. This is me being as ready as I ever will be. Looking over at Oscar, I size him up. He has stayed calm so far. Other than a few questions about the equipment, he is keeping himself together.

We have a last-minute equipment review as we check each other. Night vision will be used. The mines are pitch black, no light of any kind. Our helmets and weapons have very low output lamps, providing the faint illumination needed for the night vision to work. For a brief moment, the reassuring sound of firearm bolts shearing a round from their respective magazines and locking into place reverberates in this close space.

Mike takes point, with Held close behind. Illych pairs up with Oscar, who is now exhibiting more curiosity than anything else. This leaves me and the old man bringing up the rear. If you think taking the lead and walking point into a dark hole in the ground is spooky, try walking with your back to the darkness behind you.

The tunnel itself is wide enough to accommodate an automobile and more than high enough for upright walking. Every noise is amplified; even a kicked pebble makes a hellish racket to our augmented hearing.

Leaning close to Mr. Lark, I whisper, "How long to the facility?"

Mr. Lark replies in a low voice, "This was an exploratory tunnel approximately a kilometer long. Then it meets up with the salt mine. There, we navigate several tunnels before we arrive at the research facility. I estimate a good two-hour hike."

Breathing in, another question comes to mind. "Mr. Lark, I am curious about air quality in mines sealed off this long." This had been nagging me since we arrived. The air we are breathing is not what I would have expected.

The old man does not respond.

"This air is fresh. Any thoughts?"

"Mr. Davies, if the air was less fresh, more equipment would have been needed. Was your load hiking up the mountain insufficiently heavy?"

My response is unnecessary. His reply tells me he switched out the air via the ouiblet.

Ahead, I can see Illych and Oscar talking. A few times the Langstraad employee even chuckles. This is good. Keep the new guy calm.

The mine is in good condition, and we see no cave-ins as we move from the sump tunnel into the salt mines proper.

Other than the occasional piece of rusted and abandoned mining equipment looming out of the dark, our journey through the blackness is uneventful.

Every now and then I can see Mr. Lark close his eyes. He does not miss a step, but I know he is consulting his oculus. The old man can walk and interface at the same time. The others have to stand still, and it takes longer. Plus, it shows as an obvious activity, which is why none of them brought one along. Oscar would figure out something is up by watching the others use the scanning devices.

The light level begins to increase, and Mr. Lark quietly announces we are getting close.

The outside of our destination is obvious. The research center has gated chain-link fencing on the mine side. The research facility side is defined by a cinder block wall with a door. Above the door is a single caged light. This wall seals off the mineshaft all the way up to the ceiling.

Up until this point, with Mr. Lark's oculus to watch over us, our journey has been a casual stroll in the dark. Now it is game time.

Illych gathers us in a circle. Weapons ready, game faces on.

"Mike and Held will enter first," Mr. Lark says. "This door gets us into part of the research facility, but not the main part. However, our research at Giggle security HQ yielded useful information. Originally, Giggle planned to install security sensors everywhere in this outer ring. The sensors were never installed when they realized nothing was going to break in from a mine over a thousand feet underground. However, the data-link node they would have been connected to was installed."

"They do not have cameras installed?" I question. "Seems like a big security gap."

"Why would they have cameras watching abandoned tunnels?" Illych responds. "It is not like Sleestaks are going to come walking out of the mine."

This gets a low chuckle from most of the team. Oscar most of all. I let it go despite my ignorance of what a Sleestak is.

"We will walk this outer ring to that data node where our companion from Langstraad will connect and download the goal of this mission," Mr. Lark says. "Any questions?"

Oscar raises his hand. "What do we do if we encounter someone?"

"This outer corridor is unused," Illych responds. "It is unlikely we will meet anyone. That is the reason for our unorthodox entry path. In and out is the plan. If we should run into Giggle personnel, you will follow our instructions. Is that clear?"

Oscar nods in acceptance.

Illych gives us one last looking at and says, "We all finish this whole and go home to celebrate." He nods to all of us, and we nod back.

Mike and Held move to the door. Mike pops the locked door open in seconds, and they perform a flawless, weapons-at-the-ready entry.

Illych shepherds Oscar in.

Mr. Lark indicates I am next. Hefting my carbine, I step into the Giggle Corp research facility.

Chapter 9

The corridor walls and ceiling are ordinary beige. The floor is grey-epoxied concrete. A single overhead light is centered above the door we entered through. The corridor is not straight. Instead, it has an inward bend in both directions, like the perimeter of a circle. This reduces visibility each way to maybe a hundred feet before the curve of the hall blocks our line of sight. By the time we see something, it will be on top of us.

Mike and Held are already moving left towards the node. As soon as the spacing is appropriate, Illych and Oscar follow them.

During the brief wait for our spacing gap to open, Mr. Lark whispers to me, "The oculus is not working properly in this place. Most solid structures appear to be registering. I'm having problems with energy and some of the multidimensional bands."

This gives me a sick feeling. "We are blind?"

"Not completely. But once inside the facility, we will not enjoy the superior intelligence position we normally would."

This is not the time to quiz my employer. Which is why he probably chose this moment to inform me, to keep me quiet.

Our spacing gap now correct, we begin moving forward. Mike and Held are setting a normal walking pace. Just a stroll in the park.

Looking down at the floor, I notice long scratches and square dimples in the concrete. Must have been some heavy machinery moved here in the past.

The air has a faint off-putting smell to it. It is difficult to place. Definitely not air-freshener.

We pass a few doors. Mr. Lark tells us the ones on the left lead out to the mines. The one door on the right leads into the facility. Held rigs it with a flash-bang.

Mike signals back telling us we have arrived at our destination. The team silently repositions, with Mike watching the corridor ahead and Held watching our return path. Illych provides close-in security over us while Oscar goes to work.

The panel is a nondescript grey box. Pulling an electric screwdriver from his kit, Oscar loosens fasteners holding the cover in place in seconds. Setting the panel aside, he looks inside at the modules covered in blinking green and amber lights.

"I will link in now," Oscar says. "This may take some time."

What comes next is fascinating to watch. I am not a technology person, but our companion is obviously *the* technology guy. He connects cables with practiced hands and boots his computer up. The man's hand fly across the keyboard with surprising speed.

Code scrolls down the computer screen. Various graphs and reference gauges briefly appear and blink out. It is like watching a video game being played.

At the rate he is going, we will be done in no time. Illych is right; sometimes these missions are just easy.

Oscar's body language changes. His hands move faster than their already-disturbing blur. "There is a problem."

"How so?" inquires Mr. Lark.

"This node was never properly activated. There is no assigned bandwidth."

Taking one step closer to Oscar, Mr. Lark says, "Please clarify."

"The hardware is correct. No different than the security information you shared. This node is network connected back to the main facility intranet. Where it connects to was never properly activated. We have no access from here, and I cannot turn that access on from here."

Mr. Lark is silent, obviously considering what to do next. Whatever it is, I am sure the easy part of this mission just left the building.

Looking at Illych, the old man commands, "Alternate plan, then. We go back to the facility entrance door we passed and enter into the facility. Then locate the nearest node, and connect."

Illych nods, makes some hand gestures, and the team springs into action. Mike and Held start back the way we just came from. Oscar quickly reassembles the electrical cabinet. I walk the corridor in the opposite direction we arrived from without losing sight of the team behind me.

Standing there, I can smell that off-scent again. Very faint. Through my augmented hearing I hear the distant sound of something grinding against a concrete surface. Then a pause. Then a few more grinding noises and then another pause. The lack of regularity to whatever it is concerns me. Pumps and fans would not make such noise. People and monsters might.

The grinding noise picks up again. Longer this time and progressively louder. Whatever it is, it is getting closer.

As quietly as possible, I walk back the others. Illych notices me first and ends a conversation between Mr. Lark and Oscar with a cutting gesture.

While waving back to the way I was looking, I whisper, "I heard something up that way. Very quiet, but getting closer."

Illych grabs Oscar and his bag and shoves him toward Mike and Held.

Mr. Lark, Illych, and I stand looking towards the noise as the others continue away. Once the spacing opens up, we three begin slowly walking backward while keeping weapons pointing in the direction we are concerned about.

The faint crunching noise is not faint anymore. We keep moving, but it is obvious whatever it is will soon catch us.

Illych makes an explosion movement with his hands. Held produces one of his custom mines and places it right in the middle of the floor. We retreat until we can go no further while keeping sight of the explosive device.

The source of the noise then crunches and rolls into view. It is a gold-colored, cylinder-shaped roller machine. About as big around as a door opening is wide, with a length approximating a man's height. The cylinder is made up of discs stacked one upon the other. The perimeter of the discs is made up of large, rounded triangular studs. The discs can move off-center to the cylinder and spin independently. The triangular studs appear to be extendable away from the disks they are mounted on, as if on rods.

It rolls and shifts in fits and starts like it is searching for something. Travelling a few feet in our direction, it then shifts around by pushing with the disks and triangular studs. Now I understand where the strange spalling in the floor concrete came from.

Held holds up the mine detonator, finger on the trigger. The thing seems to finally get our scent. With some shifting and pushing, the golden cylinder centers itself in the corridor. Now it rolls toward us with no hesitation.

As it reaches the explosive device, Held activates the trigger. Our hearing is saved by the augmented audio safety cutoffs, but we are all knocked around and painfully pelted by debris. In the outer cinder block wall, an opening large enough for a two-lane road is blasted into existence. The abandoned mine outside can now be clearly seen. Propped up on the jagged and ruined wall is the golden cylinder. More than a few triangular studs are missing, and several discs are pushed out from the cylinder in a way that makes it look broken.

That blast just let everyone in the facility know we are here. At least that thing is disabled now. Based on how it was moving, my guess is it crushes its victims. Not how I would like to go. Mike high-fives Held, and Mr. Lark walks toward the precariously perched machine.

It moves.

Triangular studs extrude and push it from the wall. Crashing to the floor in a thunderous metallic racket, it uses extended triangular studs and offset discs to hurtle toward us.

"Weapons free and fall back!" Illych yells out.

Without a thought, my carbine is brought to the firing position as my thumb clicks the safety off. The others beat me to the punch as their weapons roar to life a fraction of a second before mine. The .45 ACP rounds we are firing are man-stoppers, not armor-piercers. They dent and gouge the rollers' surfaces, but I see no meaningful effect.

Illych points to a door to the mine that we are fast approaching, shouting out, "Mike, open that."

Mike slings his weapon and starts on the door lock. It is open in seconds in a demonstration of skill under pressure.

While causing no useful damage to the cylinder, our gunfire does seem to slow the construct down and confuse it. At least long enough to get the door open and push Oscar through.

"We're leaving!" Illych barks. And all of us run out into the mine, shutting the door behind us. Without pause, we rush through the chain-link fence and then turn to establish a firing line.

And we wait.

After maybe five minutes, we breathe a collective sigh.

"Why is it not following us?" I ask. "That door and even the wall are not real obstacles to that thing."

"I have my suspicions," Mr. Lark replies. "Illych, it is time to change weapons."

My ears perk up at this. The arsenal back at the Citadel has some very heavy weapons. None of them are in our current load out.

Illych drops his pack and pulls out two separate wrapped pieces and begins unwrapping them.

One part is the bolt, lever, and grip, the other is a large bore gun barrel with an underslung ammo tube. Even in the dim light the former Green Beret deftly assembles the weapon. He then pulls a long cartridge from his vest. It looks like a brass cigar, which he inserts into the breach. The bolt snaps closed with a flick of the lever action.

The SHEG is ready.

Feeling a little exasperated, I blurt out, "Just lead with that next time."

"This was supposed to be a covert operation," Mr. Lark responds. "The SHEG was included only as an emergency backup."

Mr. Lark turns to Illych. "Now that covert is no longer a consideration, please blow that door open. If that does not destroy that thing, then reload and make it happen."

Mr. Golden Cylinder is about to have his behavior corrected. The SHEG, which stands for "super high explosive gun," is a Mr. Lark creation. Unimaginatively named, it uses some sort of crystalline metal structure to store fantastic amounts of energy that can be released instantaneously. Like many of Mr. Lark's creations, I do not understand the technical part. There is no denying the weapon's effectiveness. It could breach bank vaults, if needed.

Illych moves into a firing position.

Behind us, from the black hole of the abandoned mines, the unexpected sound of sheet metal scraping grabs the team's attention.

With the speed of a cobra strike, the team's attack posture does a one-eighty. The newly illuminated tunnel reveals no obvious targets. At the edge of our vision is a ramshackle tin shed. Probably used to store tools back in the day. It is also the most obvious source of the metallic sound.

For a fraction of a second, I think Illych is going to exterminate the building. Instead, Mr. Lark says, "Stand down. Mike, check it out."

Mike immediately advances, with his weapon ready. We follow and fan out. With a pull, the door comes right off the shed and the former Ranger ghosts in.

We hear a female voice say, "Please don't shoot me."

Illych looks at Mr. Lark and then at me. "Held, watch our backs," Illych says. Held moves back to cover the door to the facility.

Illych then stalks forward, waving me to join him. With a shrug, I follow.

Inside the shed is an unexpected sight. A dark-haired woman, average height, thin, disheveled, and wearing a filthy lab coat greets us. Mike has her at gunpoint, his weapon's underslung light making her blink. Illych looks her up and down and then signals Mike to lower his weapon. I slap a puck to the nearest wall and twist, illuminating the shed.

The light reveals pitiful conditions inside the shed. The woman has made a nest from plastic sheeting and some old canvas. It looks like she has been here for some time. Still visible, embroidered on the lab coat, is a name: Jaeger, Allison.

"Allison, is it?" Illych inquires.

"Yes." She looks at us with wild, fearful eyes. She's unsure if we're saviors or bad guys.

"Why are you here?" Illych asks.

Her legs give out, and she falls down in a heap. Mike moves in, checking her eyes and pulse.

"How long have you been here?" he asks.

Her words come out slurred. "Long time."

Mike shakes his head, "Severe dehydration. I will IV a bag into her and check her out." Pulling out his medical bag, he exits the hut. "Bring her out here," he calls. Illych nods and effortlessly scoops up the woman.

A thermal blanket is quickly spread out on the ground, and the woman is placed on it. Mike inserts the saline IV and drafts Oscar to hold the bag.

Mr. Lark is observing all this from the distance. Illych looks at him and walks over. I join them . . . this will be an interesting discussion.

We huddle together, and Mr. Lark speaks first. "She is not part of the plan."

Illych looks less than pleased with that statement. "From a morale perspective, you understand we must help her."

"And how do we get her away from this mine?" Mr. Lark counters.

"We have the bag."

Wait, what, the bag? Looking at Illych, I ask, "The bag?"

"If we have wounded that cannot swim . . . or if the propeller head needs to be sedated . . . we have a single diving retrieval bag to get them out."

"And if one of the team gets wounded while we're using the bag for her?" Mr. Lark interjects. "Then what will we do with her?"

Illych shakes his head. "We will cross that bridge if we get there. Do you think she might have useful information? Like what the hell that golden cylinder thing is?"

Mr. Lark nods and comments, "Something is wrong here. Where is the security response to the explosion? And what was that mechanical construct? And why is it not pursuing us out into the mine?"

After a pause, Mr. Lark says, "Let us talk to the young lady and hear her story."

The three of us rejoin the others. Allison is now sitting up and quietly talking to Mike, who is crouching down next to her. He has given her a bottle of water and a chocolate bar.

Digging around in his medical bag, he pulls out a prefilled syringe. "Allison, I am giving you a vitamin B shot, and you will feel a lot better." He swabs her pale arm and sticks her with the injection.

She looks at him. "Thank you, Mike." First-name basis. That was quick. Even in her condition I can see she has pretty eyes. Leave it to Mike to find a girl a thousand feet below ground in an abandoned mine.

"Hello, Alison. My name is Illych," Illych begins. "This is Thomas, and Oscar there is holding your IV bag. Over there is Held." She looks at each of us in turn. Good. The IV is doing its job.

"We need you to answer some questions for us."

She nods.

"How did you get here?"

"I am a lab tech for Giggle Corp. I work here."

"Alison, this may be difficult, but we need to know how you ended up down here."

"Yes, I can tell you that." Taking a drink, she continues. "It all started about two weeks ago. When I arrived at work along with my co-workers, every morning we noticed fewer cars in the parking lot. Then a week ago, there were cars that never left or changed parking spots. The elevators were emptier than usual. We figured there was a conference somewhere or maybe offsite training. Multiple groups do research here, and we don't necessarily know each other. We share elevators, the parking lot, the cafeteria, things like that."

She stops talking for a moment, takes a deep breath, and continues. "What day is it?"

Mr. Lark shares the current day and time.

Allison looks at him, the one person she has not been introduced to yet. "Who is he?"

"That is Mr. Lark," Illych says. "Let's stay focused,. What else can you tell us?"

Allison nods and continues, "Three days ago we were in the lab assembling some modules for testing. There were eight of us. The doors slammed open, and three men rushed in. They were so fast, and their skin was grey. They wore lab coats like mine. I think they were other employees, but something was wrong with them."

Allison shudders and continues. "They each grabbed one of my co-workers and dragged them out of the lab. It happened so fast. They were screaming as the grey men dragged them away. Our supervisor, Todd, tried calling security, but the internal phones were dead. And cell phones can't get a signal down here. Andrew went running after them. We never saw him again or the ones taken.

"Todd gathered those of us remaining together and said we are leaving. We left our work space and headed for the main elevators. We made it to the main lobby where the elevators are when more of the grey men appeared. These were different. They were naked and had mechanical parts and cables attached to them. They are completely silent as they rushed us."

Allison shivers and is silent a few moments.

"Todd yelled for us to use the nearby mine exit. We ran. They were right behind us. Three of us made it through. Todd stayed to lock the door. They caught him, and we could see him taken away through the door. That left Winston, Linda, and me. We ran and ran around the outer ring. We thought we had gotten away, but then a nearby inner door opened. The corridor filled with grey men. I ran out a door into the mine. The others did not make it." She starts crying, then turns to Mike and leans against him.

Illych looks at Mr. Lark. "They won't come out into the mines," Mr. Lark says. "But why?"

"Let's take a short break," Illych counters. "We hiked, spelunked, and then dealt with that thing. We had planned on being on our way out by now."

The old man nods. "A one-hour break. Food, water, and get the woman ready to move. Then we are going in to complete this mission."

Mr. Lark wanders a few feet away from the group. Those of us who know the signs know he is using the oculus. I follow him and give him a few minutes to finish before asking my question. "Any idea what these grey men are that Allison mentioned?"

"I have my suspicions, Mr. Davies, but no evidence to make a conclusion."

The hour goes by quickly. Allison bounces back and is soon standing up and walking. The amphetamines Mike gave her probably help. Oscar's anxiety levels are also obviously up. He even asked Illych if he could have a gun. That is not likely to happen. An untrained civilian with a firearm in close quarters . . .

We move farther back into the mine and give our new companion some ear plugs. This is going to get loud.

Mr. Lark gets things started. "First things first: Illych, take down that wall and destroy that machine."

Illych smiles. "Roger that."

The SHEG bucks in Illych's hand, followed by a shattering sound and the visible detonation. The cinder block wall vaporizes for ten-plus meters in both directions from the blast. The inner wall does the same, revealing work spaces littered with newly created wreckage.

What a mess. But no golden cylinder or pieces thereof are to be seen. Must have moved on during our break.

Picking our way through the debris, we make our way into the adjoining lab.

Mr. Lark, having consulted the oculus, still pretends to have memorized the layout before the mission and gives directions to the nearest data node. Straight ahead, left at the T. Straight ahead for maybe one hundred meters. The lab is on the left.

Held and Illych take point. Allison has latched onto Mike, so the two are paired together. That leaves me to chaperone Oscar. The rear is brought up by the old man.

My theory on this being an easy in and out having been destroyed, I am switching back to default: Everything is going to hell. Complete snafu. Worst-case scenario. Any such description covers it.

The others are acting if they have come to the same conclusion. Illych has his carbine at the ready, but the loaded SHEG is dangling from his harness. We pause at every door and hall.

We see nothing.

The lights are on, but no one is home.

Held and Illych crash our destination's doors open, and Oscar is connecting to the node at the speed of light. The others position into an outward-facing circle around the frenetic engineer. My employer catches my eye and motions for me to follow.

Not twenty feet away, just out of sight, is another data point router thing. I see the wynloo in Mr. Lark's hand.

"It will be easier this time, Mr. Davies. No stabbing. Just a hard slap to the face. Ready?"

"Yes, Mr. Lark. I am ready."

The strings of gossamer light flow out of the crystal and form a bridge.

Not even a minute passes before the old man signals. The satisfying slap is disturbingly loud in the quiet room.

Blinking from the broken connection, he croaks out, "They are coming."

Grabbing my quickly recovering employer, I pull him back toward the others. Oscar is still working on the data link.

My colleagues look at me and then at Mr. Lark. My statement explains it all: "We are going to have company."

Mike shoves Allison toward me. Illych yells to Oscar to keep working. Illych, Mike, and Held take up firing positions covering all entry points. Leaving Allison for a moment, I push chairs, desks, anything to block most of the entry points.

Mr. Lark, fully recovered now, pulls a large handgun from its shoulder holder and is absentmindedly checking the round count in its magazine.

Then all is silent.

For a few brief moments the only sound my augmented hearing detects is the clicking of keys from Oscar's rapid typing and the breathing of the team around me. Slow, deep, and measured from my colleagues. Shallow and quick from Oscar and Allison.

The faint sound of shuffling feet can be heard, broken up with the occasional slap of a bare foot on tile floor. The walking sounds increase. There are many, many feet. I don't need to share my observation with the others. Everyone can hear what I am hearing.

Through the windows lining the adjoining walls outside the lab, I can see up and down both halls. Shuffling is coming from both directions. The walking noises never pause or hesitate—even as the doors at the end of the hall slam open and the enemy charges into sight.

Now I understand what Allison meant when she called them grey men. They are, or at least were, human. Some are partially clothed. Most are naked. More men than women. Some have cables, wires, or even electronic modules grafted onto them. Whatever they were, now they are dead.

Mr. Lark's voice growls in my ear. "Draugar."

Whatever that is.

The roar of .45 ACP announces the beginning of the fight. Windows shatter, and the leading grey figures go down in a hail of man-stopping hollow points. They make no sound as they advance. No calls of aggression nor any keening as they are cut down. Just a wall of silence charging ever closer.

The old man's voice calls out loud and clear, "They are essentially possessed. Headshots are the optimal choice."

Mike, Held, and Illych alternatively burn through magazine after magazine in their carbines, punctuated by the calling out of "reloading!" Mr. Lark is doing the same.

Behind me is the sound of the distinctive draugr shuffle. I rotate my body, my weapon orientationflipping one-hundred-eighty degrees. The door at the back of the lab, not ten meters away, crashes to the floor, torn from its hinges. A tide of grey-skinned, fast-moving hostiles enters the lab. They demonstrate no finesse as chairs, desks, and everything in their way is cast aside during the charge toward us.

Without thinking, I sight my reticle on a grey face, and the carbine shudders. Then I hit another and another. Beside me, Mr. Lark displays superhuman speed and dexterity. Our weapons were optimally designed for soft targets such as these. Grey men are dropping like flies.

It is not enough. A draugr slaps the carbine from my hands. Out of the corner of my eye I glimpse two grey men grabbing Oscar and Allison. Mr. Lark continues to reload and shoot bad guys at point-blank range, bobbing and weaving between attempts to physically engage him.

Oscar is trying to fight back. Allison is screaming a high, keening note and thrashing against her captor as they disappear from view.

My right hand draws my sidearm without my even thinking it, while my left pushes the draugr away. The thing slaps my hand down as I push the barrel of the pistol right to its forehead and pull the trigger. The grey man falls down in a heap as if its bones have disappeared.

The sound of gunfire echoes away, leaving just the distinctive smell of cordite. In the silence, I look around and realize the bad guys are all down. The team is reloading, and I retrieve my carbine.

"Where are they?" I ask.

"We killed them all," my employer responds.

Held and Mike high five each other, and Illych smiles.

What a mess. Broken glass, spent cartridges, grey bodies, and viscera are strewn everywhere.

"Where are Allison and Oscar?" Mike asks.

"They were taken," Mr. Lark responds.

For a moment, the five of us look at each other in non-verbal discussion.

What now?

The old man beats all of us to speaking. "We must retrieve Oscar. My organization's reputation will be damaged if we start losing people this way. I have never failed on a contract, and we are not starting now."

Illych gives a nod and some fast hand signals, and Mike takes point, with Held right behind. We walk quickly, weapons at the ready, in the direction Oscar and Allison were taken. The corridor we follow is well-lit and easily navigated. Empty labs and workshops are visible on either side through floor-to-ceiling windows.

Every door we find is locked. Figuring the draugar are likely not proficient with locks, we push on. Quickly in our search we find Oscar's helmet on the floor. After another fifty feet we find another piece of his gear. We all recognize bread crumbs when we see them.

Drifting closer to Mr. Lark, I ask, "Draugar?"

"Yes, Mr. Davies. They are possessed, of a sort. Except instead of taking over a recently deceased and still-viable corpse, the draugar possess the genuinely dead. The motivating spirit is not one of the Created, however. Instead, it is a piece of something from the other side that just happens to find a corpse. These grey men are draugar. What I do not understand is why there are so many of them. They are not a mass-phenomena and typically only appear individually."

Fast footsteps can be heard approaching from around the next corner. We spread out, weapons at the ready. Sprinting around the corner is Allison. Seeing us, she tries to stop and skids right into Mike's arms.

Sheesh, get a room.

She is trying to speak while hyperventilating. "Oscar put up such a fight. And there was only two of them. They left me behind. Then they carried him away. He kept dropping stuff, though. Those things did not seem to notice."

Or Oscar is bait and the goal is we follow them to whatever is causing all this mayhem. Glass half-empty and all that.

Mr. Lark looks unfazed. "We will continue."

Illych's hand signals indicate we are advancing. Mike hands Allison off to me and takes point again. Proceeding around the corner Allison just came from, we find it devoid of foes. Following the corridor, it eventually opens into an open-concept lobby. The space is wide and long. One hundred people could meet and move about without being crowded.

On one end is a wall of glass panels two or more building stories tall. Midpoint on one wall are three sets of elevator doors, likely the normal entry/exit point for people working here. Spreading out across the hall, we begin advancing in the direction we will most likely find our missing person. Along the way we find more of Oscar's gear.

We are almost close enough to the glass panels to see what is inside when a loud crash from the corridor behind us stops us in our tracks. Turning as one, I recognize the source of the disturbance. The golden cylinder is back. And it brought an identical friend.

After crashing through the door and part of the wall behind them, the rollers have already righted and aligned straight at us. Now they are accelerating. How quickly they achieve a distance-consuming velocity is disturbing.

Mr. Lark looks at Illych and nods. The former Green Beret takes two steps toward the death rollers while brandishing the SHEG in both hands. The firing of the weapon is underwhelming. Not much different than a shotgun going off.

The detonation is right on target. The floor shakes, and debris falls off of the ceiling and walls. Everyone except for Mr. Lark is knocked from their feet by the shockwave. The golden cylinder roller damaged in our earlier encounter is forcefully disassembled into many small pieces. The second one does not explode quite as completely. However, as the dust settles, it is apparent both machines' rolling activities are ended forever. Only broken and shattered metal remain.

Satisfied we would have no more problems from that direction, the team turns and walks toward the still-standing glass panels. Beyond the panels and through a sliding door is a control room on a mezzanine looking out over a large, cathedral-like cavernous gallery. Hanging from the cavern ceiling are cables and tubes. The poorly lit cavern floor reveals no useful details. The open space is divided by standing curtains that block our line of sight to most everything.

The sliding door is locked. Mr. Lark reveals the wynloo, which quickly extends its luminous tendrils into the electronic door lock. In seconds, the door slides back. I catch a glimpse of Allison watching wide-eyed. The mezzanine control room does not provide access to the floor below. It is just a platform with a couple of rolling chairs and panels covered in switches and buttons. There are also keyboards near large displays. Everything is dark other than a few random blinking red lights.

Illych looks around and finally says what we are all thinking: "Where is Oscar?"

We have nowhere else to look. This room is a dead-end.

Held and Mike are holding the sliding door open and watching the corridor.

Mr. Lark quickly strides over to a keyboard. Holding the wynloo in one hand, he lifts it close to a box near a keyboard. Once again the ghostly tendrils extend from the artifact to the accessory connection slots in the box, and the flatscreen comes to life.

My employer begins cycling through security camera feeds throughout the facility. Everywhere is empty. No grey men, no rollers, no Oscar. Now images captured by the cameras for the last two weeks flicker across the screen. Previously empty rooms begin showing more people, more activity.

"Interesting," Mr. Lark muses. "The system is resisting my looking at certain places." Mr. Lark's face is set in concentration. A familiar face appears on the screen and disappears.

"Wait!" I blurt out. "Go back. That was someone I know." The images slowly reverse.

"There. That man." The image of a middle-aged, athletic-looking man of average height fills the screen. Even the recorded picture of the man looks serious.

"That is Hugo Soldat. From below Castle Houska. Why is he here?"

"I intend to find out," Mr. Lark says. The flickering images begin again, this time even faster.

After a few minutes, it becomes apparent this is going to take some time. Illych and I drift to a corner. Both of us know we are not going anywhere until the boss says so.

"I don't like our staying in this one place so long," Illych says.

"What about Oscar?" I ask him.

"We have to locate him. Alive or dead, he is traceable to Langstraad Solutions. We either retrieve him or obliterate any recognizable trace so Giggle Corp can't connect him to LS. If he is lucky, Mr. Lark will locate him still alive."

Laughter ends our discussion. A deep, genuine, heartfelt laugh continues for a few seconds. A shocked Illych and I look over at the source.

Mr. Lark stands and disconnects himself from the system without assistance. Still smiling, he looks our way and laughs again. In the last year, I have no memory of this man expressing humor of any kind, and what he is doing now is genuinely disturbing. Illych looks horrified. Held and Mike look away from their sentry duties and then at each other.

"It is all about me," the old man says. "This is all about me." After placing the wynloo back into his pocket, my employer strides toward the sliding door.

"I know where Oscar is. We shall visit him, and then our mission is complete."

If the team has a collective fear, it is Mr. Lark turning out to be genuinely crazy and our getting caught up in it. His laugh was disconcerting that way.

Back in the hall and off to one side, not ten strides away, is a door hidden behind some decorations. Mr. Lark quickly approaches it and pulls the wynloo out.

Before he is able to interface, the door clicks. Looking off to one side, we see a smiling Allison having just swiped her apparently still functioning security badge. Mike pulls the door open, and we enter single file.

Gunfire ensues almost instantly, yet the shooting is over in just a few short bursts. When it is my turn to enter, I see two grey men laid out on the floor. Victims to Mike's marksmanship. No other grey men are visible.

The room has a number of soiled and gory beds. Above each of the beds is a mechanical contraption with blades and strange accessories. Only one bed is occupied.

By poor Oscar. Clearly dead.

Illych shakes his head.

"This is a kill room," Mr. Lark explains. "Where they bring the living to make them into draugar. Oscar is in process." My employer aims his pistol and dead checks the deceased man between the eyes.

"We do not need any surprises. Grab his gear. Held, rig the body with incendiary. No evidence."

Illych and Mike quickly divide up the now-useless computer equipment. Held pulls several cylindrical charges and attaches them to the body and the bed occupied by Oscar's corpse. Through all of this, Allison stays close to Mike and away from the door. Honestly, I cannot blame her. Her friends were all brought here, and if she had not escaped, she would have been converted into a grey man on one of these filthy beds.

As soon as Held is ready, we exit in tactical formation. Even through the closed door I can hear the hiss of the thermite igniting. That room is about to get very, very hot.

As we leave the main corridor and re-enter the lab spaces, I realize the mission is a bust. We did not achieve the customer's objective. And the client's asset is dead.

"Mr. Lark, what about the mission?"

"What about it, Mr. Davies?"

"How will we get the information we need? Oscar was taken before completing his job."

The team is quickly moving back the way we entered, already passing the lab where Oscar and Allison were grabbed. We find no sign of grey men, other than the ones we put down, or rollers. All I hear in my augmented hearing is silence around us.

"When I connected with the wynloo in that control room, the machinations of this place were laid bare," Mr. Lark says. "The idiots at Giggle made a deal with the devil, and now they are being punished for it. Someone sold them a bill of goods that is not as advertised.

"A terrible weapon was brought to this place," he continues. "It is unimaginably ancient while remaining undiminished in its potency. Giggle Corp agreed to collaborate because it would make their systems faster. And it did, at least until now. Unfortunately for them, the systems have begun to fail, while falling short of their goal. This will be explained to Langstraad Solutions, fulfilling our contract.

"But Giggle was deceived," he adds. "Those who provided this improved performance did so to create a super-searching ability. And they are looking for me. My organization has gained the attention of some powerful entities. Through the miracle of the ouiblet, I have managed to avoid their attentions. Thus, they dreamed up this silly idea. They recovered a weapon of apocalyptic proportions designed to exterminate all human life and brought it to this place. All because they thought it would help their cause.

"They thought keeping it deep in this mine would prevent its more hideous effects from spreading. Not only is Giggle Corp no longer receiving a boost for their systems, but the super-searching ability never found me, and now it is also no longer functioning properly."

We now pass through the doorway in the cinder-block wall where we first entered. I cannot believe our good fortune. There has been no resistance since leaving Oscar behind to burn. The team visibly relaxes as we trudge into the abandoned mines.

My employer continues, "The weapon is awakening and stretching out. The draugar are part of that. The underground location and limited resources are slowing it down, but it is only a matter of time until a nightmare situation unfolds."

"And it has a name: Legion"

That sounds bad. Apocalyptic weapon and all.

"This is why we are safe in the mines," he explains. "The broadcasting capability of the weapon is tied to the electronic systems of the facility. They are limited to the outer ring. At least for now."

Looking at Mr. Lark, I feel compelled to ask, "Should we take action?"

He shakes his head. "Thomas, as I have said before, we do not solve the world's problems. At some point the situation here will draw the attention of the government or an intelligence agency and they will deal with it."

From the way he concluded that last sentence, I can tell this discussion has also ended.

Chapter 10

We are maintaining a good pace, and Allison has no problems keeping up. The now-former lab tech is sure-footed as she stays close to Mike.

When we arrive at the entrance to the leg leading down to the sump we entered from, Held pauses as we pass, shifting to the rear of the column. Once we are all into the final downslope walk to our exfiltration point, he wires several proximity mines to protect us from anything that might be following.

The still-lit sump hums with the air pump still performing its task. The team does not pause, or slow down. We are getting out of here as quickly as possible, and the sense of urgency is palpable. Allison looks on as Mike changes into his wet suit in a flash and is out the softlock. Equipment is placed back in sealed bags that are then inflated and fed out to Mike. Once attached to the line, they will begin slowly floating up and away.

Allison tries on Oscar's wetsuit. Oversized on her frame, we apply some duct tape to take up some of the slack. Ilych is the second to leave, followed by Allison.

Despite all she has been through, the former Giggle Corp lab tech suits up without complaint and climbs into the softlock when asked.

Mr. Lark follows.

My turn then. Once out, I remain close to the softlock while waiting for Held. After what seems like forever but was probably more like thirty seconds, I see him enter the softlock and then exit into the frigid water.

For the next hour, we float upward, pulling on the line against the faint artesian current. It requires no small amount of upper-body strength. The team takes turns assisting Allison. After what she has just been though, she is demonstrating remarkable resilience. Having been in similar situations, I am guessing she is running on adrenaline for now. When this is over, she will crash.

By the time we reach the pool in the mountains, my shoulders and arms are burning from exertion. Exhaustion is also setting in. This mission has to be at least twelve hours long now. After sustaining myself on power bars and water, I am ready for a real meal and some coffee.

After those before me exit the water, it is finally my turn. The slippery ice combined with the feeling of being extra heavy make leaving the water a challenge. Standing takes a bit of doing.

Mike and Illych help with my breathing mask and air tank.

It is daytime, or at least a grey, sunless, dreary version of it. The wind is icy on my face, and a few snowflakes blow about.

Tank has prepared for our return. Boots and parkas are tied to their respective owners' rucksacks. The air tanks and masks will be abandoned and sunk. Our load walking down the mountain will be much lighter.

Allison makes do with Oscar's parka and boots. His rucksack goes to a watery grave with the rest of the gear.

Tank pulls Illych and me aside and asks what happened to Oscar. Illych draws his finger across his throat. Tank shrugs.

"Where did the girl come from?" he asks.

"They were giving them away," I reply. "Mike got the last one."

Tank shakes his head and walks away.

Our line of weary, black-clad figures begins hiking down the mountain. We have to remind our exhausted selves to put one foot in front of the other. The vehicles are still waiting when we arrive. The team splits up, four in one vehicle, three in another.

It is miles of slow going downslope before we turn onto a fire road that leads to a dirt road that then leads to a black-top road. Turns out Mr. Lark arranged for a house to be ready for us. Night has just set when we arrive at an old farmhouse in the middle of nowhere.

Tank soon has a roaring fire going in the fireplace. The house is cold enough to see our breath when we arrive but soon warms up nicely.

There is hot water and a shower. Ladies first, of course. While Allison is showering, we search for clothes for her. She left her filthy, days-old apparel in the mines when she put on the wet suit.

Mr. Lark watches our futile efforts and actually rolls his eyes. Grabbing Mike with one hand, he produces a dongle with the other. "Keep her in the bathroom for fifteen minutes," he says to the rest of us. And then they disappear.

We find food in the refrigerator and cupboards, and we all begin eating while cooking.

A knock sounds at the front door.

What the hell? We are literally in the middle of nowhere. Who could it possibly be? Firearms are brandished, and Illych gives me the signal to open the door. No porch light and the reflection of the inside illumination prevent me from seeing who is outside. Perhaps this is local law enforcement checking up on a normally dark and unoccupied property?

Opening the door, I find Mr. Lark and Mike standing there.

"Is she still in the bathroom?" my employer asks.

I nod.

"May we enter?"

I step away and make space for them to enter.

Mike shows the team what he is carrying: a collection of women's casual wear. "We can say we found them here." He then walks back to the bathroom and we hear a knock followed by Mike announcing what he has brought.

Dinner preparations continue as Allison returns from her shower. A rapid rock, paper, scissors contest ensues for who gets the shower next. Held takes his leave, and the rest of us sit down for dinner. Even Mr. Lark.

Allison, now dressed in an oversized T-shirt and jogging pants, joins the rest of us at the dining table. The hours of sleep during the drive here and now a shower have improved her condition, and she is talkative now.

"So, who are you guys?"

This should be fun to watch.

Illych steps up for this one. "We are a private organization that hires itself out for certain opportunities."

Very diplomatic, Illych.

"Like mercenaries? You have a lot of guns."

"Yes, we have a lot of guns."

"So, when can I go home?"

At this point, Mr. Lark comments, "Ms. Jaeger, you are never going home. Your employer, and more importantly, whoever constructed that nightmare back in that mine, thinks you have perished. This is to your advantage."

Silent and wide-eyed, you could see her processing what he had just said.

"Where will I go? And what about my stuff in my apartment? Oh, and my mom . . . I have not called her in days. She will be freaking out by now."

Mr. Lark calmly continues speaking. "You misunderstand the situation," he says. "If it becomes known you are still alive, you will be interrogated and murdered. This is not the sort of event anyone would want to leave surviving witnesses to."

"Who are you to make this decision for me? I appreciate the rescue, but I can figure things out for myself."

This is getting is nowhere, so I add to the discussion. "Allison, remember what happened to Oscar? That is what they will do to you. Or at the very least something similar."

"Dead men tell no tales," chimes in Tank.

This seems to register with the young woman as she pauses and her head tilts. "Like in that pirate movie. You know, I never liked that job. Why don't I work with you guys? You could use a person like me. But I do need some things from my apartment. And I have to tell my mom. She will be so worried."

This is not registering with her yet, and she is repeating herself.

My employer stands and hovers over the young woman. "You will never return to your apartment nor communicate with your parents ever again," he says harshly. "As to joining my organization, I fail to see any useful skill you could provide."

Looking directly at the old man, Allison fires back, "How can you know what skills I might have? You have not even interviewed me. There is significant room for people skills in this organization. I will start there."

Most of us at the table have to look away while we smile or chuckle. Allison is feisty, I will give her that.

Mr. Lark sits down. "I remain unimpressed, however, I have tasks that require an addition to the team and your availability, while lacking in experience, is opportune. Basing our activities exclusively at the Citadel prevents us from operating at maximum efficiency. This led to me to search for a portal in a location conducive to our operations.

"Having found such a location, I will need a supply manager, if you will, who will not trigger facial recognition everywhere they go, such as everyone at this table other than Ms. Jaeger will. Since she has witnessed some of the more extreme capabilities of our organization, she obviously cannot be released. If she is willing to join us, then the job is hers."

Allison looks at the rest of us for a few seconds, squints, and then looks back at Mr. Lark.

"Was that a job offer?"

"Yes, Ms. Jaeger. And the last job offer you are likely to receive." Now it gets quiet in the room. Only the occasional crackle of burning wood in the next room and Held's shower can be heard.

"I can never go home? My mom will think I died or disappeared."

She looks for sympathy around the group. Even Mike is stone-faced. Releasing her will get her killed, and she might give away what little she knows. This is a hard situation.

"This is like in that movie. An offer you can't refuse."

Mr. Lark nods.

The former lab assistant stands up and maneuvers around the table and shakes Mr. Lark's hand. "Thank you for the offer. I accept the position."

At this moment, Held comes out wrapped in a towel while drying his hair with another. Without looking, he starts speaking. "Hot water is out. Whoever is next will need to wait." Finally paying attention, he sees Allison shaking Mr. Lark's hand.

"What did I miss?"

Chapter 11

The day after our return from the Giggle mission and Allison joining our merry troupe is a blur of activity. The team travels back to the Citadel. Unfortunately, to Mike's disappointment, Allison only stays long enough for The Doctor to install Mr. Lark's special crown to block radiating emotions or thoughts. After that, Mr. Lark and his newest employee are off to the secret new base in plain sight, if that makes any sense. Since this all transpired, I have experienced two days of what passes for as uneventful.

Sitting in the library, I fantasize about this new base. It has now been almost a year since I came to the extra-planar fortress that is the Citadel and all its exotic strangeness. Surviving those challenges gives me nostalgic feelings about this place. Will we soon be looking back to the past as the good old days when we were at the Citadel?

My reverie is broken when Illych enters the library to fetch me. Mr. Lark is here. Time to visit Langstraad Solutions and deliver the news. During the walk to the Compass, I ask Illych about the backpack he is carrying. This is not an expected accessory for one of these trips.

"These are Oscar's gadgets," he replies. "We are returning them." I frown and nod. The adventure did not turn out well for the man.

Soon, we are in a limousine headed toward the ocean. The sun is shading red as it sets. It will be interesting to see how Boro reacts to the loss of Oscar.

Minutes pass, and our arrival confirms my assumption. Our destination is the same as last time. Illych and I share a glance and a smile. We are going back on the yellow submarine.

We enter the boathouse and descend into the submarine. At the bottom of the ladder is Langstraad Solutions CEO Boro Stipple and Chairman of the Board Virginia Allen. Once again, no sooner do my feet touch the floor than the hatch above me clangs shut. Boro shambles off to the fishbowl at the bow, leaving the four of us in uncomfortable silence.

In a few short minutes, the relatively silent electric drive of the sub announces its presence with a purr, and we begin our preprogrammed dive. Boro returns from the fishbowl at a more relaxed pace.

He waves his hand to the circle of comfortable chairs arranged on the floor. The five of us take a seat, and Boro begins the discussion. "I have not heard from Oscar. What is his condition? Was your mission a success?"

These words hang heavy in the air. Virginia and the CEO sit side by side opposite Mr. Lark. Illych sits to the right of our employer. Shifting to the left of the old man, I choose to remain standing. This could get interesting. And I can see Ilych's hand sliding up inside his coat closer to the weapon holstered there. Yes, this could get very interesting.

"Your employee perished during the operation," Mr. Lark delivers.

The silence that follows is like when players at a poker table are trying to read each other. Both sides intensely regard each other for one long pause. Then Boro speaks. "Oscar is dead? I knew something was wrong when I did not hear from him in twenty-four hours. He would not have made me wait like this."

Virginia, looking less than enthused, asks, "And the mission you are being paid a substantial premium to accomplish? How did that end?"

Mr. Lark, in a calm voice, explains, "The mission was a complete success or an utter failure, depending on your point of view."

This reply clearly exasperates the woman.

Her retort is quick. "Depending on a point of view? You were not paid to give vague responses. You were paid to deliver. The only result I see is Langstraad Solutions losing a valued employee."

"The mission was completed regardless of Oscar's circumstance," Mr. Lark replies. "My employee here has the man's possessions to return to you."

My employer continues speaking while Illych passes the backpack to Boro. "The circumstances supporting your competitors' increased performance have changed. Giggle Corp is no longer the leader they were."

Boro and Virginia look at each other. The CEO speaks first. "What have you done? This was supposed to be a peek-only mission. Sabotage was not requested. I hope this is not some strange attempt at being paid more."

Mr. Lark shakes his head. "There was no sabotage, and I will not share the technical details because I am sure you are not interested."

The old man looks directly at Virginia. "Giggle Corp engaged in a joint endeavor with entities of the most unsavory sort. For a short time, your competitor enjoyed some commercial benefits from the collaboration. Unfortunately, such things cannot last forever, and those benefits have degraded into nothing. Now the situation has changed. The performance improvements challenging Langstraad's dominance no longer exist. This is through no action we took. The change simply coincided with our efforts.

"Oscar was in the wrong place at the wrong time and died horribly from the predatory forces unleashed by the unholy pact Giggle Corp entered into. Fortunately, we were able to destroy his corpse and all traces of our presence."

Both Virginia and Boro have turned a ghastly shade of white. Gotta give it to the old man. He can deliver a message as dark and horrifying as humanly possible.

"None of this will come back to Langstraad Solutions."

My employer stops talking and waits for his clients to speak.

After a long pause, Virginia speaks first. "You did nothing? Your services were secured to peek at their technology. Instead of delivering, you tell us the valued employee we provided to assist is dead and there is nothing to report as the reasons for the mission no longer exist?"

Leaning forward toward Mr. Lark, her voice changes into something sharp and cold. "Then why should you get paid?"

I can feel my eyes go wide at that. Even Illych blinks a couple of times. She said that out loud. To Karl Lark.

Mr. Lark remains stone-faced and leans forward just a bit, locking his gaze with the woman's. "Extenuating circumstances do not nullify payment."

Sitting back, Mr. Lark continues. "You have neither the experience nor the resources to get between mercenaries and their pay. Payment is due within twenty-four hours of final delivery. I consider this final delivery."

He leans forward even a bit more. "And my opinion is the only one that counts."

The old man's eyes remain locked to Virginia's. Another long pause passes where the only sound is the faint throbbing of the submarine's electric drive.

Virginia Allen blinks.

"Giggle Corp has signed a number of contracts based on its improved performance," says Virginia as she sits back in her chair, her voice softening. "If what you say is true, your fee is an acceptable loss compared to Langstraad's stock performance when Giggle can no longer deliver on those promises. Perhaps even shorting Giggle's stock is in order."

Mr. Lark nods in agreement.

Boro slaps his hands down on his legs, catching everyone by surprise. "Then this meeting is over," he says. "Your mission is complete. Langstraad Solutions was not implicated, and Giggle Corp will no longer be a challenge. I will now change our destination and return us to the dock." The CEO quickly stands and speed walks back to the submarine's bow.

Virginia crosses her arms and legs and says nothing for the return trip. Boro stays in the fishbowl until we dock. Apparently, with business concluded, there will be no small talk. I feel cheated. A conversation on what we found or what will happen to the facility would have been interesting.

We dock, and only the CEO shakes Mr. Lark's hand before we leave. Virginia does not even stand for our exit.

The only thing left for me to consider during the drive back to the hotel is how much they paid for the mission. This prompts me to do something I have never done before.

"Mr. Lark, how much did you charge for the mission?"

Illych looks at me with an incredulous expression and slightly shakes his head.

The old man remains staring ahead. "Mr. Davies, some days you are more exasperating than others." Looking in my direction, he continues. "I fail to see the value in sharing such information with one of my employees." His line of vision then returns to its previous target.

The rest of the ride back is in silence.

No sooner do we arrive at the Compass and begin the familiar walk to the Citadel than Mr. Lark addresses me. "Mr. Davies, you are familiar with the Christian New Testament?"

Where is this going? "Yes, quite familiar. A large segment of the rare book business involves Judeo-Christian writings."

"At your soonest convenience, begin compiling every piece of information available on the demon referred to as Legion."

"The demons exorcised in the New Testament? That will not take long. There is not much more information available on Legion than there is on magi." No sooner do I say it than I know what is coming next.

"Excellent observation, Mr. Davies. Perhaps a visit to Balthazar is in order. I will arrange it. Illych will accompany you. You will have an opportunity to find out what the magus is willing to share."

"It has been months since I last saw Balthazar. I take it he still owes you some favors from his rescue?"

"Not from the rescue," Mr. Lark says. "That pool of opportunity is largely exhausted. Even though ending his three hundred fifty years of captivity earned significant goodwill, our needs have consumed it. Both in the considerable weight of gold paid and the knowledge shared. Locating his former servants and delivering them back to his residence near the Caspian Sea rebuilt that account. This request will be debited against that consideration."

"That rescue was not a clean operation," Illych comments.

"The opposition was able to trap a magus on a phantom island for three hundred fifty years," Mr. Lark replies. "Taking into account the magnitude of what we were up against, the delivery was acceptable. Our inadvertent revealing of their location was made up for by our subsequent spirited defense."

Not long after rescuing the descendants of his former servants and returning them to his residence in the non-Euclidean contraction where his ancient residence is located, we stopped our visits. Most likely to allow time for everyone involved to grieve and come to terms with what had happened. Men, women, and children had died in that operation.

After we arrive at the Citadel, the old man does not stay long. He pursues some task with Illych and then finds me at the library. After telling me to be ready to travel on a moment's notice, he leaves.

Wasting no time, I pull multiple translations of the appropriate New Testament books. After hours of reading and re-reading the few short passages referencing the demon called Legion, I have precious little to show for the time invested.

Briefly, I consider translating to a hotel and buying a laptop to access some online libraries I have researcher rights to. I quickly discard the idea. Now that it has been revealed the bad guys are using ancient malevolent intelligence to search for Mr. Lark on the internet, my searching for related topics may not be the best approach.

Disappointed in what little I have accomplished, I check the time. Where did the day go? I skipped lunch, and if I do not move quickly, my dinner will be an individual affair. Standing, I stretch then fast walk to the cafeteria. When I arrive, the others are conversing over empty plates. Quickly grabbing some food, I join the team. This will most likely be my only human contact for the rest of the day.

Mike welcomes me to sit next to him as the others acknowledge my presence.

"Thomas, you remembered to eat. We almost came to get you at lunch but figured you were deep in it."

I nod. "Mr. Lark directed me to research something. It kept me busy today."

"What did he ask you to research?" Mike asks. "I am assuming this is not some top-secret project."

"No, this is not top secret. Apparently, when Mr. Lark connected to the systems in the Giggle facility, he found something. It was brought there and connected to all those computers and the internet. Some sort of ancient weapon called Legion. The New Testament references it. Nothing useful, though. And after a long day of studying everything I have on the subject, I have little to nothing to report."

"You can't win them all," Illych joins in. "My suspicion is this Legion thing is something people would purposefully keep from the history books."

I shrug and reply, "Probably."

Illych has more to say. "Mr. Lark sent a message that instructions were waiting at the Compass. Mike and Tank picked them up a few hours ago. Arrangements have been made for you and me to visit Balthazar tomorrow morning first thing."

We knew this was coming, so it's no surprise. What I cannot explain is the giddy excitement I feel about seeing Balthazar again. Like a child who knows a gift is soon coming.

Dinner comes to an end, and I attempt sleep after some light reading. My rest is fitful. The prospect of visiting the ancient residence of the old magus and what I might learn tomorrow keeps me awake. In the end, I get fewer hours of rest than I would prefer.

Waking with cobwebs in my head does not bode well for the day. After dressing, I meet Illych in the cafeteria, power up on coffee, eat a little bit, and we leave.

Balthazar never learned of Mr. Lark's ouiblet and its ability to translate things instantly from place to place. Our employer wants to keep it that way, so we translate to a quiet location in rural Russia not far from the magus's residence. An empty vehicle sits nearby, and we drive it the two or more hours to the base of Shahgah Mountain, not far from the Caspian Sea.

This part of the world is lightly populated at best, and we see few on the road and none after the road ends as we drive cross-country to our destination.

The rumble of the diesel engine and the squeak of suspension on rough roads accompany us on a peaceful drive. Halfway to our destination, Illych breaks the silence.

"What do you think of this Allison joining the team?"

This had been bouncing around the back of my mind also. "Mr. Lark is not interested in our opinions. If he decides she is in, then it is done."

Illych pauses and then says, "She does not fit the profile."

"Neither did I. Maybe Mr. Lark has a plan?"

"He always has a plan. His plans are like nesting dolls, one within the other, with contingencies for the contingencies. And, in case you're wondering, my concern is not about her gender."

"Maybe her gender is the point. Or maybe it's because she is officially deceased. No one is looking for her?"

Illych remains focused on the road. "The rest of us show up in facial recognition databases with a big red flag. Remember when we were looking for those genetically engineered children and those thugs at that airport beat the crap out of you? They identified us both through facial recognition. If Mr. Lark is planning a move out into the world, he needs a face that won't draw attention."

The thought brings a smile to my face. "A young woman not affiliated with anything and considered dead. Just like the rest of us, she can't go back. They would find her. But they will not be looking for her."

Illych nods. "That is my guess as to our employer's most likely play."

Wondering out loud, I ask, "This new place out in the world. Do you think it will be nice?"

Illych shrugs. "Mr. Lark has a certain sense of propriety when it comes to his employees. I would guess it will be pretty swanky."

Nodding, I say, "Mike seems happy with Allison."

"He may be happy with her," Illych growls. "Hopefully Mike understands if they start feuding over a breakup or whatever interpersonal conflict might grow from them fraternizing, I will enjoy slapping it out of him."

Solving problems in the workplace through violence.

"Look at us," I say. "Gossiping like a pair of hens."

Illych grins, and the rest of the drive is spent in silence.

We stop when a singular weather-beaten and worn square stone pillar comes into view. Balthazar's front door. Illych and I exit the vehicle and walk the last few feet to stand by the pillar. Now we wait. One of his Lesser Created servants dressed as an Old World manservant will come for us. None may enter except by the magus's consent.

We do not wait long before the short, gangly, green-skinned form of a goblin appears from thin air. This is not my first experience in this place, but the creature's wide mouth filled with crooked teeth and bulging solid black eyes reflecting my own image back at me is disturbing every time I experience it.

The thing speaks in the voice of a young boy. "My master has instructed me to extend his welcome and hospitality to the servants of Karl Lark. A peace bond is offered, and no harm shall come to you in this place. Will you accept my master's offer?"

For a brief moment I considered what would happen should I decline. This thought is dismissed as soon as it manifests. Just because I can think of something does not make it a good idea.

Taking the lead, I bow my head to the ancient creature. "We accept your master's peace bond and look forward to his hospitality."

The goblin bows in return. "Then in my master's name, please enter."

The diminutive creature turns away, begins to take a walking step, and shifts from our sight, essentially disappearing. One step past the point where the goblin vanished, Illych and I find ourselves on a smooth stone road leading to a massive ziggurat-like structure in the distance. The square stone pillar is gone, taking with it the windswept Russian countryside.

Ahead of us the goblin is walking a good pace, and we briefly jog to keep up. This leaves only a few minutes to sight-see before entering the gates of Balthazar's residence. During the short walk, I can see that the fields to the left that had lain fallow for three hundred fifty years have now been attended to. To the right, the massive redwood-sized trees are as impressive as the last time. This place still feels old; ancient, really. The reason why is hard to explain, but the Sumerian-style ziggurat we are approaching certainly contributes to this impression.

The main doors are wide open. Standing in the entryway, dressed in a conservative modern suit, is Hector, former protector of the servant diaspora residing in Ehgira, Turkey, now returned to serve Magus Balthazar. Every time I have been in this man's presence he is angry. Angry at the world, angry at us. Mostly because we inadvertently led bad guys to his town, resulting in half his town's men, women, and children being murdered. That would be hard to get past.

He looks more relaxed this time. His new role serving the magus must be agreeable. Actually, I am unsure what tasks Balthazar would assign the hothead.

As we approach the great entrance, our goblin escort disappears from sight. One instant he is here, and then it is like he walks through a door to somewhere else and is gone.

Hector does not hesitate and bends slightly at the waist. "The master of this place bids you welcome and sanctuary. Peace be upon you."

Nice. Hector's manners have been seriously upgraded.

Stopping a respectful distance away, I copy his bow. "Thank you for the welcome, and peace be upon all in this great house." I can lay it on when I have to. Years of reading history gives me some skill in this area, which is why Illych is following my lead.

Hector straightens. "Please, follow me. Do you require refreshment or rest from your journey?" He turns and begins walking into the foyer, his head still half turned awaiting our reply.

"No, thank you, Hector. The journey was not strenuous."

"My master has instructed me to place you in his presence when you are ready."

Looking at Illych, we nod to each other.

"We have been looking forward to seeing the magus. Please lead us to him."

Hector sets a casual pace as we cross the great foyer to an inner door. The pale-white stonework around us is as ancient as it is beautiful. We see no other people, and it does not appear anything has changed in this place since our last visit.

Once we are past the inner door, I ask, "Hector, what is your role here now?" Not the smoothest question delivery ever, but I would like to know.

"Master Thomas, I am the major domo of the gate. Master Balthazar is instructing me in the way of my ancestors and as his personal guide to his visitors."

Interesting. Probably a good use for the militant characteristics I have seen from him in the past.

"Do you receive many visitors?" I ask.

Silence.

Illych catches the corner of my eye and shakes his head. Taking the hint, I return to enjoying the carved stone alcoves lining the hall we are walking. Each one has a scene made of both background painting and carved statuary. Some of what I see is relatable to established history. Many of them represent events that do not fit anything I have seen in any book.

Arriving at an open door. Hector steps past, turns back to face us, and with a wave of his hand, indicates we are to enter. I give the major domo a head nod as we pass on our way through the portal. Inside is a room with an array of beautiful Arabian-style carpeting and pillows to sit and rest among. In the middle is a lit brazier with a small wood fire within. Lamps placed around the perimeter of the room provide a soft white light. The lighting is comfortable; bright enough to reveal the room in every detail but low enough to comfortably relax.

Sitting upon a slightly elevated platform opposite the door is Magus Balthazar. Short by modern standards, he is lean and wiry. His scalp has what appears to be a permanently embedded golden skullcap. His forearms bear alternating gold and black rings that form tightly embedded vambraces. The ancient man sits facing the doorway as we enter and immediately stands to greet us.

Standing directly behind Balthazar is the spirit of this place. Easily seven feet tall, a hooded silvery grey robe hiding its true form. Quiet and unmoving, it has a palpable presence. During past visits to this place, only its hands and unshod feet have been witnessed, and they indicate the spirit is neither human nor humanlike. Its sinister form is never more than a few paces from our host.

Sitting to the magus's right is a man dressed in outdoor traveling clothes: hiking boots, loose-fitting trousers, and a comfortable-looking, worn long-sleeved shirt and overcoat. Lean and weathered with darkly tanned skin, even seated he appears somewhat taller than our standing host. He regards us with dark eyes.

The magus smiles and closes the gap between us. "Thomas, Illych, it is good to welcome you to my residence again." A handshake grasping both hands is exchanged with Illych and I.

"Please sit. My servants will bring refreshment." The magus returns to his seat as I take the space to his left. Illych picks a spot close to the door and comfortably reclines. Goblin manservants appear out of nowhere with Turkish coffee and a small assortment of fruits and sweetbreads. No matter how many times I see these ancient beings shift in and out of sight, it is still unsettling.

Balthazar does not introduce his guest, and whoever the man is, he watches Illych and I intently.

While Illych and I are situated and acquire refreshment, the magus consults with his other guest in low tones. The little I hear is in a language unfamiliar to me.

The first sip of the coffee brings a smile to my face. It is so good.

Balthazar sees this and says, "What brings the servants of Karl Lark seeking my knowledge?"

Looking at the strange man seated to his right, I look back at our host.

"All who enter my home must swear the peace bond, Thomas," Balthazar replies. "Nothing spoken here can be used against the speaker. To do so is an insult to the House of Balthazar."

"Thank you, Balthazar. Please forgive my concern." This would be easier if he would introduce us to the other participant.

The magus nods his head in understanding.

"Mr. Lark has sent me to ask about an ancient weapon called Legion."

The magus is silent and appears to be considering what I have just said.

"Why does Karl Lark ask this?"

"We encountered something my employer called draugar. Apparently, this Legion creates them from recently deceased humans. The name Legion was also within the data storage Mr. Lark viewed."

The magus nods. "It was only a matter of time, considering everything that has happened: my imprisonment and the disappearance of my brother magi. The enemy brings Legion into play." He pauses. "Karl Lark has performed great service for me, and if he wishes his servant to know these things, then I will explain Legion to his servants on his behalf."

"This is why I was sent here."

Balthazar sits back, and when he next speaks, his voice sounds older. "This started long ago, when those who came before were dealing with the ancients' rebellion, which is commonly referred to as the War in Heaven."

I take another sip of majestic coffee and wait.

"The rebelling ancients are what your employer refers to as the Greater Created. A group of them engaged in a rebellion prompted by the creation of the Mannu, the precursors to humanity. Assisted in numbers by their creation of the djinn, the rebels appeared to be edging closer to victory. In preparation for their perceived imminent success, they began planning to exterminate the nascent humanity they loathed. Legion is their diabolical creation. Killing a human being and then possessing and reanimating the corpse is just one of its functions. These reanimated corpses are not higher functioning in the way of the truly possessed. They act more as slaves controlled by Legion. In addition to these draugar, as Mr. Lark calls them, the weapon can do much more.

"Legion can influence living humans. Change likes and dislikes. Bend long-held beliefs. Over time, this kind of influence will drive the humans insane. But for a great while, those who are influenced will appear normal. The subjects themselves are unaware of the influence. Fortunately, only the weak-minded are susceptible.

"The ancients are few in number. Even when combined with their many Lesser brethren and their djinn creations, there are not enough to scour a planet like Earth of life. Legion allows them to control vast numbers of humanity, living and dead. An army of humans created to destroy all human life."

Balthazar pauses, giving me enough time to ask, "If this has been around for so long, why is humanity still here?"

He nods. "Well asked. Not long after initiating the creation of Legion, the rebels found themselves on the losing side of the War in Heaven . As the traitors' attempt failed, so was Legion improperly completed. It mostly does what its creators intended, but it requires more energy and attention. It is more difficult to keep operating as intended, and in the past, its consumption of humanity burns itself out without achieving extermination.

"My suspicion is you have found where this weapon is now and the strange things you witnessed are the side effects of the difficulty in trying to control the ancient monstrosity that is Legion."

Looking at Illych and then back to our host, I ask, "Can it be destroyed?"

Balthazar shakes his head. "Thomas, Legion was created by the greatest amongst ancients at the height of their power. No mortal, no matter how gifted, will ever be able to destroy such a thing. Even your current age's atomic weapons are meaningless to such a timeless thing."

The feeling of helplessness I am having is unpleasant. "We can do nothing?"

The old magus smiles. "We can do many things. There are reasons Legion has never succeeded despite many, many attempts. Legion is a difficult thing to bring to bear and even more difficult to keep focused and executing. Without herculean efforts, it tends to sabotage itself.

"Only one of the ancient masters can properly compel Legion. Not even a djinn is sufficient. Humans cannot master such a thing. Their incompetence will cause the effort to end in disaster.

"Unfortunately, until whatever or whoever is trying to wield Legion this time learns their own limitations, a misery of apocalyptic proportions may be wrought upon humanity. This cannot be allowed."

The last part of what he says catches my attention. The magi are passive observers who follow a strict policy of non-interference. Balthazar has shown flexibility in this policy since being rescued after three hundred fifty years of imprisonment on the phantom island of Hy-Brasil. Apparently, if the bad guys can put a finger on the scale, so can a magus.

"How so, Balthazar? How can we end what has begun?"

The magus reclines and unconsciously raises a hand to his chin. He nods. "Yes, I have a thought."

Looking at me and smiling, he says, "Thomas, remember how I was brought out of Hy-Brasil in order to keep the enemy from learning of my escape?"

"You have that little box or cube. The tesseract," I say. "You called it a quixault. Can we trap Legion in one of those things?"

"If properly prepared, a quixault will remove Legion from this world and hold it immobile," Balthazar replies.

"Balthazar, would you be willing to provide a quixault to trap Legion?"

The old man appears to consider the option during a long pause. "Yes, Thomas Davies, I believe providing such a thing will help even the scales. Word will be sent when it is ready, and my servant Hector will deliver it to a place of your choosing." The magus continues. "But holding Legion in a quixault will not be enough. The device must be stored somewhere safe."

The answer is obvious to me. "Why not store it here? Would it not be safe with you?"

"No, Thomas. Such an ancient evil corrupts everything it touches. Legion must never be brought here."

An idea came to me. "What about The Gyre? That place where one of your brothers went. You mentioned it was where Those Who Came Before disposed of things difficult to destroy. Let's toss the Legion-filled quixault in there."

The magus considers my words. "A possible approach, and The Gyre would be my first choice also, but only my brother Vadkeinen knew how to find it, and he is gone. There is another place where such things could be stored effectively out of reach. Referred to as Tartarus in Hellenic mythology. Those Who Came Before used it as a prison and storage vault for things too dangerous to leave lying about but not needing the permanence of The Gyre."

"Tartarus. You mean hell?"

"No, Thomas. Time and the numerous retellings of the subject have distorted what Tartarus is and changed it from its true description."

"Thank you for the guidance. Where can Tartarus be found?"

The magus shrugs. "I will provide the quixault. Mr. Lark must find Tartarus."

Okay then.

Silence settles on the room for a short while. Then Balthazar's unspeaking guest stands unexpectedly, as does our host. They share a warrior's goodbye, grasping each other's forearms simultaneously and locking gazes for a fierce moment. Then the dark man strides purposefully from the room.

The magus returns to reclining and sipping wine.

"Balthazar, I do not wish to offend you, but who was that man?"

"This is not an offense, merely a display of curiosity. That was Meili, the Traveler."

"Is he a man like you?"

"No, Thomas, he is not like a magus. He is not a man either."

Not a man? "When was the last time you saw him?

"My life is but the most recent to be privileged to carry the name of Balthazar. Magi live a thousand years, and my years number less than nine hundred. Never during that time have I met the Traveler. My last memory of him was four lives ago."

Even I can do that math. Four thousand years ago. "So you did not ask him here?"

"No one commands the Traveler. Finding him is impossible. He has no residence and is ancient beyond time, knowing even the beginning. Such beings come and go as they please. He arrived unbidden shortly before you arrived. Even today he did not say why he was here or why he had to leave."

It would be rude to ask what they had discussed. "So he just shows up at the entrance and you let him in?"

Balthazar stands, and I follow. Facing me, he places a hand on my shoulder. "Meili does not request entrance while standing outside like a beggar. He just enters. It is his way." Balthazar walks toward the door indicating our visit is over. "Now, as it was his time to continue on his journey, so must you. The quixault will be available soon. Word will be sent when it is ready." The magus steps back and bows. "Your time here is done. Safe travels, Thomas Davies, and long life."

I bow in return. Even Illych is standing now and participates in our goodbye banter. "Magus Balthazar, may you have only success in your endeavors," he says. This brings a smile to the magus.

Hector arrives right on cue to escort us out. He is good at this butler thing.

There will be a lot to consider on the trip back to the Citadel. Even if Balthazar gives us this quixault, Mr. Lark will have no intention of going back to the mines just to help out or be a nice guy. And we would need to find Tartarus.

During the return trip, I have time to replay in my mind what just happened. Who or what is Meili? And from what Balthazar explained, this Legion is a bad thing to have happen. The good news, human incompetence can inadvertently shut it down. Fortunately, there has never been a shortage of that.

Chapter 12

We arrive back at the Citadel late in the evening. Illych immediately contacts Mr. Lark with a brief description of our success. It is only a matter of time until the old man shows up looking for a complete explanation. Until then, I will get a good night's sleep. Illych and I say our goodnights and retire for the evening.

I feel someone tapping my forehead, awakening me from a deep sleep. My first sight is Mr. Lark's face not a foot away from mine.

"Meet me in the library," he says. "It is time for your report." My grey-suited employer and his oculus-topped cane promptly exit. I immediately sit up to keep from falling back asleep. A quick look at the ghastly timepiece Mr. Lark makes us wear informs me I have been asleep an hour at most. My exhaustion is actually painful at this point.

Screw propriety. Bed clothes it is, then. I am not dressing after being woken like this.

Standing, I robotically walk to the library. Illych is there already and looking as thrilled as I am.

Flopping unceremoniously into a chair across from my employer, I'm unable to focus my eyes, so I stare into the distance.

Mr. Lark lets this go for a moment, and then one of his eyebrows raises.

Time for me to share. "As instructed, Illych and I visited Balthazar earlier today. He was glad to receive us. We discussed Legion, and he even had another visitor there when we arrived."

Then I relate our entire visit in detail. In the middle of my report, Illych begins gently snoring. Mr. Lark shoots him a cross look and then asks me a question: "This visitor was already there when you arrived but left after the discussion of Legion was complete?"

"Yes, that is a fair assessment."

"And then after the stranger left, Balthazar shared his name was Meili?" The old man must be onto something.

"Yes. Does this have some hidden meaning?"

"I am sure it does, Mr. Davies. Otherwise, Balthazar would not have orchestrated it. What it is, I cannot say at this time. Perhaps with further consideration the magus's hint about Tartarus will be revealed. Until then, we are left with little to work with regarding Legion."

I nod. All I want is for the meeting to end so I can return to sweet, sweet sleep soon.

"For now, this discussion is academic. The mission is complete, and I have been paid. This Tartarus sounds interesting, though. I can only imagine what is shut away there. We may have to visit this ancient vault in the future." I wonder if Balthazar had dangled Tartarus in front of Mr. Lark for other reasons. My sleep-deprived mind is not able to fully process the concepts.

"Soon I will have another assignment for you. The details of this meeting have not yet been finalized, but I expect confirmation soon. A unique piece has recently been loaned to the British Museum for display."

Did he say British Museum?

"We will leverage your close working relationship with Dr. Chatzas . . ."

Dr. Chatzas? Mr. Lark now has my full, focused attention.

". . . to find its present location because it is not currently on public display—"

"You are arranging for me to meet with Dr. Chatzas again?"

"Yes, Thomas, as soon as possible. Maybe even yet today, after you have more rest. Please pay attention. I would not appreciate repeating myself."

He pauses and looks at me for a few moments and then over at Illych's dozing form. "Perhaps you both should return to sleeping. You will be notified when the meeting's time and place are set."

Why could he not have left us asleep in the first place?

"Certainly, Mr. Lark. Please call for me in the morning."

My employer and I leave the library, extinguishing the lights as we leave. Illych is left alone in the dark, still asleep and snoring, as we close the door.

* * *

Sleep fixes everything. I do not know if that is a saying or not, but it should be. I awaken late morning refreshed, perform my morning routine and enter the cafeteria looking forward to coffee and breakfast.

It feels like a great start to a great day.

Arriving late last night exempted Illych and I from the morning calisthenics. Held, Mike, and Tank arrive to the cafeteria just before me in sweaty workout clothes. Illych, however, is not present. He is up by now, this I know; the former Green Beret never sleeps in.

Tank comes right out with it. "Rumor has it you are meeting your girlfriend again today."

"Rumor is right. At least that is what Mr. Lark shared last night. The old man wants to make a trade."

Curiosity getting the better of him, Tank keeps going. "So, are most archeology women as friendly as this Dr. Chatzas?"

"Not my area of expertise, Tank. Before coming to work for Mr. Lark, she hated me. Not fake hate because she secretly liked me. Genuine hate. She planned my murder to facilitate her own ambitious plans."

Mike chimes in next. "I have dated a lot of women. I have even dated women who did not speak English."

"Wait, how do you date a woman when you do not share a common language?" I ask.

Mike and Tank just look at me.

"And I can't believe I just said that out loud. We are talking about Mike. Okay, continue."

"I am just saying, Thomas. None of them tried having me killed. A couple of them did set some of my stuff on fire, though." Mike pauses. "What I am saying is whatever is going on with this woman is next-level shit. You need to be extra careful."

I feel a Cheshire grin erupt across my face. "Mike, are you telling me you care?"

Tank starts laughing.

"Don't be silly, English," says Mike. "If she kills you, Mr. Lark will just find a replacement. And who knows what strange character he will inflict on us." Mike nods for emphasis as he finishes.

Illych, dressed in casual civilian attire, enters the cafeteria. This means we are going somewhere and fun time is over.

"Let's go, Thomas. Dress casual. The meeting with Dr. Chatzas is set, and we need to move. Mr. Lark briefed me already, and I will update you on the way."

Still hungry, I wolf down a few bites of breakfast and rush to get ready. Not thirty minutes later the main gate swings open and Ilych and I walk out into the cold and gloom of the badlands around the Citadel.

On the way, Ilych explains what Mr. Lark is looking for.

"Apparently, Balthazar's bringing up Tartarus really piqued the old man's interest."

"Because it is a potential warehouse of ancient artifacts or because it may contain myriad dangerous mythological creatures?"

"Those are all proper Karl Lark reasons to look into something, Thomas."

"What about the Giggle Corp situation? Legion bringing about the apocalypse?"

"We completed the Giggle Corp mission. Time to move on. However, now that Balthazar has confirmed the existence of some sort of supernatural, extra-dimensional vault that is Tartarus, I am fairly certain our employer is factoring a visit into his near-term plans."

Makes sense. There has to be something interesting to find in Tartarus if half the mythology is true.

"So, what am I discussing with Elizabeth?"

"Yeah, about that. This is going to sound weird, but it is about handbags."

"Handbags?"

"Apparently, a lot of carvings from all over the world show important people from history carrying these weird little handbags. Having a purse was all the rage thousands of years ago. Anyway, an artifact that may have been part of one of these handbags was recently on display at the British Museum. It would have been just the carrying handle from the handbag. The display called it a torc, mistakenly representing it as a piece of jewelry. Mr. Lark wants this torc and would like to know its current location."

"So we can steal it?"

"We do not steal everything, Thomas. Sometimes we buy things too." My companion is smiling at his own sarcasm now.

"Understood. I am asking Dr. Chatzas for jewelry. Where are we meeting?"

"She requested you come to her apartment."

I actually stop walking. She wants to meet at her place.

Illych shakes his head. "It will be okay. She is unlikely to have you killed where she lives."

Her killing me is not what came to mind.

Resuming our hike to the Compass, I have to address the elephant in the room "The discussions may take some time."

Illych chuckles. "We are all adults. I will find a place nearby to get some coffee, and the negotiations can take as long as needed. You don't have to leave a sock on the doorknob or anything. You can join me when you have finished your discussion."

We arrive at the Compass and translate to London. Shortly thereafter we are traveling the streets in a grey Mercedes. True to his word, Illych finds a café a short walk from my destination. He enters to enjoy a hot beverage, and I leave for Dr. Chatzas's residence.

According to my watch, I am right on time when I ring her doorbell. What is wrong with me? There are butterflies in my stomach. We were together one night, and I am losing it. This is not the time for this.

My mind flashes with images of how I want her to look when she answers the door. These thoughts bring a frown to my face; this is also not the time for juvenile fantasies.

She makes me wait long enough to consider ringing a second time before the door opens.

A professionally dressed Elizabeth Chatzas opens the door. She must have just come from the office. Her hair is down, though, so at least there is that.

She looks me up and down with a flat, neutral expression just for a moment before smiling. "Thomas, please come in. Your employer sending you improves my day."

Entering her familiar residence, I reply, "How so? Rough day?"

"Nothing out of the ordinary. Perhaps I am glad you have time to visit me." Her voice has a hint of mischievousness to it.

She guides me to a semicircle of overstuffed chairs. Everything is flowers, colors, and detailed cloth covers. Very feminine.

Elizabeth wastes no time in getting down to business as we sit in separate chairs next to each other. "Mr. Lark must have sent you for a reason."

Her left hand reaches over and grasps my right hand. Apparently, we are holding hands now. Her grasp is warm and soft. This is not helping my thinking.

"Indeed. He sent me to discuss an artifact from the recent Scandinavian exhibit. A torc. It is perhaps a foot long, made from woven metal strands. The display lists it as jewelry."

Elizabeth nods. "I know the piece. When the exhibit finished at the museum, it travelled to Tokyo for its next planned showing. Everything should be sitting in a secure Japanese warehouse. The exact location is unknown to me. If your employer can wait a month or two, he will see the object of his interest on display in Japan." Elizabeth continues, "What does Karl Lark want with the torc? Is it valuable beyond historical worth?"

I shrug. "Mr. Lark does not share his plans or opinions on much of anything. Nor does he explain why he wants to acquire something. My apologies, Elizabeth, but you know about as much about my employer as I do."

My companion gets a thoughtful look on her face and then she says, "My dear Thomas, I am positive you know things that you are not even aware you have learned. But that is a discussion for another time."

A mischievous grin appears on her face. "I greatly enjoyed your last visit." She is looking at me with hungry eyes, and her hand is rubbing my arm. Even those clueless about signals from the opposite sex can figure this one out.

Over the next two hours I find myself almost overwhelmed by her passion. Elizabeth Chatzas is a lot of fun to be with.

Our intimacy comes to an end when I realize how much time has passed. Illych will only sit in a café for so long. After that, he will begin plotting my punishment for the delay.

The visit ends with a kiss hot enough to start a fire. Why is this woman single?

My walk back to Illych is less energetic than my walk from Illych. He has been monitoring my progress on his oculus and is not surprised when I enter the café. He looks relaxed while sipping coffee and watching the few locals. The café is mostly empty at this time of day.

After taking a seat, I share what I have learned.

Illych nods. "Unless the boss is in a hurry, that should be enough information to support acquiring the piece in the near future."

He finishes his coffee and stands. "Let's go."

Chapter 13

The next few days are a steady rhythm of morning calisthenics, long hours studying in the library, and three regular meals per day. It is still several weeks until we get time off, and there is a lot to do. Mr. Lark provides a constant supply of rare texts, maps, and folios from all over the world. My regular job as a librarian is never-ending. If only I had more time.

Lunch with my colleagues is somewhat predictable. Today, Mike and Tank engage in physical shenanigans. Held eggs them on while Illych quietly watches. My introversion keeps me from getting involved. When you reside in a dimensional pocket with no television or internet access, this is what passes for entertainment.

And then our employer walks in.

Mr. Lark announces the entire team will be going on a potentially hazardous archeological expedition. Expected duration is twenty-four hours maximum. Mission launch is 9 a.m. tomorrow at the Compass.

He then turns and leaves.

Illych breaks the silence. "You heard the man. Wrap up lunch and begin mission prep. First load-out inspection in two hours."

This is not our first rodeo, as Americans like to say. Gear and weapons are already grouped and pre-positioned. The five of us move our individual gear to the open space near the main gates and begin counting. And then we count them again. Lists are checked off. Then we check our colleagues' gear. The process is rigorous.

Body armour, check. Weapons and ammo, check. Explosives, medical kit, rope, lights, high-energy food, water . . . the list is long.

This time, we do not hold back on weapons. Both Tank and Illych are equipped with SHEGs. Everyone gets a White Fang and Truestone. Just in case we run into a Lesser Created.

Dinner comes late, and it is a quiet affair. It's followed by another round of counting and inspection. Then off to bed for a good night's sleep.

The next day, the five of us show up right on time at the Compass. Normally, the walk through the gloom and the cold between the Compass and the Citadel has an element of anxiety to it. Not today; not when equipped like this. Two-and-a-half stone of hardcore military gear and weapons cover my body. I feel like the God of War marching to crush my puny foes.

Mr. Lark, clad in his ancient banded armor of origin he is still unwilling to share, is waiting to hand us our emergency dongles. The old man's armor is jet-black just like the rest of the team's. His face and head are not enclosed, however. When we are together as a group, his disembodied pale face and white hair are a little disconcerting. For reasons unknown, having his face unprotected does not bother him. It is almost as if not having a helmet for protection is not a liability. I do not understand, and my employer has shared little on the subject.

This all occurs in complete silence until Illych directs a question to our employer. "What is the op?'"

Without pause, the old man answers, "My curiosity has gotten the best of me, and we are going to look for Tartarus. I wish to see this place built to hold the more interesting of the ancients' creations."

Illych and I share an I-told-you-so glance.

"Dangerous artifacts and dangerous constructs," I interject.

Mr. Lark glares in my direction. "Since almost nothing my organization is ever involved in would be considered safe, I fail to see the value in your comment." Looking back to the others he continues. "A legend says that the Atlanteans had a map room in Atlantis that marked all the portals and non-Euclidean contractions they were aware of. I suspect the location of Tartarus can be found there."

An Atlantean map room? I have never encountered any such story, legend, or myth in all my readings. Perhaps the old man has special sources?

Held breaks his silence, his voice carrying a hint of sarcasm. "But we would need to know where Atlantis is." This is something we are all thinking.

"Finding Atlantis was something I resolved years ago. Like many of the older cities, it was largely eradicated using seismic and high-energy, delaminating weaponry. What little survived has been picked over and disappeared during the intervening twelve thousand years.

"Balthazar's Tartarus comments inspired me—no doubt his intention," he continues. "After revisiting my sources, I realized the Atlantean map room is described as being kept hidden. Perhaps a pocket dimension or non-Euclidean contraction.

"I translated an oculus to the ruins and took snapshots. To my disappointment I found no portals to pocket dimensions. There is, however, a non-Euclidean contraction. Perhaps the map room can be found there."

My frustration has been building. "Mr. Lark, where is Atlantis?"

"In Africa. Mauritania, to be specific. It is the Richat Structure. Once you understand the weapons used to destroy it, everything makes sense."

"You have known the location to Atlantis and never visited?" I say incredulously.

"Mr. Davies, thousands of megalithic structures, portals, and lost cities cover the globe. I am busy with the few I have time to visit. Should we live a thousand years, we will never visit them all. If you are finished interrupting, though, we will visit this one. May we now return to today's business?"

I nod. The world is a big place, I guess. And the old man is a little irritable today.

We cluster about the old man inside the stone circle. The translation is the usual nauseating experience. Mid-afternoon, we arrive in Mauritania.

Looking around, we might as well have landed on the moon. Bright sun and dry dust extend away from us in all directions. I had heard of the Richat Structure before. It is like a great circular eye in the middle of nowhere. Visible from space, it is a virtually lifeless part of the world. From where we are standing on the ground, I see nothing but unremarkable desert.

Thermal haze roils across the horizon. Our black full-body armor is absorbing the full force of the sun. The blazing light and heat burning through my faceplate forces me to look down.

"Mr. Lark, unless we are planning on heat-stroking the team, we need to get out of this sun," says Illych.

"Your concerns are noted," Mr. Lark responds. "The portal is close by. We will be leaving in moments. I have some last-minute information to share. The legends indicate the library is guarded. No specifics were given."

A deep-throated chuckle registers over the ComDat. Tank, I think.

Illych cuts off the complaints. "Knock it off. This is what we do. Weapons ready and get frosty."

We organize ourselves into an arrow-shaped formation. Mike at the lead with Tank and Held flanking. Mr. Lark and Illych are next in the middle center. I bravely provide rear security.

Mr. Lark makes a half-turn right from our present facing and points. "That way, less than one hundred meters."

Without hesitation, we rotate as a team and begin trudging through the soft sand. Sweat is beginning to well up on my skin. The heat has uncomfortably soaked into my armor. Perhaps this is what a lobster's last moments feel like.

Mr. Lark's voice rings clearly over the ComDat. "Here. Stop." As one, we cease advancing and wait. To an outside observer, we likely appear to be readying to charge into the open desert.

The old man removes something from his belt. One item for each hand. Mr. Lark is now moving his hands in wild gestures. It is some sort of a pattern mixed with wild arm waving. Like a wizard in a movie casting a spell.

Sweat hangs from my brow. Soon I will need to crack open my faceplate to wipe my face clear.

Mr. Lark's hands replace the items to his belt, and with a hand motion, waves us forward.

Acting like a pack of greyhounds when the rabbit is set loose, we surge forward into the empty space.

Everything goes grey, like a fog. This is not new. When we travelled to the island of Hy-Brasil, the transition from the normal world to the non-Euclidean contraction was through a mist or fog-like zone.

The fog around Hy-Brasil had monsters in it . . .

"Switch on weapon lights." Illych's voice breaks my reverie.

This does not seem like a wise move in heavy fog, but I do as instructed. To my surprise. the fog is not reflective; the light shines deep into the grey around us.

And reveals things in the mist circling the team.

Dark shapes, tall and gangly. At least a dozen of them, if not more. They move with a fast, loping gait. Their eyes are silver reflective, watching, gauging our strength. They are not acting like Lesser Created. If they were, they would not wait or delay. The Created have no fear.

Then the screaming starts.

Whatever they are, they make a shrieking noise like someone is electrocuting a little girl. Unnerving, to say the least.

Then the crescendo builds as more shrieks are piled on top of others.

Through all of this we maintain formation and keep moving forward. The transition zone should not be overly broad, and if we can make it through before those things . . .

Too late. They rush us from all sides, closing in on the team. Everyone's weapons erupt into life. Even under the armor I can feel the report of concentrated weapon fire.

I have no time to check how my colleagues are faring. I aim the reticle dot in the sight mounted on top of my carbine at the nearest creature and pull the trigger. A long burst of .45 ACP roar into the nearest charging figure. Whatever these beings are, bullets affect them. The thing goes down. I switch targets and repeat.

Two down.

Illych's voice barks over the ComDat, "Keep moving! We cannot pause. These things will overrun us."

We keep together and maintain our pace. The initial charge is put down handily. The things seem to have pulled back. The screaming is still going back and forth between them. Even through the protective filters of the helmet audio, it has a wrongness to it.

We all take the pause as an opportunity to swap in fresh magazines and keep moving.

Mr. Lark chimes in, "We are close."

Our antagonists also realize this and charge en masse.

It is at this time a little voice in my head reminds me I am bringing up the rear. This means I will be the last to exit.

Gunning down three monsters in quick succession, I begin swapping out my weapon's empty mag. Even though this a practiced activity and will only take seconds, I can see I will be unsuccessful before they reach me.

Crap.

My right shoulder is bumped as I vainly try to load my weapon in time. It is Tank. He has an MG4 with a belt feed running back to his rucksack. The muzzle flashes from his full auto sweep of the charging monsters lights up the ground like we are dancing in hell's disco.

Hot brass is flying, and I swear I can hear the big man chuckling as he punishes our charging foe.

The screaming stops, and the things retreat deeper into the mist.

Illych's voice tells us to get out of there, and the two of us rush the last few feet to escape.

The event-horizon fog disappears as quickly as it appeared, and I find myself joining the team in a large circular domed space. A quick count confirms we all made it.

The space is dark except for a shaft of orange-red light through a single entryway, a broad flight of stairs leading up to beyond our line of sight. Our weapon lights illuminate walls constructed from pale-green stone. Inside of these are polished white pillars holding up the ceiling. Overhead is fully domed. The floor is void-black with faint streaks of gold.

It is beautiful.

And old. Dust is thick on the floor, and based on the lack of footprints compared to our obvious new ones, nothing has trod this floor in perhaps millennia.

There is only one exit, the stairs up, and we begin a tactical movement toward it. Mr. Lark has that glazed look telling me he is working his oculus. So far this mission has been exciting. And no one is injured either.

As we get closer to the exit, three sets of remains become visible. They are just skeletons, really. Their clothing long since rotted away. Through the archway we see steps leading upward to something.

"Who were these guys?" Mike asks.

Whoever they were, they were tall. The desiccated skeletons are over seven feet tall. Alive, they would have been taller, maybe eight feet tall or more. What little hair remains on the skulls of these long-deceased travelers is rust red. That means something . . .

"These are red-headed giants of legend." Mr. Lark responds.

"When I was held captive by Balthazar on Hy-Brasil, he shared some books to read that talked about them," I chime in. "Apparently they are or were real."

Illych interjects, "Yeah, but what are they doing here and what killed them?"

My employer's eyes close. "Their skeletons are intact. Evidence of jewelry and tools long since eroded to nothing. Starvation or poison?"

There are other possibilities. "What about old age or illness?"

"All speculation and red-haired giants do not perish from old age." Mr. Lark says this with a confidence indicating he knows what he is saying is true.

Illych's attention moves back and forth between Mr. Lark and me, and then he says, "Perhaps you can speculate at a later time. When the situation is less tactical?"

With a nod from the old man, we re-form and advance through the arched exit and up dusty, cracked stairs. Fortunately, the steps are human-sized, and we advance quickly up perhaps a two-story climb. We clear the final archway and walk out into the orange light. Into the blasted ruins of the apocalypse. The sun overhead is an angry orb, massively larger than it should be and bearing no resemblance to the heathy yellow one back in the real world. A red-orange light bathes the landscape around us. As far as we can see in all directions are blasted ruins. The massive stones used to construct the floors around us are cracked and vitrified. In some places, long gashes can be seen melted into the hard stone.

Whatever structures were here have been broken and blasted into pieces. And then those pieces were crushed and melted. Whatever did this was very thorough—possibly to the point of overkill.

"I was afraid of this," says Mr. Lark.

This is not right. Non-Euclidean contractions are made from the real world. Their sun is our sun, their weather is our weather. I learned all this when we visited Hy-Brasil. What we are seeing here is like from another planet.

"Mr. Lark, what is with the sun? It should not be like that, should it?"

"This place was assembled from the space where Atlantis was founded. My suspicion is the weapons that destroyed the city penetrated through to this place."

Mike snarks, "You think?"

Illych looks at Mr. Lark. "Is this mission a bust?"

The old man's eyes are closed, his breathing measured. "Perhaps not."

"At least it is not hot here," Mike says. "Why is that?"

Tank retorts, "Air-conditioning?"

Illych shakes his head. "Okay, team, wagon wheel at fifty feet and check out the area."

We comply, with Illych joining us. The old man is left alone in the middle. There is nothing to find. Just dust and melted and broken rock.

And we wait, and wait, and wait.

Mr. Lark pulls the wynloo from a pouch worn on the harness belted around his armor. His right hand holds it up like a torch giving light. The crystal begins to glow and emit its ghostly tendrils. The white luminescent threads reach out in all directions. Some travel farther than others. They all form shapes like characters from some long-lost alphabet. The pale light struggles against the raging star above to be the dominant source of illumination.

We watch our employer consider each character one by one. The wynloo keeps emitting one after another while sustaining those already in place. This is concerning me because these exercises are rarely without hazard and our employer may go too far.

Illych and I must be thinking the same thing because we share a knowing glance. If Mr. Lark wants something bad enough, he will risk us all.

"There! I have found it!" His shout breaks the silence. Immediately, the wynloo goes dark, and Mr. Lark crumples to the ground. The tendrils of light and the characters they sustain begin to fade.

Illych and I break from the circle and jog to the old man. Illych calls for Mike to join us.

We meet and look down at the old man flat on his back, his eyes closed. The wynloo has rolled a short distance from the hand that held it. Reaching down, I pick it up. And immediately regret doing so. Images flash across my vision. Words in unrecognized voices and languages echo through my mind.

"Thank you, Mr. Davies, but I will take that." I feel the sphere leave my hand and find myself still standing and looking directly into the knowing face of my employer. What just happened?

Mike comes over as soon as Mr. Lark walks away.

"How do you feel?"

"I feel fine. Why do you ask?"

"You picked that thing up and stood there for almost five minutes whispering to yourself. Only after the boss revived was he able to take it from your hand and snap you out of it."

Five minutes? I remember nothing. Did he find what we came here for?

"Mr. Lark, did you find what you sought?"

"Yes, Mr. Davies. The Atlanteans were a very clever people. There was never a map here, at least not in the traditional sense. Instead, they permanently projected an attenuated gravity well topology to this location. Very clever indeed."

The questioning looks on the faces around him register with Mr. Lark.

"Instead of a written map, they just made a model of the real thing and shrunk it to fit this place's gravity topology. Like grooves in an old music record except they imprinted those tiny changes into the gravity of this place."

Nodding heads and rolling eyes confirm faux understanding.

"Are we finished here?" Illych asks.

"Yes. My goals here are complete."

"Okay, people. We are leaving. Mike, lead the way." Illych makes some hand gestures I still do not fully understand. It does not really matter. They all end with me providing rear security. Illych has explained in the past that this is an important position in the formation. He also made a comment about how Private Snuffy is always assigned this role.

Since we now know what will awaits us in our exit back through the event-horizon fog, Illych and Tank employ the SHEGs right from the start. After a half-dozen high-explosive rounds blast apart the gangly fiends from afar, the monsters retreat deeper into the fog, leaving us an unimpeded exit path.

The bright light and blast-furnace heat of the desert catch me completely off guard. Expletives from my colleagues fill my ears.

Illych quickly gathers us in a close circle. Everything goes dark, and we are back at the dimly lit, freezing-cold Compass.

As soon as the nausea passes, I ask Mr. Lark a question I dared not verbalize in the map room during the mission.

"Where is Tartarus, Mr. Lark? Where is it located?"

My employer looks my way and considers my request. "The information from the Atlantean map must be converted to determine the real-world location. This calculation will not happen instantaneously. Patience, Thomas. While I appreciate your enthusiasm, I believe our visit to Tartarus will not be as pleasant as what we just experienced."

So we will be going to Tartarus, the place that Those Who Came Before used as a prison and storage vault for things extraordinarily dangerous

It is just a matter of time until Mr. Lark return to the Citadel and tells us to prepare.

Chapter 14

My eyes open, and I consider my situation. The bed is comfortable. I have a solid eight hours of sleep behind me. It is Saturday—or at least what passes for a weekend in this place. No morning calisthenics. Not that this will stop my colleagues from doing some form of exercise. My participation, however, will not be mandatory.

The coffee in the cafeteria is calling to me.

The books in the library are also calling to me.

Unfortunately, the two cannot mix. Accidentally spilling coffee on an irreplaceable, one-of-a-kind, five-hundred-year-old text is frowned upon. Thus, I must choose.

Coffee, of course, wins. As I dress, I decide to have a quiet breakfast and then it's off to the office. On my desk sits the journal of a landowner from the city of Nuremburg in the 1500s. Apparently there were some strange things to write about around 1561.

Not an hour later, my breakfast complete, I am preparing to spend the rest of the day in my sanctum sanctorum when Mr. Lark enters the otherwise empty cafeteria.

"Good morning, Mr. Lark?" It comes out as more of a question than a greeting. Honestly, despite having been in his employ for almost a year, I have spent little time alone with the eccentric old man, so I'm caught a bit off guard.

Dressed in his grey suit and carrying his oculus cane, my employer projects a distinguished look.

Looking at me, he responds, "Good morning, Thomas."

We endure a long, uncomfortable silence while he stands halfway between me and the entryway looking bored.

"Is there something I can do for you?" I finally ask.

"Not at all. I am waiting for the others. They are finishing up exercising outside and will be along shortly." Is he just going to stand there?

After another sip of coffee, I have to ask, "Will I be busy today?"

Mr. Lark looks at me and nods. "Yes. I have some activities planned for today, and you will be included. Held, Mike, you, and I are going to Mexico today."

In my mind's eye, I see the journal on my desk bursting into flames. So much for a sedentary afternoon of immersing myself in the comings and goings of sixteenth-century Germania.

My next thought is that Tartarus is in Mexico.

The others walk in before I ask enough questions to irritate Mr. Lark. Tank finishes an off-color joke as they enter, and they all laugh. The old man stands there silently as my colleagues walk around him like a school of fish splitting around a rock. They assemble their breakfasts, and the cafeteria goes silent except for the sounds of hungry men devouring a well-earned meal.

This peculiar situation continues until the communal breakfast ends. One by one, ending with Tank last, of course, focus shifts to Mr. Lark to learn what is happening today.

"We have been busy lately," Mr. Lark begins. "The business with Langstraad Solutions was extraordinarily profitable. Visiting the Atlantean map room was interesting, and I now know the location of Tartarus." He pauses and then continues. "The latest addition to my organization is meeting or exceeding expectations. She is taking over many of the supply duties I, and to a lesser degree, Illych, have been handling.

"But none of that is why I am here today."

"Since we operate internationally, it is not unusual to be paid in the location where we execute a contract. This is also for convenience as we source our equipment and supplies globally. Allison recently placed a significant order and debited an account in Mexico. The bank declined to pay and claimed the account balance is zero. This is a long-existing account, and there has never been trouble in the past.

"Apparently, the bank has had a recent change in management. Since my accounts are not affiliated with any influential corporate or political interests, someone within the bank determined I would have no recourse if they repurposed my funds."

Someone stole money from Mr. Lark? A lot of money. Bold move. I look around at my colleagues, and their expressions cover a broad range. Illych has his usual bored expression. Held and Mike look at each other, and Mike rolls his eyes. Tank is smirking in anticipation of what should be an interesting mission.

"In every country where such accounts exist, I have attorneys on retainer," Mr. Lark continues. "This holds true in this case, and when I reached out to my lawyers, they were less than helpful. My suspicion is they tipped off the bankers.

"To be honest, my patience is challenged by this turn of events. Between bankers thieving and attorneys taking my retainer and providing nothing useful, I am feeling put out. First, we are visiting the attorneys to get the story straight. Subsequently, the bankers will need to be convinced this is an opportunity to improve the accuracy of their accounting. One of the challenges of engaging in criminal activity is protecting your assets from other criminals."

Mr. Lark pauses, looking like he is collecting his thoughts. Tank takes this opportunity to chime in, "Bankers are the worst."

Mike is right there with him. "So true. Stealing Mr. Lark's ill-gotten gains."

Illych slowly shakes his head while I watch the banter.

My employer remains stoic, quietly ignoring the irreverent back and forth.

"What is the plan?" Illych asks.

"Held, Mike, Thomas, the four of us are leaving within the hour. Our destination has already been scouted by oculus. Using the ouiblet, I was able to acquire a secretary's planner. It is fortuitus today is a senior partners meeting. The plan after that is we will begin throwing bankers from a tall building until my money is returned."

Dark humor? Probably not. The old man is feistier than usual and he may actually mean to throw bankers from a tall building. They must have stolen a lot of money.

Illych nods in acknowledgment. Tank looks disappointed.

After looking at the three of us in turn, he says, "Meet me at the gate in half an hour." We three look at each other and get up and head to our rooms. With the mood the old man is in, I do not want to be one to keep him waiting.

The only weapon I will be bringing is a large-caliber handgun in a shoulder holster. My colleagues' enthusiasm for weapons is greater than mine, and they will have knives, explosives, a taser, probably a backup handgun, the works.

During the walk to the Compass, the plan for the attorneys is shared.

"Their law office is the penthouse of a twenty-two-story building. We are translating into a storeroom on the twentieth floor. They employ considerable security at the lower levels but very little higher up. I will use the wynloo to disable the alarms shortly after we arrive. Then we take two flights of stairs up to the penthouse."

Mr. Lark looks at Held. "You have breaching charges?"

Held nods.

"The levels below the penthouse contain hundreds of lawyers, law clerks, and secretarial staff. They must not be allowed to slow us down."

Mr. Lark hands us the small brass batons that are our emergency escape dongles, and we gather close together in the center of the Compass. After a silent visual once-over, I see his hands give the final twist.

Everything goes black.

We arrive in a storeroom, surrounded by cardboard boxes on steel shelves and mops in mop buckets. The odor of cleaning supplies is strong.

A crash of metal cans falling onto the concrete floor makes us all spin to face the threat, weapons drawn.

We realize Mike took a step back due to the translation nausea and knocked a mop handle into a small pyramid of cleaning supplies. So not only did he create a loud ruckus, now, leaking containers are making an ever-expanding chemical pool on the floor.

He shrugs.

Mr. Lark, without skipping a beat, gives instructions. "The stairs are to the right. There is no one nearby to see us or hear Mr. Daugherty's racket. Let us go."

Mike is first out, followed by Held and then the old man. As usual, I provide rear security.

The hall is a typical bland office-building corridor. Beige is popular here also.

On the concrete stairs, our footsteps echo loudly as we jog up two flights, and just like in the corridor, we see no other person.

Mike checks the door. "It is locked." He points to a numeric keypad.

Mr. Lark has already produced the clear crystal sphere of the wynloo. The silver-white wisps drift outward from the artifact and toward the keypad.

"While this defeats the door's security, it is also locking the elevator at the top and disabling all security cameras in the upper half of the building," Mr. Lark says as the wynloo does it magic. "The security code for this door is now changed, and the phone system is also corrupted. No one will be calling for help. They cannot leave through the stairs or elevator. There is no escape."

The door clicks and opens an inch in Mike's grasp.

Taking a step toward the door, Mr. Lark indicates for Mike to fully open the door and step aside.

"I will lead now."

We step from the stairwell into a well-appointed reception area. A stunning dark-haired woman is struggling with a phone that I am guessing suddenly stopped working. Our appearance from the stairwell catches her unprepared. She stares at us as we walk straight toward the glass doors between us and the interior of the penthouse.

Regaining her composure, she says something in Spanish. Her voice is pleasant to the ear, but I do not know Spanish to determine what she is saying.

We do not stop or even acknowledge her presence.

Through the doors is an open-concept office. Desks are arranged spaciously. Our entrance stops all activity, and the perhaps fifty human beings within sight realize they are gawking and get back to work.

The receptionist behind us is still speaking at us in Spanish.

Mr. Lark points at a frosted glass door. "Mike, open that."

It is game time, and the former Army Ranger's body language instantly goes from casual tourist to ass-kicker. His right hand produces a large-caliber handgun. As this is happening, a tall, well-dressed, and well-groomed man, perhaps in his thirties, stands and walks a few steps toward Mike.

The man is speaking Spanish and waving his hands. Mike sweeps the man's legs and topples him to the floor. One step later, Mike's shoulder impacts the frosted glass door and pushes it open.

Held, gun in hand, watches the crowd for heroes.

As we leave, the room is silent as a grave. Just wide eyes watching four grey-suited men.

Five men in suits sit at one end of a conference table. Our sudden entry has them speechless. They look privileged, arrogant, and indignant all at once. They must be lawyers.

After Mr. Lark and I enter, Mike repositions to standing off to one side just inside the room; Held mirrors him, both with weapons in hand. The door swings shut behind us.

I stand at the end of the table farthest from the lawyers and observe.

Mr. Lark continues walking into the room until he is standing next to the men at the table.

The man at the head of the table recognizes my employer.

"Señor Lark, what is the meaning of this intrusion?"

"I secured the services of your law firm to protect my interests. The retainer was a princely sum. Now you inform me my money is lost and most likely irretrievable. This is not acceptable."

After a pause, my employer continues. "I have travelled here today to discuss the situation. Hopefully this misunderstanding will be corrected. Before we discuss the path to returning my money, I will share my thoughts on what has happened. I will explain each of the three possible reasons for what has occurred."

One of the men sitting at the table angrily barks something in Spanish.

"It is important I am not interrupted," Mr. Lark's voice thunders. "The next person to speak—in any language—will be shot." He then returns to his original topic, as if nothing happened. "The first possibility is you and this firm knowingly misled me regarding your ability to provide competent services. This would be a fundamental error in integrity and therefore unforgivable."

The man he is addressing remains stone-faced.

"The second possibility is you are incompetent and did not realize the level to which you will be required to perform. I find this unlikely as this is a very nice building your offices occupy. You have been successful over time, and this contradicts the insinuation of incompetence.

"Then there is the third possibility. That you conspired with the bankers to take my money. Just a stupid foreigner waiting to be picked clean. After all, how would I be able to get to important people such as yourselves?"

One of the men, very tall and handsome, abruptly stands and points at Mr. Lark, and begins berating my employer in Spanish.

The gunshot causes me to jump. I turn to see Held holding the fired gun. My hearing fades out from the weapon report, and everything is silent as the man's body flops messily to the floor.

The pallor of the other men's skin reveals their thoughts: Death is here.

One of the wall decorations opens inward and a gun barrel slips into view. Shots ring out, and my unprotected ears go temporarily deaf. Out of the corner of my left eye I see Held spin from the impacts. In reaction, I take aim and empty my handgun's magazine into the wall near the hole. Light can be seen through each bullet hole. Good, the walls are not bulletproof. The weapon barrel that shot Held falls back out of the opening.

Another hatch opens on the opposite side. Whoever is attempting to shoot through it is not as quick at deploying. Mike reacts and perforates the wall in the area where the second shooter's gun barrel can be seen.

The shooter is indiscriminate, and objects on the table explode from impacts. One of the seated men appears to be hit. Mike's rapid fire empties his weapon in seconds. His hands are a blur as he reloads and continues to perforate the wall around the hatch. Light can be seen through the holes.

When his weapon's slide locks open, he breaks for the door, reloading his weapon on the run.

Looking back at my employer, I see that he, in spite of the carnage around him, is having a staring contest with the remaining men at the table.

With the shooter threat being handled by Mike, I hurry over to Held. After initially falling over, he pulled himself up to a sitting position against the wall. Pain is written on his face.

"Where are you hit?"

"Left side. I think it is in my lung."

"Can you walk?"

"I can try."

More shots can be heard outside, then silence.

Mike barks outside the door, "Marco."

Held wheezes back, "Polo."

The former Ranger enters the room, his face also pale, and his left arm is hanging down straight. Blood drips from his fingers.

Dripping is better than running, but this is not the best situation to be in.

"The staff I did not have to shoot are sheltering in the offices at the far end of this floor," Mike reports. "Apparently, two of the men sitting at desks out there doubled as armed security."

Mr. Lark looks at the man at the end of the table. He starts speaking as if the shooting we just survived had never happened: "It would be most unfortunate if the third possibility is true. When we are done here, I am visiting the bank and getting my money back."

In perfect American English, the man says, "You are robbing the bank?"

"No, I am asking them for my money back. Should they refuse my reasonable request, I will begin tossing bankers from the roof of their headquarters. Perhaps they will consider it a service. Eliminating non-performing deadwood from their organization. After all, who wants to employ a banker who loses twenty million US dollars and cannot explain how?"

Twenty million? And that is just this one bank. Makes me wonder how much money the old man has.

As I pull Held to his feet, Mr. Lark addresses the sitting man again. "We are leaving now. Do not try my patience again." He turns and strides from the room. Mike slides in, and I hand Held off to him and watch them hobble away. Once again, I am bringing up the rear.

The offices have not a person in sight. Chairs are overturned, and papers are scattered. Several dozen bullet holes in the building's exterior glass bring beams of light visible as dust floats about the room.

Taking the stairs is slow going. Held is starting to cough up pink foam. We need to get him to The Doctor.

Mr. Lark pulls out the return dongle and announces we are close enough.

Everything goes black and we are back at the Compass. Held starts coughing uncontrollably. We move him onto the electric cart we use to move supplies between the Citadel and the Compass. Or as a makeshift ambulance for our wounded.

The cart can move at the same pace as a slow jog, and even in Mike's condition, he matches the pace. The long, cold, dark walk to the Citadel feels like forever. I cannot help but think about how the blood we are trailing onto the road beneath our feet may cause problems sometime in the future. Mr. Lark warned us about the creatures that inhabit this place getting biological materials. My train of thought ends as we arrive at the Citadel's gates. The bright light streaming out of the opening gates makes us all squint as we race through the entrance and slalom the cart through the chaotic layout of the buildings between us and The Doctor.

Somewhere between the gates and The Doctor, Mr. Lark leaves us. Parking the cart, Mike and I manhandle Held into The Doctor's waiting room and onto a gurney. Snatching a red stone from a shelf, I put it into the still-conscious Held's hand. His hand closes around it, his expression going slack as he passes into unconsciousness. We stand back as far as possible as the room's inner door opens and the gangly green creature we call The Doctor shambles out and pushes the gurney into its lair.

Mike sits in a chair, blood still dripping from his hand. And we wait.

The Doctor usually does his work in twenty minutes maximum. Why or how it is so fast, no one knows, but when you are waiting with a bullet in you, that twenty minutes is an agonizing eon on the edge of forever.

Looking at my colleague, I say, "That was not the smoothest operation."

Mike grits his teeth. "Not all of them are smooth. Mr. Lark picked a fight with that shoot-any-one-who-speaks thing."

"Certainly, but they made twenty million dollars disappear. This was not going to end with a hand slap."

After shaking his head, the former Ranger continues. "I think it was more than that. When there was an attempt to pay some bills from that account, it came up overdrawn or void or something. This made it look like he was trying to buy something with money he did not have or he does not know where his money is. Either way, it is an embarrassment. Especially in the circles he does business. And handling that kind of emotion is not the old man's strong point. My guess is the attorney was just the warm-up. It is the bankers who are really going to get it."

"Really? After this disaster you think we are going back out?'

"Once I am patched up, we are going back. You can bet on it."

My disbelief must show, and Mike comments, "Don't worry there, English. They are only bankers and lawyers. It is not like we are killing real people."

The pool of blood under his chair is getting serious.

I point and ask, "Are you going to be okay?"

"This is not too bad, but I would like The Doctor to bring Held back soon."

We wait a few more minutes in the dead-silent waiting room listening to the blood from Mike's hand drip into the expanding crimson pool on the floor.

I do not see why he needs to be such a tough guy. We have bandages and excellent painkillers. It would have been easy to make the wait more tolerable.

The door to The Doctor's inner room opens, and both of us breathe a deep breath in relief. The Doctor rolls the gurney out of the chamber's impenetrable inner darkness with a peacefully sleeping and very naked Held lying upon it.

After parking the gurney, the diminutive creature walks back into his chamber, closing the door behind him.

The click of the door closing is the moment Held's eyes open. He immediately sits up and swings his legs over. Mike's and Held's eyes lock for a brief second. Held shifts to standing and makes way for Mike to pile onto the gurney. We end up catching the wounded man halfway to the cart. He has lost a lot of blood—more than he is willing to admit. We carefully lie our colleague out on the padded surface. Once the former Ranger goes horizontal, I snatch the reappeared red stone from the shelf and place it into Mike's ice-cold grip.

His eyes close, and we back away as the inner door opens. What happens next is a repeat of what Held went through maybe twenty minutes ago.

As he heads for the exit, Held pauses to state, "If you are staying here for when he comes out, fine, but I need clothes and food. You know he will be ok. We can leave."

He is right. This is not like a real hospital where there are setbacks and deaths. Mike will be fine, and I need some food and coffee.

"I will come with you." And I follow him out.

As we navigate between awkward-shaped buildings while staying on course for the cafeteria, a loud catcall breaks the silence.

"Put some clothes on and stop streaking," Tank yells to us. "Some of us are impressionable." This is followed by a chuckle and a head shake. Then we lose sight of him as we pass another building.

Held peels away as we pass a storeroom. "I will get some clothes and meet you there."

Illych is already at the cafeteria, drinking what must be coffee by the smell in the air. "Just made it fresh. Help yourself."

I do so and join my relaxed-looking colleague.

He looks at me and asks, "Bring everyone back alive?"

"Barely." With that, I shared the events of the last few hours.

"Fun times. And Mike is right. You will be going back."

"Did Mr. Lark say something?"

"No, but eight years of working for Mr. Lark tells me that is what is going to happen. And our employer is very predictable."

Chapter 15

Illych looks me up and down. "You should get changed into your tactical gear."

"But Held and Mike were shot. And the bank will know we are coming."

"None of that matters. The Doctor will put our people back together, and Mr. Lark wants the bank to be ready and waiting for us; he wants them to know we're coming. It will underscore how unprofitable the theft was. We can get to anyone, anywhere. Honestly, this is good advertising. Future clients can see what we can do, and perhaps more importantly, they can see the importance of Mr. Lark getting paid."

Held enters, arrayed in tactical dress. Not the heavy armor, just the chest carapace and regular helmet with the microphone setup. He nods to Illych and makes a beeline for the food.

I head to my room, where I change into a matching setup to Held's. Stopping by the armory, I add a carbine and as many magazines as the numerous ammo points will hold.

By the time I get back to the cafeteria, the gang is assembled. The lack of horseplay strikes me. We all know round two is coming. Mike is back from The Doctor, and like Held and myself, is dressed in black with a long weapon added.

As I stand there watching and thinking, I feel a presence to my right.

A turn of my head reveals what my mind already knows. A similarly equipped Mr. Lark is standing next to me.

Without pause or even a greeting, he speaks. "Good, everyone is ready," he says. "We leave immediately."

The four of us once again head to the Compass. Mike and I walk side by side, perhaps too casually, but this is our second mission today.

"So it is the bankers' turn now?" I comment more than ask.

Mike nods. "Looks that way."

"Will we be throwing them off buildings like Mr. Lark threatened?"

"Possibly."

"Think we will arrive in a storeroom again?"

"Probably."

"You are enjoying this, aren't you?"

"Positively."

Mike is smiling now.

"I grabbed some extra mags in case this mission is more exciting than the lawyer one was."

Mike glances my way and smirks. "Look what I am bringing." With a shift of his grip, he reveals a P90 slung under his shoulder. It even has a suppressor. "Uses fifty-round mags."

Show-off.

But very cool.

"One thing bothers me," I say. "We killed some lawyers. Now we are probably going to kill some bankers. After that, what is the motivation to return our employer's money?"

"Really, Thomas?" Mike replies. "You're going to ask that question? Because if they do not, Mr. Lark will kill more of them."

I continue, "Well, I hope they return the money so we can stop with these missions. It just does not seem right."

"How so?"

"It is okay to stop monsters from murdering innocent people or killing bad people who are trying to kill us. But killing these people to get money back . . ."

"Mr. Lark already tried the polite way. He paid attorneys. The deposits were valid. He even asked nicely for them to restore the money. Sometimes the hard way is the only way."

We silently walk for a few minutes, then Mike comments, "Thomas."

"Yes, Mike?"

"Do you know what a million lawyers at the bottom of the ocean is?"

Weirdest question ever. "What?"

"A good start."

Held, some distance in front of us, chuckles at that.

Mr. Lark is ignoring our small talk.

We ghost into the Compass. Mr. Lark separates to enter one of the vaults. He returns with a satchel, which he hands to Mike. Then we group inside the stone circle.

"During our pause in operations I monitored our foes' communications quite closely. Prior to this, I was unable to identify the enterprising individual within the bank who liberated my money from my account. Upon learning of what happened to their collaborators, the responsible executive was moved to what is considered a safe house. Security is formidable.

"It is essentially a compound with a wall around it and a tower disguised as the upper stories of a house. Windows are all ballistic-resistant. Ram-resistant gates, armored doors. It is all quite impressive.

"There is even a secret tunnel that runs almost a kilometer away to the guest house on a nearby estate. The guest house is guarded at all times. We can access our target from that estate, through the tunnel.

"Mike, Thomas, you will be translated to the guest house. Immediately terminate the guard. Then, Mike, you will use incendiary grenades I just handed you. Place them around the inside of the guest house to light it on fire."

Mike's face lights up with pyrotechnic anticipation.

"Held and I will translate to the other end of the tunnel inside our target's hideout. After the guest house is on fire, please proceed through the tunnel to join us. We are not taking prisoners. Once the VP is down, we exit back out through the tunnel."

Wait, what? "Won't the guest house still be on fire?"

My employer replies, "Possibly, but that is still our exit path."

Mr. Lark hands us our emergency dongles. "The guard will be close by upon arrival. You may want to prepare your weapon now."

He does not have to say that twice. My carbine is locked and cocked in my right hand as we huddle in preparation for translation.

Everything goes black.

Christ sakes! A tattooed muscular man is sitting on a chair not three steps in front of me eating a sandwich, a sinister-looking rifle propped against his seat. He stops mid-bite, with a look of shock lasting a fraction of a second before his hands drop the food and clutch at the rifle.

My surprise exits my mouth with a squeaky grunt. The guard is now hefting the rifle. An involuntary reflex causes me to aim as my finger pulls the trigger several times. Even with the new compact suppressors, each shot thunders in the enclosed space as the flash strobes the poorly lit room. The man in the chair crumples up and rolls forward onto the floor at my feet.

The nausea from the translation and what I had just done wells up inside me, and I begin vomiting. It takes about a minute to compose myself. Mike shifts into my line of sight, P90 to his shoulder.

"You okay, Thomas?"

"I just killed that guy. He was eating a sandwich."

The incredulous look on Mike's face frames his statement. "You have killed human beings before. This is not the first time."

"Not like this."

The former Army Ranger shakes his head. "Thomas, I would like to say something comforting, but we do not have time. Get over it. Before this mission is over, you will probably kill some more."

The stairs down to the tunnel are easy to find. Mike starts tossing the incendiary grenades into every room of the guest house. They pop, hiss, and like a Roman candle, scatter burning sparks everywhere. Mike tosses the last one over his shoulder into the room behind us as we close the door to the tunnel.

Our quick pace makes a staccato sound as Mike leads the way down concrete steps. The tunnel itself is a simple square concrete tube with evenly spaced light bulbs fixed to the ceiling. We pass no cameras nor anything security-related as we jog across the dusty concrete, our footfalls echoing with every step.

A kilometer is not a short distance. The good news is the tunnel is straight and level, which makes the hike easy. That will also be bad news if a bad guy shows up at the other end with a rifle when we are halfway there. With the clear line of sight, we would be trapped with no way to hide or escape.

Just past the halfway mark, we can hear the distinctive bark of gunfire rolling back to us from our destination. Held and Mr. Lark are introducing themselves to the on-site security. A particularly long burst of a distant automatic weapon not far away marks our arrival at the stairs up to the compound. We pause, give each other a confirming nod, and with legs pistoning, we fly up the stairs.

The door at the top of the stairs is ajar and the smell of cordite is strong. Mike barges the door open with a shoulder and sweeps his P90 across an unoccupied room. The sound of more gunfire—this time noticeably closer—urges us to keep moving. We pass through the door on the other side of the room and find it opens to a hallway. Looking left and right reveals the prone forms of two men. Based on the rifles and radios nearby, they were security. Visible trauma and large blood pools tell us they are deceased.

More sounds of gunfire are coming from the right, down the hall. Mike moves fast and bold, rolling down the hall like an action-movie hero. Bringing up the rear, I am more cautious, checking blind spots and side rooms. Held and Mr. Lark did not miss anything. Everywhere we pass is only bullet holes and property damage.

The door at the end of the hall opens easily enough. Mike throws it open while we each take cover off to the sides. A courtyard ringed by buildings greets us. Two pickup trucks, a van, and a limousine are randomly parked about the space.

To our left is the gate for vehicles to enter or leave. Curiously, it is perhaps one-quarter open. Not big enough for a vehicle, but more than enough for people. We sweep the courtyard for threats and find none.

We cannot afford to wait. Every moment increases the likelihood of running into reinforcements.

"Let's go," Mike growls as he breaks from the doorway and sprints for the far side of the courtyard where the ongoing gun battle can still be heard. He moves so fast a space opens between us, and I have to full-on run to keep up. No shots are fired at us during the seconds we are exposed. Even so, the two-dozen strides in the open feel like an eternity.

A feeling of relief washes over me as we cross back into the cover of a building, and both of us instinctively plaster ourselves to the nearest wall. We are in a wide and long hall with ornate double doors far down from us at the other end. Along the hall are a number of doors on the right and left. The ongoing raging sounds of weapons firing beyond the end-of-hall doors tell us we are close to catching up with Mr. Lark and Held. Peeking through the nearest open door reveals these are luxury suits sharing a common hall. Bullet holes stitch the walls. A lack of corpses tells us security is fighting a fall-back action while Held and Mr. Lark press forward.

We advance, moving quickly down the hall, giving each open door a quick check. Past the third set of doors is a bullet-riddled makeshift barricade. Whoever they were put up a fight before falling back.

The doors at the end of the hall are stitched with bullets from the inside coming out at us. Mike and I jump away and hug the wall as we advance. The gunfight is on the other side of the doors. The walls in this place are solid concrete, so we have no worries about bullets flying through them. My only question is are Held and Mr. Lark just on the other side or are the bad guys between us? I could say something over the ComDat, but a distraction right now could be fatal.

The doors burst open, and three men back into sight while laying down suppression fire.

The door popping open like that is unexpected. Apparently, backing through the doors and finding Mike and I a few strides away is a surprise to the shooters. For the briefest instant, our two sides regard each other.

Now we play a game called the quick and the dead.

Mike's snap-action reflexes deploy his weapon with skill and takes down two of the men with expert efficiency. The third man spins around with adrenaline-induced speed, his rifle already firing before acquiring a target. I watched the fired rounds step a path from the floor to the wall; each hole is perhaps a foot apart.

As the world slips into slow motion, I realize that line will intersect where I stand. My carbine is coming in line with its target. Even driven by my will to survive, it is obvious I will be shot before I can return the favor.

With determination, I shift my focus to getting my weapon on target. My eyes follow the front sight as the first bullet punches through my thigh. My mind boxes off the pain and keeps the front sight moving. Almost there. The second round hits mid-abdomen and is absorbed by my ballistic ceramic plate.

The sight picture aligns, and my finger pulls the trigger a fraction of a second before impacts throw off my aim. My eyes do not blink as I see the bullet impact my shooter's neck and the retracting bolt of my weapon ejects a shiny brass cartridge into the air. My target fires no more bullets as he flops backward flat on the tiled floor and goes still. No sooner does the kill shot happen than the impacts from the rounds hitting my thigh and abdomen knock me from my feet.

Between the burning in my thigh and the dull, angry pain in my belly, I am unsure how to react. Sitting up tells me there is no paralysis. Looking down, I can see red spreading down my left leg. That can't be good. The carapace stopped the round that hit my abdomen, and I will have a huge bruise to show for it.

Mike walks over and offers me a hand. "That was a display of single-minded shooting. Well done. Illych will be proud. If you survive, that is." Without pause, he produces a razor knife and cuts away the part of my trousers near the wound. Once revealed, he slaps a jelly-like substance and a gauze pad on both the entry and exit wounds.

Taking his hand, I allow him to pull me to my feet. The magnitude of my injuries is beginning to register as the pain completes its journey to my mind.

"This will seal everything and reduce the bleeding," Mike explains as he adds a gauze pad. "The leg is messy, but you will be fine. And here is something for the pain."

In the ocean of discomfort I am plowing through right now, the prick of a needle goes unnoticed. The effects, however, do not. Within a minute, the pain recedes and I can think again. Then the drugs proceed to fog up my thoughts.

We turn to look through the opened doors.

To find Held standing there looking at us.

"Are you two done playing doctor?"

My drug-influenced thought process is not working well enough for me to respond. Mike just shakes his head.

Held turns while saying, "Mr. Lark sent me to get you. We have the guy, and Mr. Lark is discussing what to do with him." He turns and walks back into the room. Mike follows.

Through my drug haze, I follow my colleagues, stumbling a few times over the debris from the gunfight.

"Who were these guys?" Mike asks Held while pointing at the corpses in the doorway.

Held replies, "Security. We were herding them out the door. The body count on this is high enough, so we bypassed them while going after the target. We gave them an out, they were smart and decided to make a break for it. Apparently, they picked the wrong door."

Illych made a joke, and I would agree.

These are really good drugs.

Held leads us to a nice living room–type arrangement. At least what living rooms look like after the apocalypse. Walls, tiled floors, even the ceiling show dozens, if not hundreds, of bullet holes. Broken glass and spent shell casings cover the floor. The couch, chairs, anything with stuffing, is blown out. It is just a big mess. The cleaning person will take one look and quit.

Sitting on one of the damaged overstuffed chairs is the mission's goal. The VP is a handsome, athletic man, early middle age with just a hint of grey in his black hair. He's dressed casually, but even his casual dress says money. Mr. Lark stands nearby, pistol in hand, casually conversing with the captive.

Mr. Lark glances our way, noting our arrival. "Good. You are here. Mr. Altaro here is about to call his superiors and inquire about my money." He looks back at our captive.

The man is clearly concerned about recent events but not visibly frightened, and so far, seemingly untouched. With a nod, he picks up a cell phone from the arm of the chair and makes a call. A quick exchange in Spanish follows. Mr. Lark clears his throat, and our captive switches to English.

Mr. Altaro pulls the phone down from his mouth just slightly. "Mr. Lark, my superiors have investigated the accounting error and wish to apologize for any inconvenience," he informs Mr. Lark in a manner not unlike notifying a client of a minor problem resolved. "They are willing to provide a letter confirming the bank's misallocation, should any of your vendors need further clarification."

Mr. Lark nods. "Please share with your superiors how appreciative I am of their diligence in reviewing this matter. Hopefully protocols will be put in place to prevent challenges such as this in the future."

Mr. Altaro's brow relaxes as he realizes Mr. Lark is most likely satisfied with the outcome. "They wish you to be assured those involved will receive additional training," he replies. "This unfortunate situation will not be repeated."

"Thank you, Mr. Altaro. I will take my leave now. Enjoy your evening."

With a nod, Mr. Lark turns and walks toward the door. Held and Mike give the sitting man a menacing look and turn to follow our employer. A little voice in the haze that is my mind tells me to follow. I smile at Mr. Altaro, nod, and turn to follow my colleagues.

Our exit is a casual stroll through the carnage. We find no opposition waiting in the courtyard. We weave past rubble and various obstacles while stepping over a few corpses. Mike and Held remain alert while the old man appears unconcerned.

The edge of my vision is getting a little fuzzy, and I try to say something to Mike, but it only comes out as "gurk." Mike looks at me and frowns. "We need to get him to The Doctor." With Mike on one side and Held on the other, they keep me upright as we navigate down the concrete steps into the tunnel. At the bottom of the steps is a steel cabinet. Mr. Lark opens it and hands out fire extinguishers. Well, that is convenient. Mike and Held get one each in their free hand, and the old man carries two.

As we near the far end where Mike and I first entered, we notice smoke and a burning smell. Mr. Lark leads the way, pushing the fire door open and immediately hosing down the flames outside. As the three of us follow, we realize the small wooden guesthouse completely collapsed as it burned. In the half hour that has passed, the fire is much less formidable than I expected.

Our employer extinguishes enough flames to create an escape path. In the seconds, and in fewer than ten strides to escape the fire, I can feel the red-hot debris burning through the soles of my boots.

Except, how do we escape this place? We will not be translating. Bystanders can see us. Mr. Lark is just standing and looking at his watch. Then he pulls out a cell phone and makes a call. After speaking a few words, he tosses the phone into the flames.

The four of us stand in the wide-open space near the burning guest house. Just waiting to get shot, I guess. Then I hear a sound that brings a smile to my face. A black helicopter hovers into view and descends onto the yard nearby. It touches down without pause, forcefully blowing smoke and glowing hot embers. Held and Mike drag me onboard. Mr. Lark climbs in behind us. As soon as the doors close, the pilot applies maximum power, rocketing us upward.

The view is nice from up here.

I do not know if it is the gunshots, the painkillers, or the sudden acceleration, but I feel relaxed. The rest of the journey to The Doctor is a fuzzy memory. Almost like a black-and-white film showing the chopper landing, a short car ride, a room, translation, and the cold of the Compass.

It ends in full color as I wake up naked in The Doctor's waiting room.

Chapter 16

"I still cannot believe Mr. Lark ordered you to shoot that man at that law firm in Mexico City," I say to Held. He and I are discussing the money-retrieval mission over breakfast. Mike and Illych left early, and Tank is uncharacteristically quiet this morning. He just sits and watches as we talk.

Held looks unconcerned. "What? Shooting that guy when he stood up and started speaking?"

"Yes. Mr. Lark saying shoot the guy if he is a threat is one thing. But that man was unarmed. There was no threat."

Tank shakes his head in disagreement while still eating his breakfast.

Held's eyes lock with mine. "Thomas, you are a decent guy and a useful addition to the team. But you came in under very different circumstances. Mike was a vegetable in a VA hospital before Mr. Lark brought him in. Illych was two years into a twenty-year incarceration at Ft. Leavenworth, and I was a basket case with a brain injury. Tank won't even tell you his story." I look over at the former Marine, and he shakes his head again and continues eating.

"Mr. Lark could have left you to die in that basement in the British Museum. Or worse, left you to the Ciorii in your flat. Instead, we are doing this. Get over it."

"The truth is that we were done," Held says. "Life was over for us. Mr. Lark brought us here and gave us meaningful work. Yes, this is not far from indentured servitude, but we are using our skills and living. So, yes, occasionally we shoot somebody for not following instructions. But I am willing to bet there were no good guys in that room either."

The cafeteria is silent for many long minutes after that. Mike and Illych return from whatever they were doing, get some coffee, and join us.

Mike picks up on the serious vibe from our just-ended conversation,. "What's up with the long faces?"

"Thomas is still a little squeamish about our more-extreme activities," Held replies.

Mike looks at me. "Shooting that attorney jerk in Mexico City?" Held nods. Mike punches Tank in the arm. "Told you he would not like that." Again, no comment from Tank.

Held looks at Illych. "What's the good word? Anything coming up soon? Or is the quiet going to continue for the last few weeks until vacation?"

"No telling," Illych replies. "There is nothing planned that I know of. But when has the old man shared his plans with me?"

"I share my plans with no one."

Looking up, I see Mr. Lark in a grey suit with his walking stick in hand. How did he sneak in like that?

Illych smiles. He must have known our employer was here.

"It is good you are all here. We will discuss a potential engagement that represents a significant revenue-generation opportunity. In many ways it might be considered repeat business."

We all look at each other. Repeat business? How does that even make sense considering what we do? We do not leave anything unfinished. Or alive, in some cases.

"The brokers who often connect me with these engagements have just reached out to me. It turns out the events at the salt mine have accelerated. Giggle Corp has it bottled up for now, but the situation is evolving quickly."

"Why would Langstraad Solutions pay us to go back?" I ask. "They got what they wanted."

Mr. Lark shakes his head. "Langstraad is not the requestor. Giggle Corp is looking for troubleshooters to resolve the problem."

Mike laughs. "Troubleshooters. When we see trouble, we shoot it." His outburst awards him an icy glare from our employer.

"In a strange demonstration of serendipity, Giggle has ended up in the same place as Langstraad Solutions in regards to what is happening in those mines. The Giggle Corp CEO reached out through back channels to the brokers to learn what solutions are available.

"Giggle Corp remains unaware of our recent assault on their property. We will keep this secret from them. Regardless, the opportunity is lucrative, and we are already familiar with the terrain. This knowledge and our understanding of the foe inside those mines gives us an advantage, I believe."

"This is a done deal, then?" Illych chimes in. "We are doing this?"

"Initially, I had reservations. Returning to the mines would leave us vulnerable to ambush if this is a setup. Secondary to that would be how to deal with Legion. In another serendipitous event, Balthazar has volunteered a solution to Legion involving a quixault, which I am guessing will shortly be in our hands. All of these advantages contribute to my agreeing to take the job. An additional motivator is the fact that the mission culminates in taking the quixault to Tartarus."

Held looks at me and whispers, "He found a way to pay for the trip to wherever Tartarus is."

I agree that that is how Mr. Lark thinks.

"Are we doing that spelunking thing again?" Mike breaks in. "Are we leaving Tank behind?" Tank has a disappointed look on his face.

"No, Mr. Daugherty, the entire team will participate," says Mr. Lark. "And since we are working for Giggle Corp, we will be walking in through the front door."

We all go still for a moment and look at each other. We never get to walk through the front door.

The old man looks at Illych. "How soon until we could deploy?"

Illych looks thoughtful for moment. "We need a day to assemble the gear. Everything is here, but what about the quixault? We need that from Balthazar first, don't we?"

"Unfortunately, Balthazar did not give us a specific date when we should expect it. Prepare for the mission. Then we are ready when we receive the quixault."

Without so much as a nod of his head or a goodbye, our employer turns and leaves. This is the signal for Illych to stand and loudly clap his hands together. "Let's get started."

The next several hours are a blur of pulling equipment out, drawing weapons, making lists, checking lists, and forming piles. Then rechecking my individual pile. Then checking my colleagues' piles. This is a military thing that I am not fond of.

Late into the evening, our gear is ready. Five tired men eat a late meal and shuffle off to bed. I swing by the library to grab a book to read before I fall asleep.

After turning on a light, I shuffle through a stack of books on my desk and find a title worthy of putting me to sleep and turn to leave.

Standing not ten feet from me is the visitor from Balthazar's. The dark man is just standing there with a box in his hands.

How is he here? Inside the Citadel?

"Meili, isn't it?"

He nods and extends the box toward me. I take it, expecting it to be heavy. Instead, it is light as if empty. The lid is not latched, and I flip it open. Inside is an ornate construct made from metal and crystals. It's small enough to fit in the palm of my hand. A small piece of paper sits in the box. The few words on it, written in flowing English script, say "I only need be close."

Looking at Meili, I ask, "This is the quixault Balthazar spoke of?"

The dark man nods. He then turns and walks from the library. I follow him out, not far behind, only losing sight of him for a moment. Regardless, when I exit the library, he is nowhere to be seen. At first, I am apprehensive. An intruder has penetrated our fortress, apparently with little effort. Illych and the others should be told.

Then I realize nothing has changed. Apparently, whatever Meili is, he comes and goes as he pleases. Like Balthazar said, it is his way.

Looking at the box in my hand, I realize this should be taken to Illych as soon as possible.

Tomorrow.

After a good night's sleep.

Then all hell can break loose.

* * *

The next morning, I awake having slept surprisingly well. Looking over, I see the quixault is still where I left it on the nightstand. Without touching it, I leave for my morning hygiene ritual. When I return, it is still in place. Gathering my courage, I gently pick up the box and walk to the cafeteria. On the way, I run into Mike, headed in the same direction.

"What's with the box, Thomas?"

"It is the quixault for Legion."

"When did that get here? Mr. Lark stopped by?"

"We, or I, had a visitor last night."

"A visitor? Here? And you did not tell anyone?"

"That is correct."

"Good luck with that."

In lockstep, we enter the cafeteria together and find the rest of my colleagues already seated for breakfast. I walk straight to Illych, presenting him with the box. He looks at me with a questioning expression.

"The quixault."

"How did you get it? Did Mr. Lark stop by?"

"Meili, the quiet one we met at Balthazar's, was in the library last night and handed it to me."

Everyone is paying attention now. "We had an intruder last night and you are just telling me now?" Illych asks with irritation.

"It was late. I was tired. He disappeared as fast as he appeared. If he can get in undetected and vanish like that, there did not seem to be any urgency. What would we have done? Seriously, the guy was in and out like Santa Claus."

Illych stares at me in shock. The others look at me like I smell bad.

"Don't get angry with me. I didn't sneak him in. If he could appear here undetected, what were you going to do?"

"We had a visitor last night?"

The whole group of us rotates toward the doorway. Our employer stands waiting for our reply.

"Thomas had a visitor last night," Illych replies. "The character from our visit to Balthazar's. He brought a gift." He stands to transfer the box to Mr. Lark, who opens it to inspect the contents.

Closing the box, the old man states, "The world is a big place, and there are truly ancient things about in it. Some of them are not concerned with locked doors. Not so much because they enjoy violating a space, but rather they do not understand or value why a door must be locked. Especially when the situation is pressing."

Not sure what that was all about, but the old man apparently felt the need to share.

"Everyone is present and rested, and I take it the piles of equipment staged near the gate indicate preparations are complete?"

Illych gives a confirming nod.

"Good. With the quixault in hand, we are ready to begin. The first stage of our journey will be to the Giggle Corp compound above the mines. The corporate head of security will meet us there. Thomas, it is possible they may recognize you from your adventure at Giggle security in San Francisco. Your helmet and face covering must remain in place during the briefing."

If the corporate head of security is that tall, unpleasant guy, then yes, I should keep my face hidden.

"To maintain plausible deniability, we will travel by plane to a local airstrip relatively near the mines and then by bus the rest of the way. Once on-site, we will be briefed and then breach the mine through the main doors."

"With the quixault now in hand, we activate the travel arrangements."

Illych makes a spinning motion with his hand, and we all head for the door. Gearing up takes not fifteen minutes, and we stride out into the cold and gloom of the badlands around the Citadel.

Not one to miss an opportunity, I time my steps and shift my position until I am side by side with Mr. Lark.

"I have a question," I say. My employer blinks with frustration a few times while maintaining the pace.

"Yes, Thomas? What is your question?"

"Back in the mines, the first time, after interfacing with the computer system, you said it was all about you. Could you clarify?"

Mr. Lark maintains his stride in silence, and then, after a long pause, he says, "I can understand your curiosity." He pauses again. "What I found is truly diabolical. My use of the ouiblet is confounding Djinn Amal Halluck and at least one other Greater Created. After attempting more worldly methods to search for me and my organization, they decided to tap into more powerful tools.

"The Giggle Corp CEO was duped into believing that this artifact will give them the edge to beat their rivals at Langstraad Solutions. Legion was brought from whatever pit or vault it was held fallow in and delivered to this Giggle Corp research center..

"They were unsuccessful. In their willfulness, they opened Pandora's box, and the inherent instability of Legion began to spiral out of control. Having failed in their intended mission, they apparently shrugged their shoulders and abandoned the project. It is at this point my organization become involved, and in a cosmic demonstration of irony, I walk straight into the heart of the search for me. If there is an overarching universal deity, this may constitute one of its jokes."

I shake my head. "All those people, all those resources. Just to find you?" The moment the words leave my mouth, it registers how bad they sound.

"Yes, Thomas. It is a bit much considering I am but one old man with a fascination for ancient history. If I had to guess, our tangling with Amal Halluck set off a greater chain of events. Fortunately, my obsession with secrecy is keeping the wolves at bay, so to speak."

The Compass emerges into view through the gloom. We will translate soon.

"An American industrialist once said that only the paranoid survive," I say to my employer. "We should get a sign with that on it and hang it up at the Citadel."

Based on his expression, the old man's concentration is leaving our discussion; but not before one parting comment. "One day, we might."

After we enter the Compass, the subsequent travel to the mines follows a familiar template. Translation, nausea, vehicle to an airport, flight to a different airport, and another long drive to the mines. Due to our change in travel from the first mission, the scenery is completely different. As we drive to the mines, the mountains frame the valley around us rather than the team trudging across their frozen peaks.

The sun is bright above in clear blue skies and only few whisps of white clouds. The picturesque mountains surround us as we wind our way up to our destination. The van is comfortable and warm, and I realize some time later, after awakening, that I napped through more than half the journey. It is comforting to know that when we arrive, we will not have to dive into a frozen-over, water-filled hole in the ground. I still cannot believe we did that.

Refreshed, I ponder what we will find when we arrive. Perhaps an empty parking lot with a few security guards at one end?

A mile away from the mines one lane is blocked with concrete dividers and the other lane has a large dump truck parked across it to act as a gate.

On this side of the gate, parked along both sides of the road, *pointing away* from the mines are several black SUVs with all their doors open. From the vapor trail coming from the vehicles' tailpipes, I can tell their engines are running.

Nudging Held, I nod toward the vehicles. "What is up with those? Doors open, engines running, and pointing away?"

Our vehicle slows to a stop. "Getaway vehicles," he says. "They must be concerned about what might come out of the mines."

A soon as our forward motion stops, Tank opens the back doors and we debark. Before I step down onto the asphalt, I snap my faceplate into place.

I count perhaps two dozen men, all armed and looking very tactical. Two quick-erecting lookout towers sit on each side of the road. Men with binoculars are watching the mines. On this side of the barricades, in the road lane blocked by concrete, a tent has been set up. As soon as our feet hit the ground, the tall man who took me into custody at the Giggle Corp security headquarters back in San Francisco walks out into the sun. Now he is dressed in black tactical gear. Two armed men flank him. They pause for a moment and look at us. Then Tall Man waves us over, and he re-enters the tent.

Mr. Lark walks toward the tent, and we fall in behind him, entering under the tucked-away flap.

Several large flat screens hang along the tent walls showing security-camera views of the empty road between here and the facility. One monitor shows a mostly empty parking lot and the research facility's modern-looking main entrance. The glass and doors have seen better days. Something big and strong took out its aggression on the structure.

"There will be no introductions," Tall Man suddenly says. "I do not want to know who you are. My superiors instructed me to bring you up to speed on what we know and allow you access to the facility."

His gaze finds me and lingers.

"After the problems began, we lost all communication with site security and with systems inside the facility," he continues. "My team and I responded, and when we first arrived, we tried sending in several drones, one after the other. Not long after breaching the main doors, we lost contact. A six-man team was then sent in. They made it to the elevators and stairways down to the mines before losing contact. Their audio feed remained operational for a few minutes longer than video. From that, we determined they were attacked, could not retreat, and were quickly overwhelmed. A second, larger team was sent in. Twelve men, heavily armed, similar results. "We then set up a perimeter outside the main entrance while we considered our options, and then this happened."

Tall Man nods to a team member, who activates a monitor. It shows the parking lot with the security perimeter and main entrance behind it. Dozens of security officers are in view. The main entrance is also undamaged.

The black-and-white feed does not have audio, only visual. A construct of sorts, the size of an automobile, bursts out from inside the main entrance doors, causing the damage now visible. Mechanical in nature, its proportions are all wrong, displaying a strange asymmetry. It moves via long piston-like rods cycling quickly in a perverse version of walking. The distance to the security perimeter is covered in seconds. Fast-reacting guards are already firing their weapons at the thing.

The construct targets the security guards. But instead of crushing or skewering them with its piston legs, it roughly gathers them up. The machine is unconcerned with broken limbs or severe injury. Each man is quickly snatched up and pinned to the construct's form. Even with the visual feed's poor quality, the carnage is shocking. Terror and desperation play out as those harvested remain alive and screaming. The horror continues until its form is covered in tortured and writhing forms.

Then, as fast as it appeared, the construct bolts back into the mines sheathed in living cargo.

Now I understand the vehicles pointing away with their doors open and engines running.

"Now you know what we know," he says when it ends.

"One other thing to note. Corporate also wants to convey the value of this facility. Whatever is loose inside there needs to be put down before this reaches government ears—and to keep the collateral damage to a minimum. Do you have any questions?"

Mr. Lark's expression is nonchalant despite the horrors we just witnessed. Everyone else is quiet. We were ready when we arrived.

"One last thing, just so we are clear," Tall Man says. "If you call for help, we are not coming."

Another pregnant pause ensues.

Tall Man gets the hint. "Proceed, then." The sound of the dump truck firing up signals the way is open.

Time to go slay monsters.

Chapter 17

Held drives us the remaining mile at a relatively slow speed with the rear doors open. Just in case we need a quick exit.

The van rolls to a slow stop in the middle of the abandoned parking lot. While this is a warm, sunny day and we're within a remote wilderness area, there are no birds in the sky or nearby trees. My augmented hearing array hears nothing that does not come from the team.

We spread out in a skirmish line and slowly advance on the abandoned main entrance. Equipment from the previous security presence is scattered randomly about in the aftermath of the smash-and-grab attack from the thing in the mines. Several firearms can even be seen in or near the smashed barricade. The machine monster's piston-and-long-rod method of locomotion left gouged divots in the blacktop where it stepped while pursuing its prey. Between the divots, the smashed barricades, and the wrecked main entrance, the visible evidence of that construct's physical capacity for destruction is impressive.

Mike's voice comes over the ComDat. "Why would it grab those people like that? To make more grey men? If the thing in the mine can make machines like that thing, why bother?"

"Humans represent a greater array of resources to Legion than just the grey men," Mr. Lark replies. "My guess is our raid inadvertently depleted its on-hand stock of material. That machine was sent out to replenish badly needed biological inventory."

As we approach the shattered main entrance, I am heartened by the firepower on display. Illych and Held both have SHEGs. Tank has his belt-fed MG4, which despite being a sizable piece of hardware, looks like a normal-size rifle cradled in his massive arms. Mike and I have carbines. Mr. Lark looks under armed with just a single holstered handgun.

The tension increases the closer we get to the main doors. Night vision won't help us see into the dark main lobby until we get clear of the sunlight we are currently standing in.

"We rush it," Illych says as we reach the entrance. "Three, two, one, go, go, go!"

All six of us storm the gaping hole the monster machine tore into existence. Mike even vaults one of the crushed doors. Between the hole and broken windows off to both sides, our rush to enter is unimpeded.

Clear of the sunlight, the night vision kicks in, and we get our first view of the interior. It is truly dark; no lights. The lobby furniture, security checkpoint, and reception area have been shredded. Piston-foot divots are evident in the punched-through floor tiles and spalling concrete beneath. Devastation is everywhere. Dried blood splatters trail from entry to elevator shaft.

Mike's voice comes over the ComDat. "Property values are going down."

"Stop the chatter," Illych snaps back. "Stay focused."

Spreading out, we check the side offices and the dark spaces above what is left of the false ceiling.

Illych finally calls it. "Nobody is home."

"No traps?" Held chimes in.

"Mr. Lark, is there anything on the oculus?" Illych calls out.

"Strangely, no," Mr. Lark responds. "There is no proper interference, but at the same time, only solid objects are observable." He continues, "This thing sent a machine out to collect people against their will. I do not expect obstacles to our entry. The spider will only ever welcome the fly."

Looking around, I see two ways down to lower levels. Three sets of elevator doors. No joy there with the power out. Plus, taking a metal box down to whatever is waiting at the bottom is unappealing. When I look over at the stairway, I see Mike looking inside past the door half ripped from its hinges.

Shuffling over, I look in. No lights, no emergency lights. Just a pitch-black stairway down a one-thousand-foot shaft to the mines.

Mike and I look at each other. I speak first. "This is Castle Houska all over again." Mike's helmet nods in agreement.

Illych's voice provides instructions. "Mike, you take point. Then Held, Tank, myself with Mr. Lark, and Thomas on rear security."

Illych has not even finished speaking before Mike is through the door and down the steps. I stay in place while the others pass in order. Illych slaps my shoulder on his way down, saying, "Don't let them sneak up on us, Thomas." Then Mr. Lark passes and it is my turn.

As we descend, the faint light from the reception area above fades out. Night vision requires some light to function, and we are forced to activate low-output illuminators on our chest harnesses. The stairs go down forever, and soon we are deep underground with only pitch back around us.

One thousand feet translates into approximately a one hundred–story building. That is a long way down. There is no rushing, and we keep a steady pace.

The stairwell shows no signs of the piston divots. Besides, how would something as big as that machine fit into the confines of the spaces we are currently traveling? If it had, we would see more damage.

"Excuse me, but how did that machine thing get back down to the mines? These stairs do not look like it went through here. Could it have used the elevator shaft?"

"I share your concern," replies Mr. Lark. "Those elevator shafts would have also been too small for the dimensions of that mechanical beast. I have been consulting the oculus continuously, and while the mines are shrouded, I see nothing out of the ordinary in our path or regarding the elevator shafts."

Two-thirds of the way down we find a ghoulish surprise: a corpse. A Giggle employee in a lab coat is slumped against a wall. The blackened pool of blood shows whoever it was bled out in place. The process of decomposition is well underway, and I am thankful for the breathing filter built into my helmet and facemask.

We are probably ninety-plus floors down when the light levels begin to increase. The night vision registers it first, and as we descend farther, it becomes obvious lights are on somewhere down there.

From our first visit, I know the stairs open near the elevators in a great hall. It will already be a mess from when we blew up those roller contraptions what seems like forever ago, but it has really only been a few days.

Mike's voice comes over the ComDat. "I am down. The door is open. From what I can see, nobody's home."

"Keep in cover and enter," Illych responds.

We had spread out a bit during the journey down. Now, as each of my colleagues pause before entering the great hall, we catch up with each other. Soon, only Mr. Lark and I are waiting on the stairs side of the doorway.

We are greeted by a spectacle of change. Whatever is down here has been busy since our last visit. Most of the lighting is gone, but our night vision gives a clear view. The walls all have a shallow honeycomb scaffolding running from floor to ceiling. A low fog, no more than a few inches, really, floats across the floor. Looking up, the same fog obscures the ceiling.

To our right is the control room Mr. Lark previously did his supernatural hacking in. My guess is that will be our first target.

Illych's voice calls out, "Mr. Lark, are you seeing this?"

"Yes," the old man replies. "The oculus is useless in here. We will make for the control room and see what we can find there."

"Roger that." In my mind's eye I can see Illych making hand signals and the team responding.

Mr. Lark breaks my line of thought. "Let's go, Thomas." He walks out into the gallery. I follow two steps behind, the fog swirling about our feet. Other than the click and scuffle of the team's walking, the augmented hearing is finding no sounds to amplify.

Falling into a familiar wedge formation, the team advances quickly to the control room. Closing in on our destination, it becomes obvious the glass overlooking the open bay beyond is now filthy or painted. Only a faint green glow can be seen.

The helmet mic picks up a distinct clack sound from behind us.

And above us.

As the rear guard, I spin, looking for a foe.

And one appears. Falling from the fog above us and slamming down in front of me, perhaps halfway down the gallery, is the machine from the security video. The recording did not do it justice. In person, the unnaturalness of the thing makes your eyes hurt. Terror rips through me. My feet are already walking me backward toward the team.

Illych's command is loud in my ear. "Drop, Thomas, drop!"

Terror drives my instant reaction as my feet kick straight back and I fall face down and prone. I can still see the machine beast as its piston legs begin to actuate. Then the report of a SHEG. Farther down the gallery behind its missed target, the explosive round detonates with sufficient force to shake debris loose from the walls and ceiling.

In a second, the distance between that thing and my body is cut in half. A second report sounds. This one detonates on the machine beast. It is too close. I am driven backward across the floor while high-velocity pieces of machine painfully impact my body. A cry of pain comes across the ComDat.

Even as I roll and slide backward, I can see how the explosion blows the murder machine apart, throwing chunks of it in random directions.

For a moment, I flex my hands and wiggle my toes, feeling for injuries. While I am doing this, debris bounces off the ceiling and rains back down. The good news: Everything on me still works.

Pushing to my feet, the fresh silence is broken by Illych calling out, "Sound off!"

"Tank here."

"Mike here."

"Thomas here."

Mr. Lark is already standing and looking around. He ignores our check-in.

Illych's voice comes back. "Held?"

After a long pause, Held replies, "I'm here. Something is stuck in my leg, though." The pain in his voice is palpable. So that is whose sound of pain came across the ComDat a moment ago.

The rest of us are up and moving. Covered in thick dust, we start brushing ourselves and each other off as we locate Held. We find him a distance away from us down the gallery, virtually at the control-room door. His left thigh has an ugly chunk of metal impacted into it.

The crash of a concrete block falling down onto the floor grabs our attention. One of the machine beast chunks is moving.

Now I see four chunks dragging themselves free from the wreckage.

Tank's MG4 roars to life with the sound of tearing linoleum. Armor-piercing rounds take a toll on the nearest machine. With a cyclic rate in the hundreds of rounds per minute and the granite stance of its wielder, the target of its violence visibly withers under the hail of rounds. Sparks fly and pieces of metal are violently separated.

The murder machine collapses. Tank does not pause, just rotates to the next-nearest target. Machine two is already in motion, but the MG4's stream of machine death catches it quickly. AP rounds cut away its ability to move. A long center mass burst of fire finishes it.

Illych steps into the edge of my left field of vision, SHEG in hand. I see the flash and recoil while keeping my eyes on what is coming at us.

Too close.

This one is about the same distance away as the original construct. The detonation shatters the charging machine. When I finally realize what happened, I look up at the ceiling as concrete chunks, dust, and machine bits cover me. For the second time today, I am wiggling my fingers and toes to confirm that I have not been seriously injured. Everything works, but my body aches from the shock wave.

The team is not the only thing repositioned by the explosion. Machine number four was thrown over us through the glass overlooking the bay behind us. It must have been leaping when Illych blew up machine number three.

We are a mess. Dirt, dust, and debris cover everything. Pieces of wrecked machinery are everywhere. Illych's helmet took a big hit; the left side of his face is a bloody mess. All of us are missing gear. The shockwave actually tore things from our harnesses. Mike was huddled with Held and rode out the storm better than most of us. Tank had a chunk of concrete wall fall on him. He struggles free without assistance. Somehow his MG4 slowed the descent of the slab, preventing any serious injury. Unfortunately, the weapon is now bent into a non-functional shape.

Where is Mr. Lark?

After scanning around, I find him not far away, looking at the hole in the glass. The green glow shines through the penetration no longer dimmed by the filthy glass. The path the machine beast took through the glass was overhead, above floor level. The bay on the other side is a good twenty feet down. Hopefully the thing smashed to pieces wherever it landed.

Tank loads his backup weapon, a short-barrel shotgun with a rotating drum. Not much use against killer robots, but very effective against soft targets. Illych removes his now-useless helmet and tosses it aside. Mike removes the object from Held's thigh and bandages him up. With the painkillers taking effect, he can stand and slowly limp.

Gathering outside the control-room doors, we prepare to enter.

"That is what I would call a guard dog," comments Illych.

"Yes. The approach was unexpected but effective," Mr. Lark interjects. "The SHEG at close range is problematic. Hopefully—"

The sound of explosives detonating cuts the old man off. The elevator doors are blown off into the gallery. All three sets of doors blow simultaneously.

"Those are breaching charges," Tank calls out.

Illych quietly adds, "We have visitors."

I snap my carbine to ready. To my surprise, Tank sprints off to hug the wall the elevators doors are recessed into, getting as close as possible. The others, including Mr. Lark, drop prone and ready weapons. The SHEG is out of the question. Another explosion in this place, and some of us will die.

Tank and I cover maybe half the distance when men begin running out of the elevator shaft openings. Average height, curly hair, robust build. These are Amak Halluck's goons.

Mr. Lark's voice comes over the ComDat. "Looks like we are not the only ones here for Legion."

Illych, Held, and Mike open up with their carbines. Tank and I keep going for a few more feet before sharing our position with the arriving goons. The bad guys have body armor, which will slow down the rate at which we put them down. But the numbers arriving is the most concerning thing. They must be speed-rappelling down the elevator shaft in close formation, because they are exiting one after the other in close succession.

The goons themselves have short-barreled assault rifles of an unfamiliar make. As soon as they are clear of the bodies piling up in front of the elevator doors, they take a kneeling firing position and begin shooting back.

The dust and fog make identifying targets difficult; more so for our foes than us. The last of the arrivals trip over the corpses of their comrades, stumbling into view and making easy targets. The flow of goons ends.

The bolt on my carbine locks back, empty. At this point, Tank slaps another drum reload into his shotgun and strides forward, blasting the few remaining goons at point-blank range. The last remaining goon gets a clear shot at me as I reload. The bullet does not find a solid target and glances off a piece of my carapace's hardware, causing me to spin and fall down. A blast from Tank's shotgun prevents a second shot from the goon.

A few more shotgun blasts later and the gallery goes silent. I unsuccessfully try to sit up. Tank's broad form comes into view above me as he extends a hand to me. I take it, and the former Marine effortlessly pulls me to my feet.

We walk through the fallen goons to make a count and dead check them. More than a few have to be assisted to the afterlife before we are done. The total ends at twenty-six before the echo of the last shot fades from the gallery.

Tanks calls it out. "I count twenty-six."

"Where did they come from?" I ask.

Illych's voice, tired and filled with more than a little pain, replies, "Could have been choppers dropping them right after we arrived. Or they are working with Giggle."

Mr. Lark's voice cuts through the discussion, speculating out loud, "Perhaps Giggle was to hire us so Amal Halluck would know right where we would be? If so, why such an awkward ambush?" The old man pauses, then orders, "Search the bodies. Look for something unusual."

Tank shrugs, and we start back through the corpses. What we are looking for is obvious to me as soon as I see it. One of the goons has a strange little box strapped to his chest. It has a simple latch holding it closed. Reaching down, I flip it open. Inside is a weird-looking metal and crystal construct. A quixault?

"I think I found it. Looks like they brought a quixault."

"Do not touch it," Mr. Lark quickly replies. "They are here for the same reason we are. To collect Legion."

The shattering of glass interrupts the discussion. The fourth mechanical beast segment leaped from inside the warehouse space on the other side of the windows to perch at the edge of the gallery. In doing so, it shattered several massive panes of glass outwards onto the gallery. Mr. Lark is standing so close, he is showered with shards of glass like a storm of transparent blades.

Unharmed, my employer is within a single leap of the killing machine. With a swift movement, his right hand plucks something from his chest harness and tosses it toward what can only be his near doom. Even in the dust and dim light I can see a dot of black arcing away from my employer. Swiftly finding its target, it blossoms, extending strands in a weblike pattern. Gossamer threads wrap themselves around the construct. Once plastered to its surface, they glow orange, then red, then white hot. The machine, apparently forgetting its nearby prey, struggles against the bright lines crisscrossing its form. The web begins to contract, white-hot wires slicing inward. Rivulets of molten metal splatter to the floor in a shower of sparks. The smell of burnt hot metal fills the corridor with a strength even my facemask filters cannot keep out. In just a handful of seconds, the threads meet and reform into the small object Mr. Lark originally deployed. The killing machine, now diced into numerous smaller, motionless chunks, falls apart. The cross-sections of the pieces still glow from the cutting. Metallic clanging sounds resonate though the gallery as the pieces crash down, coming to rest on the floor.

Mike's voice is in my ears. "That was exciting."

"We must remain vigilant," says Mr. Lark. "There will be other obstacles to our success."

The old man picks his way through the machine's dismembered corpse to recover his weapon from the floor. Mr. Lark always has the best toys.

The team gathers together to check weapons and assess our status.

Held can barely walk, and the painkillers he is on will make him less than reliable in a fight. The right side of Illych's face looks terrible. It is swollen, purple, and bloody. I am not sure he can see from his right eye. Tank's MG4 is no longer functional. Our ammunition status is good, though. Both for the SHEGs and the carbines.

Mr. Lark looks at Illych. "You and Held will remain here. Take cover, and keep any stragglers from coming up behind us." Illych nods and starts building a fighting position from debris.

Our employer looks at those of us remaining, "You three are with me." He turns and walks toward the control-room door. We fall in behind him while giving Illych and Held a last visual once-over. Illych returns our nods with a thumbs-up.

Without hesitation, Mr. Lark opens the no-longer-locked sliding door. Since our last visit, the controls and computers in the room have disappeared. In their place is a crudely constructed stairway down to the bay floor. Appearing to have been welded and bent into place, it is an incongruous construct. Mr. Lark takes the first step down, waits for a moment, and then jumps up and down in the most undignified way. Despite its ramshackle appearance, the stairway is solid.

We slowly make our way down to the bay floor. The space under the roof must be the size of an American football field. It is dark except for that unhealthy green glow from the center. Our line of sight to everywhere is blocked by ridiculously tall cloth dividers. Once down to the bay floor, it becomes obvious the cloth dividers were white at one time. Now they are dingy grey and spattered with who knows what.

The dividers are everywhere. If there is something in here with us, we won't know until it is literally on top of us. Line of sight is broken in all directions.

"Keep tight together," Tank instructs. "If something jumps us, we need to be close to help each other."

If there is a mechanical killing machine in here with us, the only thing closeness will get us is dead.

Mr. Lark seems to know where he is going and drifts indirectly to the center of the room. The dividers obscure a direct route, so we just wind back and forth. The deathly silence of the place gives way to the sound of breathing. There is an unhealthy, distinct wetness and hesitation to it. It quickly becomes obvious the sounds are coming from more than one source.

"Does anyone else hear the breathing?" I ask.

"Roger that," Mike confirms.

Tank sounds relieved. "I was worried I was the only one hearing that." Mr. Lark continues walking without speaking. We round another divider and find the source of the green glow. In the center of the bay is a haphazard collection of coffins or sarcophagi. Cabling hangs down from the ceiling to each one, and within each cable bundle is at least one line with a faint green glow emanating from it.

Cautiously, we move in closer, and I get my first look at what is inside. Each one of what I count to be twenty-eight sarcophagi has an emaciated, naked human form inside. The exposed brain matter of the open skulls of men and women connect to a forest of fine wires terminating in a cable connected to the sarcophagus.

Feeling ill, I ask, "Good God, Mr. Lark, what is this?"

The old man deploys the wynloo in the palm of his hand. "This is how Giggle Corp crushed Langstraad Solutions in performance," he says. "Human minds have been incorporated into the processing matrix. The increased processing speed was primarily used in the search for me and my organization. The leftover bleed off was made available to Giggle's efforts."

The crystal ball in my employer's hand starts glowing white. "Thomas, I am going to interface and attempt to locate Legion. Please stand ready to help me disengage."

Stand ready to slap or even stab him? What can I say, I am here to help.

Glowing threads stream outward from the wynloo, connecting with the occupants of the sarcophagi around me. Other luminous threads link with the hanging cables. White light illuminates the scene, revealing more detail of the horrors dealt the victims around us. My employer's eyes actually roll back in his head. As if that was not creepy enough, the living corpses around us begin to convulse in their open-topped coffins. Pale, abused flesh ripples, and atrophied limbs feebly shake. The white glow of the artifact in Mr. Lark's hand increases as Mike, Tank, and I draw close, weapons at the ready.

In a faint voice, Mr. Lark says, "Thomas, now."

With a heavy gloved hand, I forcefully slap the old man right across the face. The sound has a satisfying note to it.

The glowing threads fade away, and Mr. Lark's posture briefly personifies exhaustion.

While Mr. Lark recovers, Tank remarks to me, "Wait, what? Did I see that correctly? You just slapped him. How do I get that job?" If this comment was heard by our employer, he does not show any sign.

The old man whispers, "They are coming." No further explanation is needed. We know what is coming. The three of us form an outward-facing triangle around Mr. Lark. At least all these sarcophagi will be obstacles to our oncoming foes.

My helmet's microphone array picks up only the labored breathing of the suffering contents of the sarcophagi around us. I find myself looking up and around while considering unconventional approaches for our enemy.

Now, out of sight and blocked by all the cloth dividers, I hear the slap of bare feet on concrete floors. Through the occasional tear or small spaces around the dividers, I see glimpses of the approaching chaos.

One thing I am certain of. They are fast, and we only have seconds before they arrive. A quick look and listen reveals no other opponents approaching from a different direction.

"They are only coming from that direction." Mike's voice startles me.

Without comment, Tank and I shift a few sarcophagi for cover.

"Suppression fire," Tank barks. "Let's try to slow them down."

Lifting my carbine to my shoulder, I place my sight's reticle in the general direction of the chaos shambling toward us and fire a burst. For perhaps two seconds, the three of us shred cloth separators. It feels good to be doing something versus waiting for a virtually unseen enemy to get within arm's reach.

I just finish reloading when the draugar break free from cover. The same grey, nude, near-corpses, moving with an unnatural quickness. I put one down with a head shot. From the corner of my vision, I see Tank and Mike doing the same.

Then they are upon us. Slapping hands, punching fists, and slamming bodies physically push me to the ground. My carbine is gone. One of them pins my right hand down with painful force. In seconds, I am scooped up by four draugar, who begin shuffling away with me. Looking back, I can see Tank physically punishing any grey man who gets close.

I see Mike close by with his combat knife out. A few quick stabs demonstrate how six inches of steel are as effective as a bullet in putting these monsters down. Despite their energetic defense, Mike and Tank are getting knocked around by draugar.

Where is Mr. Lark? Twisting in my captors' grasp, I look to the sounds of renewed gunfire. I can just barely see my employer moving quickly, handgun in hand, shooting his way through the press of grey foes. One draugr goes down with each shot. Perhaps by luck, he has fewer of the near-dead chasing him. Or maybe he is just killing them faster than the rest of us. Regardless, the last thing I see as I am marched away is Mr. Lark putting down the last of his attackers and rushing to help Mike.

Now the dividers block sight of pretty much anything. My silent captors have me in an iron grip as they march back in the direction they came. They did not search me or remove any of my gear. I still have a pistol and grenades. As soon as a hand is free . . .

The end of the cathedral-like space has been converted into a shrine of sorts. The focus is a pedestal with cables running away from it and then up the wall behind. Constructed from an eclectic collection of electronic parts, unidentifiable mechanical bits, all mixed with something that makes my eyes hurt even through the helmets vision filters.

The draugar bring me close and force me to kneel, facing the pedestal. The two grey men keep my hands and arms firmly restrained. One of the others who carried me here stands behind me and removes my helmet.

The pedestal thing is giving off heat.

My head hurts.

Now it hurts more. A voice is whispering.

Inside my head, combined with the pain, is a voice.

"Take me from this place."

The voice is smooth and crisp, almost soothing, yet it still causes pain with every word.

"There is so much you can know."

The force of its intrusion into my mind has rendered me mute and unable to put two thoughts together. Images of things I have wanted flash through my mind. Fantasies of what I have coveted surface inside my consciousness. Feelings of desire and lust. All mine for the taking and more. All I need to do is reach out my hand.

The draugar have released me. All I have to do is reach out my hand.

The loud report of close-proximity gunfire breaks the spell. The images and the pain rush out of my mind, leaving me weak and sick. Falling forward, I catch myself before I go down face-first. With a push and twist, I roll onto my back. The draugar are dead around me.

The voice is faint in my head. Now Legion is trying to entice Mr. Lark.

"You can have what you seek."

"The tools, the history. There is more than your portals and pocket dimensions. So much more. Just take me from this place."

From where I am lying, I can see the old man facing the pedestal with that peculiar green glow illuminating his face.

"What you found. What you are. There is more. Weapons can defend as well as attack. With Legion, you will be unassailable."

Mr. Lark's expression is unreadable and blank.

Then the old man removes the quixault from his belt.

"I cannot be destroyed, only wielded," the voice barks. "If we do not join, another eventually will join me. Take the safer of the paths. You can be so much more."

Mr. Lark nods, steps forward, and places the quixault on the pedestal. In an instant, the green light disappears, and the sensation of something in my head stops.

Tank walks into my view and offers me his hand. As I take it, he pulls me up so I am standing. Looking him and Mike up and down, I find they appear to be uninjured.

Mr. Larks puts away the ouiblet and says, "We are done here. It is time to leave." While walking back to Illych and Held, the feeling something has changed is palpable.

As we climb what passes for stairs up to the gallery entrance, I ask a question that needs an answer. "What about the people back there? In the sarcophagi. We are just leaving them here?"

The old man stops at the top of the stairs and turns to look down on me. "As I have stated in the past, Thomas, I am not in the business of saving the world. Your empathy for your fellow man is commendable but eminently impractical.

Regardless, there is no saving them. They are doomed to a slow, painful death now that Legion has been taken away. The only saving grace is they no longer have a never-ending life of suffering to look forward to."

He then turns and walks through the door into the gallery.

Mike and Tank are right behind him. I stop at the doorway and look back over the bay. Most of the forest of dividers has been knocked over. The sickly green glow is gone. A few pin pricks of individual lights remain, the last gasps from the life-support equipment the only illumination. In a few hours, this place will be a tomb.

Chapter 18

Getting Held up a hundred levels of stairs takes so very long but is uneventful. The dark of night and twinkle of starlight greets us upon exiting the ground-level lobby. Tired and wounded, we shuffle out into the cool night air, thankful to have open sky over our heads.

Once we reach the van, we speed away from the nightmare mausoleum a thousand feet below us. At the security roadblock, Tall Man is waiting. Mr. Lark is riding shotgun and does not exit the van when Tank brings it to a stop, forcing the security leader to walk over and engage with our employer.

"You guys made it out."

Mr. Lark nods.

"You must have been inside maybe an hour, maybe a little more, when a dual-rotor helicopter landed in the parking lot. On the camera, we saw may two dozen guys get out. They entered the lobby, and we never saw them again."

Tall Man pauses, perhaps waiting for an answer. None is given.

"After fifty minutes, to be precise, the chopper powers up and flies away," he says, and then he pauses again. "Now, hours later, you bunch come walking out."

Mr. Lark says nothing.

Another long pause, then Tall Man continues, "Did you figure it out?"

Mr. Lark nods. "The problem has been solved. It is safe to enter the mines. Notwithstanding the structural damage and the large number of corpses that are potentially a health hazard."

Tall Man's face almost softens for a moment as if he finds something humorous. "Health hazard, you say." Taking a step back, he waves us through. "Enjoy your evening."

Our journey back to the Citadel is quiet, and we all take time napping. Mr. Lark secures the Legion-containing quixault in one of the steel vaults surrounding the stone circle and promptly leaves. Now five tired men trudge through the cold gloom. Held and Illych visit The Doctor. The rest of us clean up, and our wounded join us for a quiet meal.

* * *

Waking up the next morning, I realize I have no assigned tasks. With yesterday's nasty business behind me, a full day of reading and working on the library's collection await. Cheered by the thought and with a spring in my step, I head to the cafeteria for breakfast. A good day indeed this will be.

My colleagues are all present when I arrive. All four dressed in exercise sweats and looking like they just finished a run. Thankfully, they did not try to include me in their calisthenics the day after the mission we just had.

With no reason to rush to a next assignment, we sit and relax.

"Is Mr. Lark keeping whatever that Legion thing is?" Mike busts out.

Illych shakes his head and replies, "No. It will eventually go to Tartarus, which Mr. Lark hinted is in the Pacific Ocean somewhere."

"Somewhere warm, I hope," Tank chimes in. "There are other options in the world than in swimming in freezing mountain water or crawling around deep underground."

Mike looks at Tank. "What are you talking about? You didn't do any swimming. We did the work, and you took a nap."

Tank smiles and nods.

"What do you think will happen to the mess in those mines?" I ask.

"Giggle will go in and clean it up," Illych responds. "It is their problem now."

"That was a lot of dead bodies," Mike comments wistfully. "We may not even be responsible for most of them."

Held leans in. "You know, we took down a bunch of those Amal Halluck goons. I bet he is even less thrilled with us then he already was."

The conversation pauses with that comment. Making that djinn upset is something we are good at. We keep dodging the bullet on retribution for that, but someday . . .

On that positive note, we end our breakfast and go our separate ways. My path leads me to the library, where stacks of books await. It feels so good to be sitting, reading, and writing that I skip lunch.

This is where Illych finds me. At some point in his waiting for me to acknowledge his presence, he gives up on the passive approach and clears his throat. I look up to find him watching me patiently.

"Uh, hello, Illych. What can I do for you?"

"Just received word from Mr. Lark."

Good Lord, can I not have one day undisturbed? "What task has our illustrious employer assigned to me?"

Illych smiles.

A feeling of dread mixed with interest wells up inside me. "No, it can't be. So soon? Is it her again?"

Illych nods in an exaggerated way while smiling.

"What now? Some new trinket I need to learn about?"

"Not this time. She has a request to make of Mr. Lark. The boss is sending you to learn what it is and report back."

"What could she possibly want from Mr. Lark?"

"Thomas, what is with the hostility? A beautiful woman wants to talk with you. Just go with it. Held will be nearby if things go sideways. Okay?"

"When is the meeting?"

"Tomorrow morning at the British Museum in London."

"At the museum? The one we robbed? This is her idea?"

Illych smirks. "Mr. Lark's. Normal business hours, and it is a public place. Hear her out, report back. Maybe he thought you were having too much fun during your visits."

I acquiesce. "Fine." Tomorrow. At least I get a whole day in the library today.

"Oh, and take this." He hands me a key card. "This is left over from when we robbed the place. Maybe it will be useful." With no more to say, he takes his leave.

Alone now, I have time to consider what her request could be. This will be my third meeting with her in a month. That must mean something. Is she trying to say something without saying it? Communication with the fairer sex has never been my strong point, but I do know they often do not say what they want.

Regardless, I will find out tomorrow.

* * *

The next morning begins as an uneventful trip. Held and I travel to London by the usual route, and he drops me off near the museum. As I exit, he shares he will be nearby watching me with the oculus. Then he drives off, leaving me feeling very alone while I look at my final destination. The last time we were here we robbed the security vault, kidnapped Dr. Chatzas, and simulated a car bombing in the parking lot. Now I am supposed to just walk through the front doors.

My entry is uneventful. Security ignores me. I was half expecting posters with my face on them and large lettering saying I should be arrested immediately. For just a moment, I pause and realize I am in a place I would normally go before I met Karl Lark and everything changed. This is a small piece of my life from before.

It seems so long ago.

Pulling myself together, I notify the information desk I am here for my morning appointment with Dr. Chatzas. While I wait, I people watch. The museum visitor traffic is light this morning. Individuals and couples, all spaced out. None look threatening, and no one has bushy curly hair.

The young woman at the information desk interrupts my observing. "Mr. Davies, Dr. Chatzas will see you now. Please follow me."

"That will not be necessary. I know the way." I walk away, leaving the confused-looking woman behind me. It is true; I do know the way from my previous life. The walk is short, and the key card brings the elevator and opens the office's main doors. Useful. Soon, I am standing in an open doorway looking at a sitting Dr. Chatzas focusing on her computer screen.

"Dr. Chatzas."

She stops and looks up at me. A warm smile thaws her serious expression.

"Thomas, I asked you to call me Elizabeth."

This makes me smile. "Elizabeth."

She waves me in, and I take a seat across from her.

"It is unfortunate your employer insisted on our meeting here. Business is business, though, and I have a request for Karl Lark."

I nod. "That is why I am here. What is the ask?"

"How would an interested party hire your employer's organization?"

I have to think how to reply to that. "Honestly, I do not know. Is this a serious request? What could you possibly need for my employer's particular brand of . . . skills?"

"It is not for me. An archeological team found some interesting artifacts and even bribing the right officials has not been successful in getting them released to take outside the country."

"They want to hire Mr. Lark to smuggle artifacts? That might be overkill."

"These are not culturally significant, and they would complete a collection on representations of the underworld. Hades, Gehenna, and similar."

"Would Tartarus be covered within the collection?" I wonder if Amal Halluck is looking for something?

"The collection is not exclusively Greek, but yes, Tartarus would be included."

"I will pass your request along to my employer," I say. "Your friends will need deep pockets, that much I know."

Dr. Chatzas nods. "You know how complete collections can be exceptionally valuable? If Mr. Lark is able to facilitate this happening, the people involved will have no problem paying his fee."

Our business apparently complete, we sit quietly while looking at each other.

I break the silence. "When should I expect your next request to meet?"

Her smile is radiant. "Just as soon as I can arrange another reason for you to visit. Until then, I wish you well, Thomas Davies."

I stand and nod. "You as well, Elizabeth." With one final locking of our eyes, I turn and leave.

My steps are light on my way out to meet Held. It was good seeing her again. I doubt Mr. Lark will have any interest in her request, but if I am lucky, he will send me to deliver the message.

No sooner do I clear the building than the grey Mercedes with Held piloting glides into view. With only a brief stop for me to hop in, we are then off.

Held wastes no time in commenting. "That was quick."

Shrugging, I respond, "She or someone she knows is interested in hiring Mr. Lark."

"She is asking about hiring the team? All of us?"

"She more specifically spoke of hiring his organization. I take that to mean all of us."

Held shrugs. "Never a dull moment."

We return to the Citadel by the usual route. Mr. Lark is not waiting, and Illych debriefs me upon my return.

This leaves me with an afternoon and evening to retire to the library while looking forward to undisturbed hours.

Chapter 19

The five days after my return from visiting the British Museum are a blur of activity. Illych informs us Mr. Lark has located Tartarus in a megalithic site known as Nan Madol. Referencing maps in the library, I quickly determine Nan Madol is located on an island in the South Pacific People live there, and the place is open to tourists.

Illych also shares that we will be traveling on the yacht we used to rescue Balthazar from Hy-Brasil. A contractor is prepping the boat to be ready in twenty-four hours. We here at the Citadel are to also prepare. The plan is for Illych and Tank to pilot the yacht out to sea beyond the presence of prying eyes and then translate themselves and the boat to a point approximately a hundred miles from Nan Madol.

That one day passes quickly, and Ilych and Tank leave Held, Mike, and I to finish organizing the gear. This is when the real work begins.

Normally, translating to a moving object is not possible. The ouiblet only supports moving between defined points in Earth's gravity well. The exception to the rule is if Mr. Lark installs what looks like a scaled-down version of the Compass at the destination. This was done a year ago when we were first exploring Hy-Brasil. Now, if Mr. Lark provides the right dongle, we can translate right to the boat.

The boat is a converted aging yacht, so old it is made of steel. Nowhere near as sleek or futuristic as modern yachts, but Mr. Lark requires a steel ship for protection in a firefight.

Propulsion is provided by recently installed oversized marine turbo-diesels. The Godzilla-level horsepower available changes the heavy ship into a speedboat now capable of an impressive fifty knots.

The original reason for Mr. Lark acquiring an ocean-going vessel was the exploration of the phantom island of Hy-Brasil. In the utilitarian way typical of my employer, the ship was never christened and named. Apparently, those who work around boats are a superstitious lot, and this lack of a name drew unwanted attention and comment whenever the converted yacht was docked. So much so that the old girl now has a name: *Esmerelda*.

Hustling back and forth between the Compass and the *Esmerelda*, loading gear and supplies onto our new temporary home takes time. Preparations complete, Illych points the bow toward Nan Madol. The rumble of the monster diesels, as much felt as heard, announce the action is about to start.

And Mr. Lark finally shows up.

The ship has autopilot now, and Illych sets it for twenty knots. The six of us gather on the sun-drenched deck under the clear blue sky. There is nothing around us for miles in every direction. As we cluster in front of the pilot house, Mr. Lark steps out in front of us.

"Now that we are ready, it is time to brief you on more of the mission details," he begins. "This is a straightforward portal entry. Tartarus is a special case of a pocket dimension similar to what we have at the Compass or Citadel. The portal is close to the ocean with no roads nearby. Most of the buildings and nearby terrain is flooded, as Nan Madol is somewhat sunken into the water. Hence our ocean approach."

This does not make sense to me. "Mr. Lark, why not just translate straight in? There have to be places we can remain unseen. How about a night mission?" Honestly, why do we need a ship at all? Not that I am complaining about having some time in the sun.

"Nan Madol is popular with tourists, many of whom specifically travel there at night," Mr. Lark says. "If we are seen with no means of transport apparent, maintaining plausible deniability becomes a challenge. This mission has a high probability of interaction with bystanders. The good news is there are no authorities nearby. Any police interference will be very delayed, if at all."

Civilians in the zone of operations. Good to know.

"What do we do when we run across the random sightseer?" Held asks.

"Nothing," Mr. Lark replies. "We simply ignore civilians. Our faces will all be covered, and we will not talk to them. We take the rubber dinghy and float into the city through a flooded channel, getting as close as possible, debark, and navigate the remaining distance on foot. Time to the portal will be less than an hour from the time we leave the ship."

"Who is staying behind with the ship?" Mike breaks in.

"No one," Mr. Lark responds. "We lock it up, and everyone debarks. We should only be gone for a few hours. It is unlikely anyone nearby might be a threat. That said, I will be leaving a deterrent behind, just in case someone should decide to tamper with the boat while we are gone."

"Why all of us?" Held asks somewhat impatiently. "Why the whole team? Seems overkill to deliver a trinket."

Mr. Lark nods. "Assembling the whole team and the high level of preparation do perhaps seem a bit extreme. But please keep in mind Tartarus is an ancient storage site for high-risk artifacts, dangerous creatures, and even Lesser Created. It is not a place, based on its reputation, that we should enter lightly."

"If there are no other questions, then I suggest everyone get some rest. At our current speed, we will arrive close to sunset."

The meeting breaks up. Mr. Lark enters the pilothouse and then climbs up into the armored pillbox that passes for a crow's nest.

With nothing further to concern myself with, I locate a comfortable spot near the pilothouse. Sitting on the warm deck, I lean back against the superstructure. My eyes close while the heat of the sun brings out a smile. The sway of the ocean relaxes me, and the last thing I remember is the rumble of the diesels as sleep takes me.

Chapter 20

My colleagues left me to sleep the afternoon away. An abrupt change in the vessel's orientation shakes me awake. For a moment, I do not remember where I am. The sun sits low on the horizon, and the sky glows red in the fading light. How does that saying go? Red at night, sailors' delight; red sky in the morning, sailors take warning? I take the red sunset as a good omen.

As I stand and begin stretching, the splash of the anchor announces we have arrived. Sleeping while sitting on metal plates has left me stiff. Looking around, I see Illych in the pilothouse with Mike. No one is near me in the front of the boat. Shrugging my shoulders, I walk around to get a view of the stern and find all the action.

Tank and Held are working the dinghy out and down onto the ocean surface. Mr. Lark is not in sight. The scraping sound of metal not quite aligned announces the opening of the pilot door. Still a bit warped from the Hy-Brasil incident, it is serviceable compared to its prior barely functional state. Mike calls out from inside the pilothouse telling me to gear up. I wave in acknowledgement and walk toward the door. Mike leaves it open, and I nod to my colleagues as I shuffle through and then down the stairs to belowdecks.

This open space consists of a single level taking up two-thirds of the *Esmerelda*'s internal volume. There are steel shelves and cabinets, two sets of triple bunk beds, and an efficiency kitchen. One door leads to the head and the other to the mechanical space at the stern. It is all very minimalist.

A smaller version of the stone circle at the Compass dominates the middle of the room. A dozen black-stone cylinders rising to mid-thigh in height define the perimeter.

I am alone in the room.

Mr. Lark instantly appears right in the middle of the circle. Startled, I jump back and make a high-pitched noise. Having never before witnessed translation on the arrival end like that leaves an impression. The effect is quite unnatural.

Mr. Lark notices my shock and leaves it unaddressed. He just walks past me and up the stairs. Regaining my composure, I quickly step to my reason for coming down here—my gear pile—and reassemble it on my person. Now, almost two stone heavier, I step to the stairs and head up.

Everyone other than Illych is back at the stern, waiting. As soon as I exit the pilothouse, Illych is locking the door behind us. Time to go.

The dinghy is large enough for a dozen. This leaves plenty of room for the six of us. The stern outboard motor roars to life, and we are soon leaving the *Esmerelda* in our wake. Being anchored less than a mile offshore, the ride to the sunken ruins is short.

Mr. Lark is standing at the bow, demonstrating considerable dexterity as he remains upright without support while the dinghy bucks and weaves. He looks his usual stoic self, yet his expression shows just a hint of concern.

In the fading light, Nan Madol reveals its ruined glory. The entire megalithic site is curiously made up of lengths of hexagonal basalt stacked atop each other like a stone log cabin. The mystery of it is that the thousands and thousands of tons of stuff used to construct the site were not sourced locally. With acres and acres of stacked basalt structures organized in a semi-grid fashion, nobody knows how it got there.

My suspicion is Mr. Lark's dour expression is not caused by the prospect of getting our feet wet. Something about this mission is bothering him. I figured the prospect of opening Tartarus would be a more positive experience for the old man.

Assuming nothing trapped in there kills us . . .

Held is piloting the dinghy and slows down to a walking pace to navigate one of the waterlogged and sunken roads. In the dimming light, the basalt structures around us have transformed from mysterious and unknown structures to the outlines of shadowy skulls with windows and doors for eyes and mouths. As darkness falls, this place does a great imitation of a graveyard. The only sound to be heard is the put-put of the idling outboard motor.

The silence is pierced by a squealing alarm. The sound is not all that different from a car alarm. Reflexively, I join the others in scanning the surrounding ruins for the source.

Except the shrieking is coming from Mike. Or, more specifically, from the Mr. Lark-provided unique timepiece worn on his wrist. I vaguely remember the alarm means something bad. What was that?

Then Illych's timepiece begins screaming. Then mine. Now everyone's wrist is shrieking. Any chance of surprise playing a role in this mission is gone.

The outboard motor stutters, recovers, and then dies.

This pushes Mr. Lark into action. "EPS! Break and run. The effect is short-ranged. We only have maybe 30 seconds." His last words can barely be heard as he leaps from the bow and parkours from rock to rock. In just a few leaps that would put a mountain goat to shame, my employer reaches the nearest building and disappears inside.

Several splashes follow in quick succession. Held just dove right off the stern and is rapidly breaststroking away. Mike and Illych are off to starboard, and Tank's bulky frame wallows away to port. Mr. Lark had jumped to the nearest dry surface. His escape pushed the dinghy from the closest dry land, but I figure why not try to duplicate his escape. But the push of my legs just shoves the boat away from underneath me, doing little to move me closer to my goal. In a maneuver lacking any dignity, I flop into the water.

And stand up. It is only waist deep. No big deal.

Wading toward the building Mr. Lark disappeared into, I reach an elevated stone walkway along the channel. I use it to pull myself out of the water and onto my chest.

Facedown. I remember being facedown. But now I am face up. The canopy of stars above is beautiful, the lack of light pollution having left the heavens open to the naked eye. The stars are so bright that, even on this moonless night, it is possible to see without night vision.

Mike shifts into view above me. "Thomas, can you hear me?"

I nod. My mouth does not seem to be working.

"Okay, you took the full force of the EPS. I just found you lying here facedown. Tank caught the edge of it, but not as badly as you. Snap out of it. We have a situation here. Illych hit a flip-trap and disappeared. There is no sign of Mr. Lark or Held. It is the three of us for now."

My mouth might just work now. "Ambush?"

Mike nods. "Looks like it. Someone or thing was waiting."

Functionality is quickly returning to my body, and I sit up. Tank is about twenty feet away using a pocket in the stone construction for cover. Rolling onto all fours, I crawl to the nearby wall.

Looking at Mike, I ask, "What is the plan?"

"The oculus barely works, and these ruins are a mess. The portal to Tartarus dominates everything I can see. I did find the flip-trap Illych is probably in and a few others."

"What about Held and Mr. Lark?"

"Forget it. Finding any single person in this mess is beyond me."

Mike looks too concerned for that to be all.

"So, what are you not telling me?"

"I can't find individuals, but I can see groups of individuals. There are other people or maybe Created in the ruins. We are not alone."

How bad can it be? "Like a dozen, two dozen?"

"At least a hundred, I think."

One hundred? That is bad. "How close?"

"Close and coming this way. They appear to know where we are. The only reason they have not made it this far yet is all the sunken roads and confusing terrain. We fell back to here to see if anyone else made it. Then we found you."

"Okay, so what is the plan?"

"We fall back to the nearest defendable structure on higher ground and make our last stand."

Not an optimistic plan. "Where is the dinghy? What about returning to the ship?"

"Thomas, you were out for more than an hour. The dinghy floated away."

I nod and stand up. Legs are working; that is a good sign. Looking over at Mike, I can see he is interfacing with his oculus. Unfamiliar male voices drift over from the far side of the building we are leaning up against.

Mike shakes his head to clear it from the oculus interface and points down the sunken road the way we were originally going in the dinghy. "The channel narrows about a hundred meters up, and on the other side is an elevated structure probably better for defense than these others."

Tank nods and begins shifting from shadow to shadow, moving quickly in the direction Mike indicated. Falling in behind, we occupy each shadow in turn, following in Tank's footsteps.

The male voices are getting closer. We are moving lateral to their advancing line. Crossing the water-logged channel may be a too much of a delay. This could be a close thing. Too slow and we will be caught out in the open.

Tank crosses first. Slipping into the waist-deep water without making a sound, he shuffles to the other side. The channel water in the dark takes on the unnerving appearance of a river of black ink. I find myself tensing up as he crosses, and then relaxing as the former Marine climbs back out and Mike begins his crossing.

The voices are too close now, so I enter the water before Mike completes his crossing. Halfway across, the far-too-close bark of someone calling out to his comrades shoots a bolt of anxiety through me. In my mind I picture a man pointing at the vulnerable librarian out in the middle of the channel, exhorting his colleagues to come so they can shoot me together.

After looking back for signs of whoever is advancing on us, I return my vision forward and find Mike and Tank have disappeared. This is not good. Tank told me a joke once about two men coming upon a bear in the woods. The bear promptly begins advancing on the men. As one man turned to run away, the other says to him, "You cannot outrun a bear." The running man yells back, "I only need to outrun you." For just a moment, another flash of doubt and anxiety course through my body. Did my colleagues just leave me as a speed bump to our pursuers?

Mike's voice surprises me from the top of the basalt-cylinder pile that is our goal. "Thomas, around the back, the stones form a passable ladder. Hurry up." I finish my crossing, climb the improvised ladder as instructed, and find myself on the square roof perhaps a good ten meters up from water level.

Mike is setting himself up in one corner. "Watch out for the floor. There are holes that are hard to see in the dark. I almost fell in one."

Tank rumbles from the other corner, "If they have a mortar, this will be over quick."

The situation is grim. Mr. Lark did not hand out emergency dongles for this mission. And where is our employer?

Mike calls out instructions. "Thomas, watch that ladder and the rear of the structure in case some of them try to sneak around."

Another mission with me watching our rear while the others are in the real action. Right about now is when some monster would sneak up behind us. This thought of this has me looking everywhere at once.

Why is there no gunfire yet? The way the bad guys have been advancing, they know we are here. There has been more than enough time to get this party started.

As if reading my mind, Mike comments, "They are waiting for something. The oculus counts more than fifty combatants, with more on the way. That is plenty enough to punch our tickets."

The quiet waiting is broken by the sound of gunfire from back down the channel where Mike found me. The weapon report is distinctly familiar. Someone with a carbine in similar calibre to what I am carrying is shooting. It is unlikely Illych escaped the flip-trap. The only one of us with a carbine and not accounted for is Held.

The also-familiar sound of AKs firing responds. Mike shares from the oculus that our antagonists have taken up positions in a crescent shape, trapping us between them and the ocean. Whoever is shooting is doing so on the far flank tail of that crescent.

Unfortunately, we can do nothing to help. The nature of the terrain, hard cover provided by the strangely constructed basalt structures separated by open spaces and waterlogged paths, makes movement impossible. For us and our foe. Once in position, the surrounding spaces become a suicidal no man's land for both sides.

Mike is back on his oculus. "It's Held. He is working his way up the line."

Shouting erupts from the bad guys in the dark. From one end to the other, up and down their lines, voices sound off.

Mike narrates what the oculus is telling him. "They are withdrawing."

Time passes slowly as we wait.

"Held is coming."

A familiar voice calls out from the shadows down by the channel we crossed getting to our current position.

"Marco!"

Tank bellows back, "Polo."

A few minutes later, Held climbs up onto the roof with us, looking none the worse for wear.

Handshakes and back pats ensue.

"Where have you been?" Mike asks.

"When the EPS started and we scattered, I swam down a channel and then ran for what I thought would be far enough. I then went to ground to evaluate my situation. Night vision is working, but the ComDat and microphone array are down."

"Yeah, we have the same problem," Tanks says.

Held shrugs. "Then I started backtracking to find the team."

"That was over an hour ago," Mike says.

"The return path was not clearly defined."

Tank looks at Held. Even in the dark, I can see the big man's eyes narrow. "You were lost?"

"Hey, this place is rough at night. No lighting, no visible landmarks. It is like a graveyard full of open mausoleums."

"You are a Green Beret," Tank continues. "I thought you guys can navigate by the stars."

"That was fifteen years ago. Navigating by the stars is not a skill I have been using much."

While the others are bantering back and forth, a thought enters my mind.

"What about the batteries?" I blurt out.

The others go silent and turn to look at me.

"The ComDat and microphone array; they run on batteries," I continue. "We could try taking them out and putting them back in. I had a television that was like that. Every now and then you had to disconnect the power for a few seconds. Then you plugged it back in and it would work."

"Our night vision sets run on batteries, and they are still working," Mike replies.

I shrug and pull my ComDat from my chest harness. The batteries are inserted into a circular hole filled with a threaded plug to hold them in. After unscrewing the plug, I tip the two cylindrical batteries out into my hand. They look fine, and I re-insert them and screw the plug back in.

Mike follows my lead. No sooner does he reinsert his batteries than the click of the earphones in my helmet alerts me to our success. Tank and Held follow suit, and we can now communicate in low tones instead of yelling at each other.

Emboldened by our success, we collectively take off our helmets and remove, examine, and re-insert the small batteries powering the microphone array. This proves a successful as with the ComDat.

Having all of our gear back to full functionality improves our spirits.

"But why did the ComDat and the microphones go out?" Mike questions. "Why not the night vision? This makes no sense."

Held fills in the blanks. "This may be an insight into why Mr. Lark is so electronics averse."

Yes. I think I also understand better now. Another eccentricity justified.

Mike looks at Held, the most senior of our team. "What do we do now?"

"With all of our gear working now, we can outmaneuver the bad guys. We need to look for Mr. Lark."

"About the bad guys," Mike begins. "Did you get a good look at who they are?"

"It is those same curly-haired bastards from the mines and San Fran."

This is incredible. "How did they know we would be here? Now?" I ask. "This does not make sense."

Held shrugs. "Let's go ask. If we manage to capture one alive, that is."

With Held and Mike watching through their oculi and our night vision and super hearing back in action, we begin to advance. The oculi tell us the goons have fallen back to the near center of the Nan Madol complex, forming their own security perimeter. It is not solely human mercenaries. Mike can't make a precise determination, but whatever it is is moving and man-sized.

Half an hour later and halfway to getting a view of our opponents, Mike's voice informs us over the ComDat that better than half of the security forces are moving east, to our right. Who or whatever is in charge just improved our chances of making a decapitation strike.

Whoever they are, security is not one of their strengths. There are no outlying observation posts and no ring of sentries. Not much more than one hundred meters from the gathering, we find a stone ramp that would give us an elevated view. The four of us crawl up the ramp and peek up and over at the top. The scene before us is unexpected.

The curly-haired goons have assembled in small groups that are spaced out in a rough circle around an area where all the vegetation is scraped away from the bare basalt rock beneath.

An altar-like stone platform has been installed in the middle of the platform. Off to one side is a vertical cylindrical pillar with a smooth half-sphere top. A large dark-skinned man dressed in khakis, nearly seven foot tall and muscular, has two hands on the half-sphere surface, and he appears to be concentrating.

Several hexagonal basalt cylinders are on top of the altar. Fluorescent blue string-like lines of energy rise end first from the altar's surface. The lines encircle and whip the basalt surfaces. The whipping motions bring the lines across the basalt cylinders where they instantly shear through the stone. The scrap tailings clatter away onto the altar. Nearby goons are using hooked poles to quickly snare and pull the shards free.

Only now do I notice that the ground surface around the altar is covered in a gravel made up of these cast-off pieces. My guess is this is not the first operation like this.

As the basalt is shaped, many of the blue strings insert themselves straight into rock, and pieces begin to rise and align themselves to each other. A vaguely humanoid biped form takes shape. The joints between the stones glow blue from the energy strings binding the construct together.

Glancing at my colleagues shows my concerns reflected in their faces. We are equipped to go head-to-head with goons all day. Our current loadout does not include the tools for dealing with monsters literally made from stone.

Looking back at the altar, I catch the final moments of the basalt construct's creation. The leader lifts his hand from the pedestal and slumps back to sit on a nearby basalt surface.

The blocky construct takes one step and then another. With disturbing vigor, it marches away into the dark. The glow from its joints makes a pool of blue light around its feet.

"What was that, and where is it going?" Mike says in a heavy whisper.

"Not toward us," Held responds. "They had us pinned down back there and then left. That thing is meant for someone else."

"Mr. Lark?" I say.

"That is my guess," Held replies. "Our employer is out there somewhere causing trouble, and those things are being sent to deal with him. No wonder they are lax about security. Anyone drawing attention to themselves will probably get some glowing blue love from whatever those constructs are."

While listening to Held, I visually scan the encampment laid out in front of us. The organization is haphazard and looks like they have not been here much longer than we have. Off to the right edge of the deforested space is a man reclining on the ground in the shadows. I tap Mike with my left elbow.

"You guys see the figure on the ground to the right? He is difficult to see in the shadows."

"The lights are making the contrast too extreme for night vision to compensate for the shadow," Held comments. "Is it Illych?"

For a minute, we all strain to see. The figure finally moves, adjusting his position. For just a brief instant, a stream of light plays across his face.

Mike says it first. "That is Illych. They must have collected him from the flip-trap."

Back at the encampment, the level of activity increases. Teams of goons are manhandling basalt cylinders to the altar. The big man is looking reinvigorated. Looks like another of those golem things is about to be in the works.

"Once they start making this thing, my guess is the leader will remain focused and won't stop," Held says. "That last one took more than fifteen minutes. I will work my way over to Illych. When I give the signal, hit them with everything you have and then fade away. Fall back and set up an ambush, and then fade again. There is a lot of space between here and the ocean."

"And when they send one of those rock monsters after us?" I ask.

"One thing at a time," Held replies. The former Green Beret crawls down the ramp, melting into the black night of the surrounding ruins. We three remain spread out along the ramp's edge, tucking ourselves behind individual basalt rocks jutting out. At least we have good cover.

While waiting for the signal from Held, I watch the big man.

"Say, Mike," I begin. "That big man looks a lot like Leveque from back at Castle Houska."

Mike responds, "Can't be. Mr. Lark ended him."

"He was a possessed. What if Leveque likes a body type? He could have found another man fitting his preference."

Silence.

Held's voice clicks in my ear. "Almost there. Should be ready in five."

"I have a count," Tank replies. "Forty-six goons. Keep to your respective lane. One magazine and then we fall back. No heroics."

My eyes are glued to Illych's reclining form. The clutch of bored-looking goons tasked with watching the prisoner are not all that engaged in their responsibilities. Instead, they appear fascinated with the rise of the stone construct happening in front of them.

Held's voice is in my ear again. "I am in place. Light'em up."

Tank calls it. "On three. One . . . two . . . three."

The last syllable is barely spoken when we three bare down on our targets. Half the magazine is gone in less than two seconds. With minimal effort, I pivot and drop my sight reticle on a shocked-looking group wildly looking around while lifting weapons into a firing position. The last half of a magazine roars down range. My bolt locks open on an empty weapon at almost the same time as my colleagues.

With a half-roll and body slide, I bring the target I now represent away from the ramp edge and begin working my way down. To my right, I see Mike and Tank joining me. This is not the time for stealth. We run for our lives. Loud yells and barked commands can be heard behind us. Soon we hear short bursts of gunfire as our foes organize and begin moving in our general direction.

We run straight into a dark alley between two of the blocky basalt structures.

"Here!" Tank calls out. The former Marine points to a pile of long hexagonal basalt cylinders haphazardly stacked and scattered in the space between the next row of structures over. We run over, spread out, reload, and push ourselves into as small a space as possible for cover.

There is only the briefest pause before the alleys around the first building we passed is surrounded by a sea of goons chasing after us.

"Now!" Tank shouts. The three of us expend our mags in a single continuous burst. No aiming is needed. The bad guys are so close we can see their faces in the gunfire's strobe.

Our closeness is a liability once we need to reload. Our muzzle flashes gave away our general location, and dozens of AK-47s share their version of what we had just delivered. Dashing from cover and away from the bad guys, I run for my life. A bullet glances my helmet, knocking me off-balance. Falling down, I roll up onto my feet and keep going. Adrenaline is driving everything now.

My comrades do the same and the three of us are running while trying to put obstacles between us and our antagonists.

My forward motion is accelerated by a painful shot to my middle back, stopped only by ballistic plating. Bullets are whizzing around and ricocheting from the basalt, sending stone fragments everywhere. Anywhere I have exposed skin is painfully scratched and bleeding from sharp and abrasive impacts.

My colleagues are getting it as bad as I am, if not worse. But we keep going. We dart between two structures relatively close to each other. This pinches off most of the bad guys' line of sight for now.

Tank's voice, filled with pain now, rings in my ear. "Behind this wall." He jogs straight to a low wall and throws himself over it. Mike and I follow suit. Space out, squeeze into cover, reload.

Tank says what we know at this point. "Last stand, guys. If we try running after this, they will just gun us down."

After what just happened leaving that last position, I agree.

The goons are right on our heels, and there is no pause. While we may have night vision and body armor, our opponents have numbers and an apparent lack of the fear of death. They understand basic tactics, though, and soon establish alternating advances and a virtual storm of suppression fire.

There are noticeably fewer of them, though. Our previous efforts have taken a toll. They are no longer a river of bodies flowing toward us.

My head throbs and my vision blurs from bullets glancing off my helmet. The goons are starting to flank us. Tank and Mike both have bullet wounds to their arms and shoulders from breaking cover to get off a shot.

In spite of the constant fire, a distinctly different report than an AK can suddenly be heard. A different weapon is being fired off to our right flank.

"Did you miss me?" Held's voice over the ComDat makes me smile.

The appearance of more opponents throws the goons into disarray. Mike, Tank, and I take advantage of the lull in suppression fire to light up nearby targets.

The remaining goons begin falling back. Their return fire tapers to random bursts.

In scant minutes, our foes exit the field, and a quiet falls. With no small effort I push myself up to standing. I can't say for sure how many gunshot impacts my armor stopped, but my comfort level with being shot helped me keep my cool. Remedial training indeed. However, I know that when I wake up in the morning, it will hurt.

Held and Illych materialize from the shadows and approach our position. The goons removed everything from Illych. Gear, weapons, armor. It is all gone. Both of them are smiling though.

Mike's voice, strangely soft in sound, comes over the ComDat. "Guys . . ."

Turning, I find Mike kneeling next to a reclining Tank. The former Ranger has removed Tank's shattered helmet and is checking him for a pulse. The expression on his face tells all.

Shuffling closer, we see a gash above the big man's right temple. The fatal wound.

Tank is gone.

Mike stands, and he and Held link arms side by side and touch their foreheads together. Illych's expression shows his grief. Tank was just here, fighting.

"Thomas!" Illych's voice breaks my reverie. Looking around, I realize I had walked some distance away in a daze. Turning, I walk back to the others.

Mike sees it first. "What the hell?"

A blue glow reflected on the walls is moving toward us from the direction the goons retreated. This is not good. Barely has this thought registered when the unnatural form of a stone construct, moving with that same unnatural vigor, marches into view. The thing is quick.

I prop my carbine against the nearest rock, leaving it behind, and start walking toward the advancing construct.

Illych notices and comments, "What are you doing?"

"I have an idea."

"Perhaps you should share it before getting close to that thing."

Honestly, as fast as the golem is moving, it will reach us momentarily regardless. Now it will just reach me first.

My guess is this thing follows the rules of the Created. There is no explaining why I believe this. Perhaps desperation or insane optimism. It does not matter with that thing seconds away.

We all received Truestone and a White Fang as part of our loadout. My right hand secures the rare white pebble while my left draws the White Fang from its sheath. If I am right, this could qualify as a stroke of genius.

If I am wrong, that thing will crush my body will little effort.

Stumbling, I almost mess up the approach. The golem is closing too fast. With a toss of my right hand, the Truestone sails toward my target. The throw is not that bad either.

I feel a surge of victory as I witness the Truestone begin to incandesce just before impacting its target. It *is* a Created of sorts. The point in the center of the golem forms a bright-white light that the Truestone homes in on. The projectile of white acts like a magnet seeking steel and adjusts its flight path for the perfect landing.

All I need to do is stab that incandescent point with the White Fang and this thing's attachment to our world ends. Thankfully, the Truestone paralyzes the Created, making the job much easier.

Everything goes according to plan. Except that instead of being paralyzed, the golem is only slowed down dramatically. The thing is still moving. And the Truestone's effects do not last forever. Now I have to get to the glowing point on a still-moving killer statue before the only thing slowing it down burns out.

A strange dance begins where I am faster, staying close while looking for an opening, and my slower foe with its much longer reach is trying to crush my puny human body.

Seeing my chance, I lunge, White Fang first.

While the golem is slow, a hit from it would be like being struck by a slow-moving car. There is no give; you just lose. A stone arm glances me when I am just inches from success. The force of that one impact is frightening, and I save myself by rolling instead of just falling flat on the ground. Seeing stars, I roll back onto my feet, looking for a new opening. Taking a deep breath, I wait for the monster to take a step and bring an arm back for the swing.

When I get that opening, I charge White Fang first, extending forward like a knight jousting. My peripheral vision makes me aware of the stone arm en route to pulverize me. My forward momentum drives the Fang right into the glowing star at the monster's core.

Things in motion remain in motion. Newton was right, and I receive a violent physics demonstration even as my efforts succeed. The White Fang instantly unravels the golem's connection to the physical world. This leaves me standing very close to more than a ton of carved basalt rock obeying gravity and falling to the ground. Before gravity serves me my doom, the inertia of the moving arm piece hits me like a freight train, knocking me clear from the path of the falling rocks.

I find myself lying flat on my back, looking up at the starry night. Everything hurts, and I am not inclined to move and find out what else is injured.

Illych walks into sight and stands over me. Soon he is joined by Held and then Mike. They stand there looking at me.

"Very brave or very stupid, Thomas," Illych comments. "Well played, though."

While I am considering this comment, Mr. Lark joins the constellation of faces looking down on me.

"Yes, Thomas, well done. I had not considered a White Fang solution."

"Where have you been?" I croak in hoarse tones.

"After we became separated escaping from the EPS, I encountered one of the glowing constructs. Since then, I have encountered three more of them. Battling them while exploring Nan Madol has kept me away."

"Wait . . . if you were not using the White Fang, how are you defeating those things?"

"The cutting web I used back in the mines is effective in neutralizing them. Unfortunately, it requires time to recover between uses, which forced me to spend more time than I would have liked just staying ahead of these things."

Mike extends an arm and helps me to stand. Once on my feet, it becomes obvious the sore part is not waiting until tomorrow.

Together, the five of us shuffle back to Tank's unmoving form.

Mr. Lark takes it in quietly. Honestly, I cannot read his expressions or if the quiet means something.

"It is time to finish this," our employer announces. "Our foes have set up on top of the portal to Tartarus. We will go there and encourage them to leave."

Illych looks at Mr. Lark. "And if they do not feel like leaving?"

My employer begins walking toward our new destination. "My cutting web is fully recharged," he says. "An appropriately enthusiastic application of force should produce the results we desire."

The sound of bolts locking in fresh rounds echoes from the stone surfaces of this place.

"What about Tank?" Mike asks.

Mr. Lark pauses his walking. "He will be okay while we resolve the mission. Then we can move him somewhere more dignified."

Mike nods, and we resume moving back the way we just escaped from. The path is now littered with the corpses of our foes, their weapons still clutched in their hands. Whoever these curly-haired men are, they are not treated well by Amal Halluck.

It is a short walk back to the clearing, and the big man is bringing another golem to life on the strange altar. Only a handful of guards remain, and they show no stomach for a fight. As soon as we appear, they hesitantly shuffle away, putting the potential Leveque between them and us.

Illych makes some hand motions and he, Mike, and Held spread out and take cover with weapons ready. I do not feel like taking cover. Tank's death has left me feeling a little foolhardy and I will stand here in the open for now.

We are only a stone's throw away and the giant's facial expression shows he knows we are present, yet he concentrates on the stone monster taking shape on the altar.

Mr. Lark apparently decides this will not happen and waves a hand to Illych. Almost as one, the three men open fire. The barrage lasts a full two seconds as they empty a full magazine. The goons huddled on the other side of the altar flinch and crouch.

And nothing happens.

The bullets do not reach their target. In the dim light, it is difficult to tell, but they seem to have been stopped or deflected. This is not good.

Things gets worse as the stone construct reaches completion, stands, turns to face us, and jogs almost straight at Mr. Lark and me. At this distance, we have seconds, and I am out of Truestone. My legs are already moving me sideways when I notice my employer's right hand clutching something. Sure enough, once the golem has covered half the distance between us, the old man makes a tossing motion and an object flies true to its target.

The web cutter expands elegantly as thin gossamer strands billow forth, forming a tight grid pattern in a fraction of a second. In another instant, this web wraps itself completely around the golem.

Out of the corner of my eye I can see the giant at the altar with an almost human expression of disappointment on its face.

The web lines burst alight, incandescent white. This close, I can feel the heat. The lines begin to constrict and section the stones making up its body. But unlike the swift conclusion back in the mines, it is obvious that whatever magic or science this thing is made from is sterner stuff than the mechanical monstrosity previously witnessed. Regardless, with rivulets of magma running from the cuts, the beast is sliced up, falling into a heap of hot stones. Mr. Lark walks the few feet and recovers the web cutter.

Does he have another one of those I could have?

My employer bends down and picks up a stone and casually tosses it at the big man. The stone sails half the distance and strikes something invisible, which stops it.

Instead of the rock bouncing off, the barrier just absorbs the forward motion and the stone rolls back down to the ground.

The giant laughs. "Not now. This is a new body, and I will not give it up today. Last time you surprised me."

It *is* Leveque.

"The barrier will keep you from me for now. Unfortunately, it keeps me from you as well."

The possessed looks at me. "Thomas, we meet again, as I said we would. Have you reconsidered my offer? There is much for you at my side."

I just shake my head. This conversation is a bit too surreal.

Looking at Mr. Lark, he continues, "You have Legion with you, I see. I suspected as much. Thank you for collecting it. These things make a mess whenever they are used."

Mr. Lark looks unfazed. "And its purpose?"

The big man laughs a warm, full laugh. "You know this already. We are looking for you. Who is 'we,' I'm sure you're wondering? You will learn in time. Even now we have not really found you yet. My associates, yes, let us call them associates, and I appreciate the challenge you represent. A mystery. When you have seen the sun rise and set many millions of times, you learn to appreciate a true mystery. It is a rare thing.

"You are too limited to understand, but your kind is predictable to a fault," he continues. "It is tedious to suffer this for eternity. But not you, Karl Lark. We have not found you. Not yet."

Illych, Mike, and Held have come forward and joined us at the edge of the invisible barrier.

"Now I must go. The barrier in front of you does not last long and today's efforts are done. The field is left to you. Tartarus and Legion are yours. For now." Looking straight at me, he says, "Elizabeth Chatzas has failed us for a third and final time. You will not see her again." Turning from us, he strides away, disappearing from sight between two structures.

The barrier is down in maybe a dozen minutes. We just keep tossing rocks until one gets through.

While our employer inspects the pillar and the altar, his prizes to take from the field of battle, the rest of us have time to feel what has just happened. Tank is gone, and Elizabeth is done for. And we survive to fight another day.

Chapter 21

With Leveque gone, we walk back to Tank's body. Using Green Beret ingenuity, the four of us construct a way to carry the big man away. Turns out, while Mr. Lark wandered the ruins trying to not be crushed by glowing rock monsters, he found the dinghy. We agree on a place to meet, and the old man goes off in grab the dinghy.

We arrive at the channel just as Mr. Lark and the dinghy idle into view. Gently placing our friend in the bow, we navigate out to the *Esmerelda*. As we clear the ruins onto open ocean, the sun breaks the eastern horizon. The morning light illuminates our destination.

She is right where we left her.

Tank is moved belowdecks. We still cannot translate this close to potential prying eyes. The engines rumble to life and Nan Madol is soon in our wake.

Mr. Lark is on the deck watching the sun rise, and I join him.

I nod to him. "Mr. Lark."

"Thomas."

"What about the mess back at Nan Madol? Just laying around are a hundred corpses that obviously died violently, not to mention an arsenal of abandoned weapons."

The old man's expression does not change. "Not my problem."

"What about Legion? Where is that going?"

After a long pause, he replies, "Leveque just demonstrated Tartarus is off limits. Whatever we put there he can just come back and retrieve. There is another place it will be safe."

"Are you sure?"

"Yes, Thomas. There are places so ancient, dark, and deep even Leveque has no knowledge of them."

That seems unlikely. An immortal creature who has been trapped here since not long after the Earth began spinning around the sun probably knows. But it does not seem a good idea to debate Mr. Lark right now.

He continues, "You understand we cannot attempt to rescue Dr. Chatzas. Leveque making such a statement makes it almost a given the situation is an ambush."

"I was not going to ask." After a moment, I ask, "How did they know we were coming here?"

Mr. Lark turns to look at me. "When you last visited the curator, what did you discuss?"

"She shared that someone she knows is interested in hiring you. We made some small talk about our relationship. She is working on a display of mythological underworlds throughout history. Hades and such. I mentioned Tartarus as a possible addition, but I never discussed what we are doing. I only mentioned it because I had recently read up on it."

Only now do I make the connection. "Wait, do you think she figured this out just from that conversation?"

"Her request to meet was most likely a ruse. The doctor and her employer knew Legion needs storage in someplace hell-like. She brought up the subject, and you spoke what was most recently on your mind. It was not an absolute guarantee we would be going to Tartarus, but as possibilities go . . ."

Oh God. "I gave away our mission destination? What about Tank? Does this make his death my fault?" The realization is making me sick.

"Inadvertently, and your role is minor. I assigned you to the visit. Let this be a lesson in how subtle our foe can be."

I need a drink. Probably more than one.

Once we reach the middle of nowhere, the whole boat, with us still on board, is translated thousands of miles away. Mr. Lark set up a long-term berth in Perth, Australia. We dock after dark. The *Esmerelda* is tied up and shut down. After locking the ship from the inside, we gather in the belowdecks's stone circle and translate away.

* * *

Now we are a funeral guard. From the dark and cold of the Compass, the whole team translates to the Valley, a spot high in the Rocky Mountains hundreds of miles from anything. Only accessible by helicopter or ouiblet, we use it as a firing range. Oval-shaped, a kilometer long, and a half kilometer wide, it will be the final stage of Tank's send-off.

Standing here, on the other side of the world from Nan Madol, it is afternoon. The Valley is above the tree line; only short grass grows here. In the past, Tank shared his desired parting ceremony: a Viking-style funeral. We do not have a long ship for this, but a funeral pyre is in order.

Despite our exhaustion and hunger, we translate multiple times to bring in the needed lumber to construct an epic pyre. I learn Illych is skilled with a chainsaw and that the nausea from repeated back-to-back translations does not get easier.

Once we complete our task, we lay the former Marine atop the massive construct of logs and lumber. And just in time, as the sun sets behind the nearby mountains.

I am unsteady after not sleeping for two days, being injured, and the hard labor of assembling probably two tons of wood. Regardless, we silently wait in the chilly evening air.

Upon reaching a predetermined time I was not clued in on, Illych lights a flare, and I realize that Mr. Lark has joined us.

Illych tosses the flare, and the kerosene-soaked pyre ignites. The flames spread, and in moments, we find the need to back up from the raging inferno's heat.

Mr. Lark's voice breaks the silence. "Goodbye, Leslie Patrick Hensen."

Wait, what?

"Tank's first name is Leslie?"

I look at my comrades. That son-of-a-bitch. He gets the last laugh.

"You knew?"

Illych and Mike nod their heads. "He liked to be called Tank," Held says. "He was not embarrassed by his given name. The opposite, actually. It is a family name with a great history. But jerks would say something the first time it came up, and then a fight would start."

And he never told me.

"What about how he came to be with Mr. Lark?"

Mr. Lark is standing apart and is obviously not going to get involved in this.

The three of them look at each other, and then Illych says, "He was a quad amputee. We found him at a VA hospital. It was not a hard sell to get him to join."

Illych pauses and watches the roaring fire.

"I think the loss of his original limbs is what drove the power lifting. He was not like that before."

We turn back to the roaring pillar of fire.

Farewell, Tank.

Chapter 22

It is almost noon the next day when I wake, and wow do I hurt. The bruising on the side of my body where the stone golem hit me is disturbing. Red, purple, and black covers most of my left side from shoulder to hip. The marks are so bad I might have Mike look at them.

After slowly and carefully going through my morning ablutions, the next destination is the cafeteria. What on most days constitutes not much more than a short walk is now long and painful. I desperately need painkillers; no one should feel this bad and still be alive.

Entering the cafeteria, I find my colleagues already there. Yet not seeing Tank in the mix adds another twist of the emotional knife to my morning's misery.

Looking at my watch, I correct myself. The afternoon has already begun.

Mike and Held sit across from each other. Mike is speaking. ". . . Belize has these beautiful beaches. We can get nearby villas. You will not regret it." I tune the rest out. Mike is trying to convince Held to join him in Belize for the upcoming time off. This just serves to remind me my usual destination of San Francisco is no longer desirable. Being caged, chased, and shot ended that.

Illych is reading some papers at the same table a bit apart from the others. I collect my breakfast and coffee and sit across from him.

Illych glances up at me. "You look like shit, Englishman."

Nodding, I reply, "We are two days away from vacation. Should we expect any surprises?"

Illych gives me a wry grin. "While you were enjoying extended beauty sleep, Mr. Lark visited. We have to close out one last detail before we get 30 days to do whatever we wish."

"And that detail is?"

"I am leaving it a surprise. The good news is you have until this evening to rest up. Mr. Lark wants you in a suit, ready to travel, at seven tonight. Check in with Mike a half hour before. There are some special considerations prior to your appointment."

That is cryptic.

I pursue another line of questioning. "What was it like in a flip-trap?"

Mike and Held go silent.

"It was dark," Illych responds. "Not much different than translating. Completely black. You are standing, but I could not tell on what or if I just felt like that while being held up. Shining a light in any direction just showed black. Nothing reflected. When they pulled me out, it was the same as entering. In an instant, I was back in the world and the goons grabbed me."

Good to know.

I spend the rest of my breakfast discussing recent events and savoring the scent, heat, and flavor of my coffee. In spite of several more attempts to clarify this evening's events, Illych reveals nothing. Mike provides the requested painkillers, and I retire to the library for a long, slow afternoon.

When it's time, I put on the signature grey suit and find Mike. Apparently, I need to be disguised for tonight's festivities. He bandages my head, including adding a splint for my nose. This is not a loose, casual, easily removed disguise. Using rubber glue to hold the whole thing in place, he comments, "Mr. Lark was specific this disguise was not to fail."

Looking in the mirror, I find myself unrecognizable. There is no way to figure out who I am. Unfortunately, it itches.

At seven, I am at the Citadel's gates. They soundlessly open, and Mr. Lark, in a matching grey suit, walks in.

Looking at me for a moment, he comments, "The disguise is acceptable. We do not want our hosts tonight recognizing you." My employer turns and walks back out and onto the road to the Compass. This is my cue, and I briefly jog to catch up. The painkillers are barely containing my discomfort.

"And who are our hosts tonight?" Seems a reasonable question.

"Jak Regal, CEO of Giggle Corp."

This is a red flag for me. "Those guys put me in a cage."

"Your disguise will prevent your identification."

"And why am I going on this trip?"

"Honestly, I find these meetings tedious at best and often irritating. A companion seems to keep me on good behavior."

He is bringing me along because he is nicer that way? Does he boil people in oil when he is solo?

"Where are we meeting Mr. Regal?"

"On a ship in international waters."

"That sounds . . . unsafe."

"It is. This Jak enjoys intimidating people. His security detail is quite impressive. Organized and trained by former French Foreign Legion, most of them are former child soldiers. A truly terrifying group."

"And why are we going to this place?"

"Giggle Corp is a client, and they have requested a final update on the contract. That is all."

"And if they get uncivilized?" I ask.

Mr. Lark retorts, "I do not have time for 'what if' games. Perhaps you should be more positive."

We translate to a hotel. A car drives us to an airport for a chartered three-hour flight. We exit our plane and immediately embark onto a large corporate helicopter, which promptly lifts off and heads out over the ocean.

So far, so good.

The ship is big. Much bigger than I had anticipated. The helicopter lands and powers down. Two tall, muscular, serious-looking men with sidearms march up and open the door for us. Mr. Lark and I step out and find ourselves overshadowed by our escorts.

A smartly dressed athletic man more our size walks up, and in a French accent, requests we follow him. Mr. Lark nods, and we fall in behind. We walk into the superstructure and down a hall and completely out the other side to the open deck of the ship's bow. The space has been set up to entertain. Comfortable chairs form a large circle. Of to one side is a small bar with an attendant.

Standing in the middle of all of this is a tall, broad-chested, well-dressed man. Perhaps fifty years old with grey-streaked hair, Jak Regal's posture says it all. This man is in charge.

I am taller than Mr. Lark, and the guards and Mr. Regal positively tower over me. My employer is almost childlike in comparison. Jak waits for us to approach him. No hand is extended. The Giggle CEO just stands there glowering at us.

His gaze settles on me. "What the hell happened to you?" His voice is strong, with a tinge of anger blended in.

"I fell down the stairs."

My reply does not improve our host's mood.

Now his eyes fix on Mr. Lark.

"I need answers, Lark. My people went into those mines after you left. The place is a wreck. Close to one hundred million dollars of investment gone. You were hired to get the place under control, not conjure up the apocalypse."

A long pause passes before my employer replies. "The facilities were in poor condition upon our arrival. The threat profile on this mission did not come close to representing what was confronted and defeated. Regardless, the mission was a success, and all resistance to Giggle regaining control of the facility ended. This met the requirements of the contract."

"Contract details are for lawyers," Mr. Regal sneers. "You were reckless, and people died. So far, Giggle has kept the government out of this, but the FBI is snooping around. Some employees have gone missing, and their relatives have reported it. This may go badly for you."

That sounded like a threat. This should be interesting.

Mr. Lark closes the remaining distance between himself and the Giggle CEO. He is now standing well within the personal space of the football player–sized executive who is looking down on him.

"This is an unfortunate turn of events," Mr. Lark retorts. "You hired an outside consultant to improve performance using methods that at the very least qualify as crimes against humanity. This consultant then contaminates the entire operation with something so toxic nothing can be saved. And you point fingers at me?

"You are experiencing buyer's remorse," he continues. "It is a hazard in my line of work. The challenge when this happens is in getting your point across without injuring the client. The primary obstacle to overcome is the client's belief they are in control. Unfortunately, the only way to make this point is through lethal violence. One option is to sink this ship. But that is perhaps too extreme."

The old man pauses and then continues. "Let us leave it up to you, Mr. Regal. What would be the least destructive way to convince you this path you are considering is less than ideal? Should I blow something up or just kill one of your people?"

Mr. Lark turns completely around, placing his unprotected back within arm's reach of a now confused-looking executive. Yeah, Mr. Lark does that to people.

After another long pause, the old man takes a few steps away and turns to face the Giggle CEO again. He cocks his head as if asking a question.

This CEO is probably someone who has built a career out of getting inside people's heads. There is genuine confusion playing out on his face. I can tell he's wondering if Karl Lark is really that bad ass or if this is a bluff.

"Consider this negative customer feedback, Lark. You have been paid. Nothing more is to be discussed regarding this matter. You may leave."

Mr. Lark nods to Mr. Regal and walks away toward me. I fall in beside him, and the French-sounding man walks us back to the helicopter.

The return flight is uneventful. The whole trip back I remain tense, waiting for something to happen. Only when the cold air and nausea hit me upon returning to the Compass do I finally relax.

Vacation is soon, and hopefully this was the last bit of excitement before then.

Chapter 23

The day before the team leaves for quarterly vacation is usually festive with everyone in high spirits. Leave falling in December is emotionally challenging, though. We have all lost contact with our families in order to be inducted into Mr. Lark's organization, so we have no one to visit for the holidays. And this particular season's melancholy is amplified by the loss of Tank.

So instead of pranks and laughter, preparations this time are a bit on the somber side.

It is not unusual for our employer to run a last-minute operation just before vacation. His prerogative, I guess, and we all keep an eye on the door.

Dinner is winding down, and as the military men say, all we have left is a wake-up. I drift to the library for some evening reading. The quiet of this place is conducive to complete immersion in the material. Illych and Mr. Lark enter without my noticing until they settle into nearby chairs.

Neither looks stressed or impatient. Closing my book, I move it to the nearby table and give them my full attention.

"I wanted a last meeting before the team leaves to rest and rejuvenate," the old man begins. "Upon your return, changes will be implemented. My organization's efforts over the last several years have created a significant monetary endowment. This has been globally invested and will be more than sufficient in supporting our activities. While we may take a particularly unique opportunity under consideration in the future, we will not do so out of just monetary considerations."

This sounds like a positive development, I guess. No more pimping ourselves out.

"My only wish is that this had been achieved sooner," he says. "These most recent contracts have been exceptionally violent. This, combined with the recent loss of a valuable employee . . ." He pauses. ". . . has motivated me to seek a different path for the organization. The first change is to find a proper residence where we remain secure while being able to watch a sunrise. This has become imperative with the induction of Ms. Jaegar. After significant effort and at great cost, the team now has a more human living experience to look forward to."

How does that work?

This prompts me to ask, "How can we be secure out in the world?

Mr. Lark nods. "A valid concern. The world is a big place with many players. In such a complex environment, some people see my organization as an asset. Or perhaps as a deterrent or just extraordinarily useful to have around."

"Have you considered this new place could act as bait?" I ask.

Mr. Lark considers my question for a time and replies, "As I have said before, only the paranoid survive, and I plan on surviving for a very long time."

Illych looks barely awake as our discussion continues.

"Is the new place nice?" I had to ask.

My employer gives the tiniest of head shakes with a hint of a frown. "Yes, Thomas. It is nice. The library is much larger and will contain almost my full collection."

This brings a smile to my face. The library here in the Citadel is too small. Cataloging the complete collection will be wonderful.

"These changes will be nice, I am sure," Illych begins, "but I have a question. Where did that Legion thing go?"

Mr. Lark takes a breath before answering. "After what happened at the Tartarus portal, it obviously could not be left there. It is too dangerous to be kept here at the Citadel or at the Compass. I am unsure how it would interact with the Lesser Created wildlife in this place."

That is a scary thought. If that thing could gain control of Lesser Created or even just influence them, the spaces around the Citadel would become even more dangerous.

"There is another place it can go where it will be undisturbed," Mr. Lark says.

"How can you be sure?" Illych presses.

Mr. Lark smiles the most minimum of smiles. "I am absolutely sure of few things in this world. However, the prison Legion is to be interred into forever is one of those sure things. This I know. It has been tested."

Neither Illych nor I wish to delve into that comment, so we do not ask any more questions. Hopefully we are done with this conversation.

"Is there more to discuss?" I ask.

Mr. Lark stands. Apparently not.

He looks briefly at each of us and nods. "We meet again in thirty days." The old man strides from the room and is gone.

Illych lifts himself from the chair, saying, "Good night, Thomas," as he heads for the door.

"Good night, Illych."

That is that, then. It is late, and I am tired.

Time for bed and a wake-up.

Epilogue

There are secrets so ancient, they are beyond knowledge. Mr. Lark knows that what he must do next can never be shared. There is a place Legion will never be found. A prison created by the enemy so long ago it has passed beyond all memory.

Except Mr. Lark knows. He found it.

An oculus translated to the state park he is to visit takes a snapshot that tells him no one is there.

He was driving during his last visit. Now he translates close to his destination.

Choosing broad daylight seemed prudent. The last time he was here it was summer and warm and green. Now the light of day is pale and weak under an overcast sky. A frozen wind blows fine snow across frozen ground, and the forest floor resembles dried sticks poking up from the snowy earth.

Mr. Lark absentmindedly pats the fanny pack at his waist. Time to put this somewhere safe.

With sure footing, he walks straight into the forest toward the portal at the heart of this park. A portal positioned at the almost exact center of the park's perimeter. It is almost like it was planned that way . . .

More agile now then the last time he walked this path, he stalks through the dense forest. This area was logged bare of old forest more than a century ago. Now, young growth competes for space. Even in the dead of winter, this makes for a dark and claustrophobic walk in the woods.

The portal is right where he remembers it. The location is not marked in the outside world. Just a side of a hill no different than any other in the park. It is only there for those who know how to look.

He realizes this is exactly where he stood nine years ago in his last minutes before everything changed.

This time, there is no crude manipulation to open it. Pulling the wynloo from a pocket, he holds it up. It glows, and luminescent threads extend toward something. It only takes seconds, and the threads just fade away.

With a few steps forward, he is in. No human has set foot here in eons, if ever. Other than the last time he was here. The dust on the floor shows his steps entering and exiting. Nothing else is to be seen except for fine dust of untold years evenly covering every horizontal surface.

Time to give Legion a permanent home. And what better place than a pocket dimension built as the ultimate stealth prison.

This place held an angel captive, undetected and isolated, unable to escape for a length of time almost impossible to comprehend. It is a fitting place for Legion's final resting place.

Passing through lightless kilometers of passages and open spaces, Mr. Lark finally arrives at the prison. There is no light here, and the illumination he brought with him is swallowed by the vast darkness in front of him.

A ledge, perhaps the width of an automobile, rings the void. There are no considerations for safety, such as a hand rail. The black stone of the prison walls is only the barest shade different than the dark void it surrounds. Just walking the path requires paying attention or you could miss where the ledge ends and the drop into the void begins. And it is a long way down.

Mr. Lark is surprised he successfully made this journey back in the day. When he was just an old man spelunking this place.

His destination is on the far side of the void, requiring walking the half perimeter around. Reaching the far side from the entrance platform, he finds the controls to the prison. The dust on the floor is a mess. He had fallen here back then. His efforts to free the angel almost killed him. Black stains on the floor still mark the blood loss. It had been a close thing.

Turning to the square stone pattern on the wall, he begins punching in the sequence to put something in the prison cell. Soon, it is ready.

Now for the easy part. He withdraws the crystal-and-metal construct that is the quixault from the fanny pack. Without delay, he tosses it out into the void. The darkness swallows the device. Even without seeing it, he knows the extradimensional storage device is suspended in the exact center of the open space.

This place was built to keep an angel imprisoned and undetectable, forever.

Legion will enjoy the same long rest.